JACKIE
MANTHORNE

LAST RESORT

gynergy
books

Cover illustration: Brenda Whiteway

Printed and bound in Canada by: Best Book Manufacturers

gynergy books acknowledges the generous support of the Canada Council.

Published by:
gynergy books
P.O. Box 2023
Charlottetown, P.E.I.
Canada, C1A 7N7

Canadian Cataloguing in Publication Data
Manthorne, Jackie, 1946-

Last resort

"A Harriet Hubbley mystery"
ISBN 0-921881-34-7

I. Title.

PS8576.A568L37 1995   C813'.54   C95-950196-7
PR9199.3.M36L37 1995

*To lesbians who are true to themselves,
their friends, their lovers and their communities.*

Contents

It was time to begin counting lesbians, Harriet Hubbley thought whimsically as she drove over another bridge spanning the Atlantic Ocean on her left and the Gulf of Mexico on her right, came to the end of U.S. 1, and entered Key West. It was gratifyingly easy to identify them. There were individual lesbians on foot or riding bicycles or mopeds, and couples and groups loitering on the sidewalk or cruising in cars and vans. There were a few on North Roosevelt, more as she approached the centre of the city and Roosevelt became Trueman Avenue, and even more when she reached downtown. She turned left on Duval and became mired in the interminable traffic jam that plagued Key West's main street from one end of the island to the other. Not that she minded; it gave her more time to scrutinize the parade of out lesbians and gay men. Key West was exhilarating, not to mention a fabulous winter destination during March break, when temperatures were often below freezing back in Montreal and blizzards were still as common as sunny days. She wound her window all the way down and hot, humid air filled the car.

Harriet — better known to close friends as Harry, and called "The Hub" by the teenage girls in her high school physical education classes — had been in Key West several times before, but she had never quite become used to its untamed, rowdy nature. Southern good old boys and gals, straight tourists, expatriate Cubans, gay men in leather and lesbians in denim, or vice versa — all of them congregated in the southernmost city in the continental United States, where they mixed freely with the frequently eccentric natives of Key West, also known as Conchs. After all, the island was less than two miles long and four miles wide, so everyone was flung into the same cauldron. On Duval Street, gay businesses like the open-air 801 Bar and the Treetop Bar at La-Te-Da existed side-by-side with predominantly heterosexual establishments like Sloppy Joe's.

Harry was on her way to visit Barbara Fenton, her first woman lover. She and Barb had met in university, when Harry had been a young, naive and terribly passionate first-year student from a coastal village in Nova Scotia and Barb had been a cosmopolitan third-year student from somewhere splendidly urban. Opposites had attracted, the proverbial sparks had flown, and they had nearly been kicked out of residence and suspended from university for their conspicuous consumption of each other. When she and Barb had been discovered in each other's arms, Barb had lied outrageously to deflect their inquisitors, realizing early on that those in authority hadn't wanted to know the literal truth. In fact, it seemed that they were willing to go quite close to the ends of the earth to avoid a scandal which would have a negative impact on alumni donations. Lesbians in the women's residence? Heaven forbid! Better it be silverfish, cockroaches or even a man or two. So they had escaped censure, although rumours had swirled around them like blackflies in late spring. Their love affair had actually waned long before the gossip. And while they had both gone on to other lovers, they had remained close friends.

Harry turned left on Catherine Street, drove two blocks, and pulled into the tiny parking lot next to Barb's guesthouse. The parking lot was hedged on three sides with red bougainvillea that had been allowed to run wild. The lot was crowded with the ubiquitous mopeds and bicycles that could be rented at dozens of outlets on the island, and Harry felt suddenly conspicuous in her over-sized rental car with its power this and power that. She would have preferred to drive Bug, her aged Datsun, but that would have meant spending most of her March break on the road. Besides, Bug's cranky transmission and quietly deteriorating body might not have survived the trip, and she hadn't wanted to squander half her vacation waiting for repairs. Neither had she wanted to be at the mercy of unscrupulous mechanics who would take one look at her and understand that she knew nothing about what was under Bug's hood, except that it was old and rusting. So she had parked Bug in a corner of the lane behind her apartment building, flown to Miami, picked up her rental car at the airport and driven south.

Harry got out of her car and removed her suitcase from the trunk, breathing in hot air thick with the scent of tropical flowers. Her nose twitched and she held her breath for a moment, waiting to see if she was going to sneeze. The feeling passed, and she sighed with relief; perhaps her allergies would leave her alone this trip.

It had been three years since she'd been in Key West, and much had happened since she had last visited Barb and Barb's lover, Karen Lipsky. Two years ago, Judy Johnson, who was Harry's partner of twelve years, had gone through what Harry now regarded as a mid-life crisis. This had resulted in Judy insisting that their relationship be open. On a disconcerting vacation to Cape Cod, Judy had become reinvolved with a former girlfriend, while Harry had become lovers with a police officer she had met while investigating the suspicious death of an elderly innkeeper.

Then, last summer, Judy had taken her close friend Sarah as her lover — an act which had devastated Harry. Shortly thereafter, Harry had attended a high school reunion in her Nova Scotia hometown and had become entangled in a relationship with an old classmate while solving yet another murder. The relationship with the classmate hadn't lasted and Harry hadn't been with anyone but Judy since then, partly because the classmate had been HIV-positive. Harry had gone for a test upon her return to Montreal and then six months later. Both tests had been negative, but for the six months between tests Harry and Judy had utilized safer sex practises — which had been sometimes frustrating and sometimes amusing. Eventually, they had grown comfortable with safer sex, although Judy had professed relief when they'd been able to stop. Harry had then suggested that Judy and Sarah get tested, at which point things turned sour and she had dropped the subject. Privately, though, Harry still thought this was a valid suggestion and there were certain things she no longer did in bed with her lover, although neither of them ever alluded to the mysterious disappearance of certain acts from their sexual repertoire.

Meanwhile, Judy maintained that she was perfectly capable of being involved in two monogamous relationships at the same time, while Harry had never wanted their relationship to be open or to deal with the complexities of having a lover who had another full-time lover. Perhaps this vacation in Key West would help them sort things out; when they were at home, they rarely had time to talk. She had flown down alone because Judy and Sarah had already been in Key West for nearly a week. Tonight, Judy would join her at Barb's guesthouse while Sarah would spend another few days at Alexander's, an exclusively gay and lesbian guesthouse, before flying back to Montreal. Maybe then she would have Judy's undivided attention and they'd be able to resolve some of their differences. And she could hardly wait to talk things over with Barb in person rather than over the phone.

Harry wheeled her suitcase along the sidewalk and climbed the short flight of stairs to the main building of the guesthouse. She knew from previous visits that this was where the office was located. Barb had purchased the old, wood-frame house, with its decorative gingerbread carving, seven or eight years ago. When she had informed her startled friends that she intended to open a guesthouse, everyone had assumed that she would name it after herself. But, to Barb, that would have been the epitome of banality. She had always envisioned herself as a cross between the free-spirited dancer Isadora Duncan and the disciplined, ethical, socialist feminist Emma Goldman, and she had spent weeks debating the merits of "Isadora's Hideaway" versus "Emma's Lodge." Since Barb herself was more eccentric than conventional, more artistic than political, more outspoken than reticent, it was no surprise to anyone that Isadora's Hideaway won out.

Harry entered the guesthouse and leaned against the doorframe. "Hello there, stranger," she said with a smile.

"It's about time!" Barb exclaimed, rising from the chair behind her cluttered desk. Harry suspected that the desk was an antique, but it was so obscured by letters, files and scraps of paper that it was impossible to tell for certain.

"I got caught in traffic up around Key Largo and it was slow the whole way down," Harry replied. Key West could theoretically be reached from Miami by car in under four hours. But, like most of Southern Florida, the Keys tended to suffer from a boom and bust economy. When it was booming, traffic on the two-lane highway proliferated like the palmetto bugs that clicked eerily along sidewalks after dark.

"I meant that three years is too long," Barb corrected her.

"You're right," agreed Harry, and as they hugged she realized how much she had missed Barb. She *always* missed her, she understood suddenly, but not enough to plan her life around Barb's, although she might not have felt so adrift nor nearly half as lonely these past two years had she and Barb been living in the same city. Carrying on a long distance friendship just wasn't the same. "This is nice," she commented as they moved apart and she had the opportunity to glance around the office. "You've fixed it up since the last time I was here." The office had been painted a warm coral and had a built-in, wooden, floor-to-ceiling bookcase at one end. Every surface was covered with file folders, letters and old, yellowed newspapers, pamphlets and books.

"Well, you know how it is — you always do your own space last. It's a bit small, but it serves the purpose," Barb commented. "There's even a closet-sized bedroom and a full bath with a shower for when things are too busy to leave. And believe me, I've spent more than one night camped out here."

"Your own personal doghouse, do you mean?" Harry joked.

"You could say that," Barb responded, her tone ambiguous.

"Anyway, I've saved the best room in the house for you and Judy," Barb said as she opened the top drawer in her desk and removed two keys. Harry appraised her fondly. Barb was big-boned, busty and wide-hipped, with faded auburn hair. Her clothes, on which she spent what seemed to Harry to be a fortune, were normally exquisite, and today was no exception. She was wearing a silk teal tunic over black leggings, topped with several gold chains of varying lengths and drop-dead gold earrings which dangled to her shoulders. Harry knew the clothes were mere window-dressing; Barb had genuine presence.

"I assume you're alone, at least for the moment," commented Barb as she handed Harry the keys.

"Yes," Harry responded. "Judy's supposed to be joining me tonight. She and Sarah are at Alexander's."

"I suggested they stay here, but she didn't seem to think that was a good idea. I got the feeling she felt shy about being here with someone other than you. Anyway, we can talk about it over dinner," Barb said. Just then, a tall, handsome and impossibly blond woman entered the office. She was dressed in white walking shorts and a white tank top and was deeply tanned.

"Oh, sorry, am I interrupting something?" she asked, removing her sunglasses and looking from Harry to Barb and back again. She had a slight British accent and her green eyes were frankly appraising, making Harry want to squirm.

"I guess you two have never met," Barb said with a curious smile.

"No," Harry said. "I think I'd remember if we had."

"I'm *sure* I would," the blond woman remarked. "I'm Pearl Vernon."

"Harriet Hubbley — but call me Harry."

They shook hands and it was apparent that Pearl wasn't in much of a hurry to let go.

"What is it that you wanted, Pearl?" Barb inquired, amused.

"Good question," Pearl laughed. Her voice was husky. "I'd almost forgotten why I dropped by. Karen was acting rather the petulant ninny again, so I thought I'd come round to cry on your shoulder or at least complain bitterly." She released Harry's hand after giving it a gentle squeeze. "But that hardly matters now. Tell me, where have you been hiding this treasure?"

Harry blushed when she realized Pearl was referring to her, and she looked to Barb for assistance.

"I've been meaning to introduce the two of you for quite some time," Barb remarked.

"But you never did, you naughty girl, you," joked Pearl. "Luckily, I'm perfectly capable of making up for lost time."

"I'm afraid she's taken," Barb proclaimed, as if Harry were a passive commodity.

"Aren't they all," Pearl said tragically, her hand sweeping through the air in a gesture of despair. "But you will give me a chance, won't you?" she suddenly beseeched Harry.

Harry opened her mouth and closed it again. This woman was too much — an actor extraordinaire, and extremely attractive to boot.

"Now look at what you've done," Barb scolded Pearl. "She's just arrived after a long, exhausting trip from the northern wilds of Canada and you've scared the bejesus out of her."

"Who, me?" Pearl replied innocently.

"Montreal is not located in the northern wilds of Canada," Harry managed to declare.

"All right, so I deviated slightly from the truth," Barb conceded. "But you are tired, aren't you?"

"Well, yes," Harry admitted.

"Try again later. Like tomorrow," Barb suggested to Pearl.

"Certainly," Pearl replied, giving Harry a warm smile and then leaving the office.

Barb stared after her for a moment and then shook her head.

"Pearl's a very attractive woman, isn't she? Would you believe that she was my first lover?"

"What, are you collecting former lovers for March break?" Harry asked dryly, although she wasn't surprised by Barb's disclosure. Half the woman Barb knew were former lovers, and she claimed, without even a hint of apology, that she had always possessed a large appetite for wine, women and song — with the emphasis on women, of course.

"It seems I must be, doesn't it?" Barb chortled, pleased with herself. "I met her in England when I was studying over there — you remember, I told you about spending a horrible year feeling like the dumbest student in the known universe and hating every minute of it, except for Pearl, of course. That was a revelation that changed my life, but I still came back to Montreal to finish my degree."

"And that was when we met."

"Yes," Barb said, glancing at her watch. "Let's put your suitcase in your room so we can go to dinner. I reserved for six, and if we're more than a couple minutes late, they'll give our table away."

"Is Pearl always on the make?" Harry asked, picking up her suitcase.

"Not really," Barb replied as they left the office. "You obviously made quite an impression on her. Now why do I have the feeling that it was mutual?"

"She is quite attractive," Harry admitted.

"So are millions of other women," Barb pointed out drolly.

That might be true, reflected Harry, but she hadn't met the vast majority of them. She abruptly changed the subject. "This is wonderful, Barb — you've done so much work!" she exclaimed as Barb led her through the main building and out the back door to the patio. The grounds had been professionally landscaped with tropical trees, shrubs and flowering plants, and the paths leading from one building to another had been paved with patio stones. Deck chairs, padded recliners and plastic patio tables circled a medium-sized swimming pool with a large sun deck and a whirlpool in which two topless women were seated. They were so absorbed in each other that they didn't even turn at the sound of Harry's voice.

"I bought the other buildings and made them into a compound so no one can overlook us," Barb explained.

"How many rooms do you have now?" Harry asked. She followed Barb into another building which ran parallel to the one they had just left. It had a central hallway with doors down each side.

"Thirty," Barb replied with evident pride. "And we're booked solid for the whole winter."

"That's fabulous."

"Isn't it, though?" Barb said, giving Harry an engaging grin. "Who would have thought that I'd turn into a hotel manager? What a lark! Although Karen does quite a bit of the work, too. And here's your room," she announced, opening the door.

Harry walked through the living room, past the kitchenette and into the bedroom, where she deposited her suitcase on the bed. Then she rejoined Barb in the living room. "Barb, this is a whole suite, not just a room. I don't know if I can afford it," she protested.

"What do you mean, *afford*? Who said anything about paying?" Barb replied. "I wanted to put you in my building. My apartment's right next to this one, you see, and this is the smallest building — there are only four suites plus a kitchen and a storage room. I generally reserve them for friends. Karen has the suite across from mine and Pearl is currently installed in the one across from yours. It's private enough so that we can leave the doors open and run back and forth in our sweet nothings like we used to in the old days."

"You and Karen have separate suites?" Harry asked, grinning in spite of herself. Sweet nothings, indeed; Barb had always been too proud of her body to cover it up, and with good reason.

"We didn't have quite enough room for all my stuff and her artist's studio in one apartment, so we've spread out," Barb explained. "Do you like it?"

"Of course I do. It's marvellous. But I intend to pay, just like any other guest," Harry responded firmly.

Barb shrugged. "In lieu of cold, hard cash, a big hug would do."

"Well, you can have that, too," Harry chuckled as she turned to her friend.

Barb's hugs were as uninhibited as ever. Harry's face was showered with kisses, and Barb's hands explored her back and then patted her hips. "You've put on a little weight," she commented.

"I'm nearly fifty," Harry said with chagrin.

"It's lack of exercise, not age," Barb remarked. "At least that's what they tell me." She laughed as she casually planted a kiss on Harry's lips.

Karen Lipsky's indignant voice filled the room. "How many times do I have to ask you to close the door when you're in flagrante delicto? You don't have to advertise your affairs to the whole world!"

Harry flinched and backed away from Barb.

"But it's just Harriet," Barb protested to her lover, holding out her hands.

"Hi, Karen," Harry said feebly. She wished Barb had picked some other time to kiss her fully on the lips or that Karen had chosen another moment to wander into the apartment. She had no reason to feel guilty, but it looked bad.

"It's good to see you again, Harry," Karen said, although she didn't sound like she really meant it.

"You too, Karen," Harry replied. She glanced warily at Barb, who was staring at the wall over Karen's head with an impartial look on her face. A couple they might be, and a long-standing one at that, having lived together for nearly fifteen years, but they always seemed to be arguing about something, be it money, women or a topic as mundane as the weather. If one of them said it was sunny, the other would swear it was overcast. They were also as physically different as two women could be. Karen was short and thin, and was most comfortably dressed in jeans and a tee-shirt stained with the proof of her profession as a not-so-successful artist.

"I hope you'll enjoy your stay at Isadora's Hideaway," Karen added with stringent formality as she wheeled around and retreated from the room.

"Phew," Harry uttered. "There's certainly nothing like getting off on the wrong foot."

"Don't worry about it," Barb said reassuringly. "You know what she's like."

"But there isn't anything to be jealous about," Harry protested.

"Of course not," Barb agreed. "And don't think she doesn't know it. Now let's go eat."

"I'd better give Judy a call first and let her know I'm here," Harry said. She took out the tiny address book she kept in her purse, looked up the number for Alexander's guesthouse and dialled. There was no response in Judy and Sarah's room, so she left a message that she would expect to meet Judy at the Hideaway around midnight that evening unless she heard otherwise.

"Tell me, do you find it difficult coordinating your life these days?" Barb asked as they left the apartment.

"Does a dog have fleas?" Harry quipped. "But never mind. Where are we having dinner?"

"At the Rooftop Café at Front and Duval," Barb replied. "The food there is not only wonderful, it's healthy. That's not always an oxymoron these days, thank god. But it's too far to walk, so we'll take my car."

Harry had forgotten how noisy Key West was at night. Barb grasped her arm and they walked together from the parking lot along Front Street to a crowded section of Duval. It was hot enough to melt the pavement under their sandalled feet. They strolled past several stores that sold tee-shirts exclusively, and Harry wondered how they managed to stay in business when there were so many of them in Key West. They passed the saloon doors of a popular bar and loud tex-mex music issued forth. Harry wrinkled her nose as the pungent smell of beer and the harsh odour of American cigarettes drifted to the sidewalk and made her sneeze. As they moved aside to let several bearded, long-haired men pass, she remembered that Key West was one of the last remaining hippie bastions in North America.

"Here we are," Barb said. They walked up an exterior flight of stairs, arrived at the Rooftop Café on the dot of six and were seated almost immediately on the narrow outdoor balcony overlooking the street. Harry stared out over the water and breathed deeply. The sun was dipping low in the sky, and the light had that pre-sunset aura which infused everything with brilliant detail.

"You know, I wish you and Judy would get your act together and join us down here for part of the winter instead of just dropping by for a couple of days every few years," Barb commented once they had ordered a rum and Coke for Harry and a white wine spritzer for Barb.

"But I'm staying for ten whole days," Harry protested. "And Judy's been here for a week. She told me that you'd already been to dinner twice."

"Let's be frank, Harriet; I enjoy seeing Judy, but it's you I'm friends with," Barb said.

"I know," Harry nodded.

"And a couple of days, a week and a half — what's the difference? You never stay long enough," Barb claimed as their drinks were served and menus placed in front of them by an obviously gay waiter.

"There's a big difference, especially when I have to work to support myself and my job happens to be half a continent away," Harry responded dryly.

"There is that, I suppose," Barbara conceded grudgingly.

"Unfortunately."

"To friendship," Barb said affectionately, raising her glass.

"To friendship," echoed Harry, touching her glass to Barb's and sipping her drink. It tasted like a double, and the rum went straight to her head. The effect was probably enhanced by the heat, for although they were on the balcony facing the ocean, the breeze that ruffled their napkins was hot and scented with odours from the dozens of restaurants in the vicinity and the distinctly maritime tang of tar, salt water and seaweed.

"Perhaps we should order," Harry murmured.

Barb nodded and spent a few seconds studying her menu. "I always have the catch of the day. It's invariably fresh and perfectly prepared," she said, tossing her menu aside. It teetered on the edge of the table and fell off. "It comes with a salad and lots of vegetables. You know, all that healthy, fat-free stuff we're supposed to eat once we reach a certain age."

"Sounds good," Harry agreed. "I think I'll have the same thing."

"Are you all right? You seem so subdued," commented Barb.

"I suppose I am," Harry sighed.

"I assume that's because of what's going on between you and Judy," said Barb.

Harry nodded. "Why don't we eat first and talk later?"

"What, have you lost the ability to eat and converse at the same time?" Barb teased.

Harry snorted into her drink and made a face.

"Yeah, I love you too," Barb retorted as the waiter returned. Barb ordered for the both of them, gave him Harry's menu and moved her feet so he could search under the table for hers.

"You and Judy have been together for a long time," Barb said after the waiter rushed off with their order. "Weren't you ever tempted?"

"You know very well that I was," Harry responded.

"But you never did anything about it," Barb surmised with a knowing smile.

"You know the answer to that, too."

"You've always been such a cautious woman."

"I'd rather think of myself as a faithful homebody," Harry sniffed. "I wouldn't insult myself to that degree if I were you," Barb retorted crisply.

Harry bit back a response as the waiter placed a basket of bread and two plates of mixed greens on the table.

"The world's changed, you know," Barb told her, lathering a crust of French bread with butter. "People don't necessarily stay in one relationship for life or even for half a life, for that matter."

"You and Karen have," Harry pointed out.

"Yes, but we've never been monogamous. I made it clear right from the beginning that that was out of the question."

"Then why has Karen always been so jealous?" Harry asked as she forked several pieces of lettuce and a yellow flower petal into her mouth. She always felt sophisticated when she ate flowers.

"She's not really jealous," Barb responded. "Well, maybe a little, but that's habitual, not deeply felt. But take it from me, she's more concerned about appearances than anything else. She'd rather we keep our affairs behind closed doors, but that's never been my style, so it's been a recurring bone of contention between us."

"Yes, but what I don't understand is the purpose of staying together if you're going to go off with other women all the time," Harry protested.

"Look, you told me about the two women you had affairs with," Barb said, pushing her salad plate away. It was empty except for three pieces of tomato. "Did you love Judy less when you were involved with them?"

"No," conceded Harry.

"Well, don't think you're any different from anybody else, because you're not."

The waiter chose that moment to remove their salad plates and serve the main course.

"Give me a break, Barb," Harry complained as soon as he turned his back. "I never said I was being logical about this."

"At least that I can understand," Barb acknowledged. "But you've got to grow up a little."

Harry was exasperated. She shook her head and looked down at her dinner. The filet of red snapper was exquisitely broiled, the rice pilaff aromatic and the modest servings of vegetables perfectly steamed.

"So Judy's pushed you in a direction in which you didn't particularly want to go," Barb said quietly as she finished her wine spritzer and waved at the waiter to bring her another. "That happens sometimes. Just because you're a couple doesn't mean that you're in perfect sync, or that one of you won't have needs the other can't fulfil."

"I know that," Harry said. The sun was dropping below the horizon, its lingering rays reflecting off the clouds, painting the sky with crimson.

"Of course you do," Barb agreed with equanimity. "Isn't the snapper beautifully cooked, by the way?"

"It's just that I can't accept it," Harry admitted. "And yes, the fish is marvellous."

"You're not without options, you know," Barb said, looking up at her with more curiosity than Harry thought was proper for a good friend to display.

"Yeah, sure," Harry moped, slicing off another piece of red snapper.

"You obviously don't want to break up with her, but you could renegotiate your relationship. You've been letting Judy call the shots. She's been telling you how things are going to be," Barb pointed out with a wave of her fork. Several pieces of rice dropped on the tablecloth. "But you've got some rights, too, and one of them is to put your foot down."

"But where will that get me?" Harry responded. "I don't want Judy to leave me."

"Is your relationship that close to the brink?" Barb asked, startled.

"I don't know," Harry admitted.

"Don't you think you'd better find out?"

"We haven't been communicating with each other all that much lately," explained Harry, placing her knife and fork across her plate.

"Karen and I argue all the time, but at least we're talking about what's important," Barb said. "No one could possibly be as unreasonable as she is, and I'm certain she feels the same about me. In fact, I *know* she does because she repeatedly tells me so. But if you and Judy aren't even discussing things, then you're in real trouble."

"Tell me about it," Harry said, trying to grin.

"It doesn't have to be that way," Barb said.

"I'm a coward," Harry confessed.

"Do you think that nothing worse will happen if you bury your head in the sand?"

"I suppose so."

"It doesn't work that way," Barb said. "One morning you'll wake up and find you and Judy have nothing in common or that you've lost interest in doing things with her or that she's changed jobs, found a new lover and won the lottery and you never even noticed."

"That's not funny," Harry said.

"It wasn't meant to be," Barb replied, staring at her. "You used to have more gumption than that. What happened?"

Harry had trouble meeting her eyes. She didn't like seeing the disappointment in them.

"Promise me you'll use this vacation to sort things out," Barb requested.

"I will," Harry assured her.

"Good. Now, why don't we talk about something else? Lots has happened since the last time we spoke on the phone, and I've got a few surprises, too," Barb said with an enigmatic smile.

"Really?" said Harry, raising her eyebrows.

The waiter picked that moment to check on them. "Finished, ladies?" he asked.

"Yes," Harry said rather impatiently, annoyed that their conversation had been interrupted. She watched in silence as the waiter deftly cleared the table.

Barb glanced at the sky and then commented, "We should have gone to Mallory Square to watch the sunset."

"There's always tomorrow."

"True," Barb said enthusiastically. "Yes, let's. I haven't done that for months, and it's such fun. You've been there before, haven't you?"

"Yes, although I think we missed it the last time Judy and I were here. It was cold and it rained the whole time, remember?"

"How could I forget?" Barb laughed. "That was when we watched lesbian porn videos for two days and nights."

"Erotica," Harry corrected her.

"Whatever," Barb said with a dismissive wave of her arm. "Anyway, the sunset ceremony is as hokey — and as moving — as ever. The bagpiper has put on a little weight but he still flirts with all the girls and plays a mean 'Amazing Grace' as the sun goes down. And the tightrope walker still hasn't fallen off, the juggler is as much of a showman as ever, and then of course there are the usual hawkers of jewellery and tee-shirts."

"Are the conch fritters as good as they used to be?"

"What's your cloresterol level?" Barb retorted.

"Not low enough to mention in mixed company," Harry sighed. "But what were you going to tell me before?"

"Dessert? Coffee? An aperitif?" their waiter hovered, giving Harry the impression that there was a long line-up.

"Why don't we go to the tea dance at La-Te-Da?" Barb suggested. "We can have another drink and continue our conversation there."

"That sounds good to me," Harry replied.

They split the bill down the middle and strolled back to the parking lot to retrieve Barb's car. "I have a moped, but I assumed you were too tired to use one of our rentals," she commented as she opened the doors.

"I've never driven one," Harry confessed, fastening her seatbelt as Barb switched on the air conditioning.

"You're kidding."

"I'm afraid not."

"Well, we'll have to remedy that," Barb said. "I imagine you've ridden a bicycle at some point in your life."

"Yes," Harry answered, adjusting a vent that was blowing cold air in her face. "But not for years." She didn't mind driving Bug through the streets of Montreal, dodging pot holes the size of bomb craters, coping with erratic drivers who had never heard of turn signals or rearview mirrors and avoiding jaywalkers whose purpose in life seemed to be to ignore the existence of traffic lights and intersections, but she'd never had the nerve to take up cycling in the city. Besides, there were too many hills.

"That doesn't matter," Barb assured her as she turned left from Duval onto a side street. "It's like making love — you never entirely lose the ability. I'll take you out for a lesson the first thing tomorrow morning."

"Great," Harry said with as much enthusiasm as she could muster.

"Don't sound so excited," Barb said wryly, glancing at Harry and then pulling into a parking space a van had just vacated.

Harry got out of the car, gasping involuntarily; it was like stepping from a walk-in freezer into a blast furnace. "No, I'd appreciate it," she said. "And don't go all polite on me," Barb grumbled, taking her arm as they walked back toward Duval Street.

"You know me too well," Harry conceded with a laugh as she wiped sweat from her forehead. It was true. Barb had always been able to read her like a book. This had disconcerted Harry when they'd been lovers, because she'd never been able to hide her feelings and this had placed her at a distinct disadvantage. But knowing that there was someone other than Judy who cared enough to think about her when she wasn't around was somehow comforting. She resolved to write Barb more often and to call her regularly, aware that she'd made similar resolutions in the past and hadn't kept them. Why did her closest friend live so far away?

"Dolt" Barb said affectionately as they rounded the corner.

"It takes one to know one," Harry retorted, suddenly feeling cheerful. She was on vacation, she was in Key West and the weather was hot, hot, hot, and she was strolling arm-in-arm to a tea dance with a friend with whom she was close enough to trade amicable insults. What more could she want? "Can I get you a drink?" she asked Barb, before she had time to think about what might be wrong with the equation she'd just made.

"Another white wine spritzer," Barb requested once they had found a table at the edge of the empty swimming pool. "But make sure he puts a slice of lime in it, not lemon."

Harry stood in the swiftly moving line at the bar, tapping her foot to the dance music and looking around. Vines, shrubs, tropical flowering plants and even several small palm trees had been planted throughout the patio, which was filled with gay men and lesbians. Men outnumbered women by about eight to one. Most of the men were dressed in jeans and short-sleeved shirts or shorts and tee-shirts, but a few were flamboyantly attired in leather chaps and vests, and one young man wore nothing but a loose pair of faded denim overalls. The gaudier the costume, the more outrageous the flirting, she noted. There was just enough flagrant cruising to make her wonder whether this reckless abandon extended to sex. The women scattered throughout the crowd were generally in groups, with a few couples holding hands or standing close to each other. The younger women tended to be dressed in shorts, while the older ones wore pants or jeans. None of them were dressed in leather, and more than one seemed bemused by the ostentatious clothes and accompanying antics of some of the men.

Harry asked for a rum and Coke and a white wine spritzer — with a slice of lime — and returned to the table, where she found Barb deep in conversation with a young man sitting beside her. An older man hovered behind them with an impatient look on his face.

"Harriet, you've never met my brother, Peter, have you?" Barb asked as Harry placed their drinks on the table.

"No." Harry looked curiously at Peter Fenton as she sat down. His hair was a darker auburn than Barb's, and while his facial features clearly resembled those of his older sister, the strength so evident in Barb's countenance was completely lacking in his. "It's nice to meet you, Peter."

"The same here," he said. He gave his sister a petulant glance and rose from the table.

"You don't have to leave on my account — " Harry began.

"There are friends waiting for us," Peter's companion said in a voice full of tedium.

"Ta ta, sis," said Peter lightly. "See you soon."

Harry watched him put an arm around his companion's shoulder and then they strolled off. "I didn't know your brother was gay," she commented. "Does he live in Key West, too?"

"No, thank god," Barb replied, quickly finishing her drink. "He and his boyfriend, Ross Hunter, are here on vacation."

"It must be nice to see him."

"He only comes when he needs money," Barb frowned, "which he thinks I possess in great abundance. Let's go upstairs. Talking with Peter and Ross always depresses me. We'll have another drink and then a few dances."

"That sounds good to me," said Harry. They picked up their glasses and strolled past the swimming pool. The sun had completely set and the sky was a uniform dark blue. Recessed lights provided enough illumination to see but no more. They climbed the stairs to the largest second-storey deck and found an empty table. It was all very romantic, Harry thought, as they watched several couples dance. She wondered again what Barb had been intending to tell her.

"I think you may have to drive me home," Barb commented a few dance tunes later. She had switched to scotch on the rocks and was drinking methodically.

"I'm not sure I can," Harry replied, looking at her empty glass. "Barb, what were you going to tell me?"

"Why don't we have a nice, long chat over breakfast tomorrow morning?" Barb suggested with an affectionate smile. "I'm a bit tired, not to mention fairly inebriated. Lord, listen to that music! Let's dance!"

"Sure," Harry responded immediately.

It had been too long since she and Judy had been out dancing, Harry thought as she and Barb took to the dance floor. The music was loud but not overpowering and its repetitive rhythm soon transported her to a state of grace. It was the gentle, tropical breeze, the southern sky overhead, the freedom to be gay, to dance with another woman in the company of others. Sweat poured down her cheeks and gathered under her breasts and in the small of her back, but she ignored it.

"Harry?"

Harry opened her eyes. "Sarah," she said, feeling her senses return to earth with a dull thud as she recognized Judy's other lover. Sarah Reid was a short woman in her late thirties with brown, medium-length hair. "How are you?" Harry asked, pausing in her dancing. "How's your vacation been?"

"Just fine," Sarah responded. She gave Harry an uncertain smile.

Harry stuffed her hands in her pockets and gazed down at the floor, feeling as uncomfortable as Sarah looked. Before Judy and Sarah had become lovers, Sarah had been one of Judy's closest friends. Harry had liked her, but once Judy had fallen in love with her, Harry's affection had become tempered with caution, a fair amount of ambivalence and just plain fear.

"Hi, Sarah," Barb said. "Come dance with us."

"I was just on my way to join Judy at the bar," Sarah answered.

"I think I'll go talk to her, if you don't mind," Harry said, spotting Judy at the bar and knowing that Sarah wouldn't protest even if she did object. As she walked towards Judy, she heard Barb begin to engage Sarah in conversation.

"Hi," Harry said.

"Harry!" Judy replied. She was holding two brimming wine glasses in her hands, and she now carefully deposited them on the shiny bar.

"I didn't expect to see you here," Harry said inanely. They'd only been separated for a week, but Judy looked good enough to eat.

Unfortunately, Harry didn't know whether it was appropriate to say something so intimate when Judy was still with Sarah. These days, the boundaries always seemed to be muddied.

"It's a small town," her lover replied evenly. "Would you like some wine?"

"Thanks," Harry replied, picking up a wine glass and downing half its contents. "How've you been?"

Judy's shrug surprised her.

"Missed me, did you?" Harry asked, shifting closer.

Judy gave her a look and then drained her glass, but she didn't move away.

"Sorry I asked."

"It wasn't all I thought it would be," Judy commented with a sigh as the bartender refilled her wine glass. "And then I found out something which threw me for a loop."

"What?" Harry asked, emptying her glass and holding it out before the bartender could disappear. It looked like she and Barb would be walking home tonight. It was a good thing it wasn't far.

"Maybe I should just leave the bottle," the bartender suggested.

"That sounds like a good idea," Judy responded with a smile.

"What did you find out?" Harry repeated, but before Judy could answer, Barb had joined them.

"I guess you'll need another glass, too," the bartender commented.

"Not for me," Barb told him, holding up her hand. "I'm drinking scotch and no, I don't need another just yet. Good lord, it's hot," she added, wiping sweat from her face.

"I left a message for you at Alexander's suggesting midnight. Is that okay, Judy?" Harry asked.

Judy nodded and they moved apart just as Sarah arrived.

The four women stood and chatted until Barb had finished her glass of scotch and Harry, Judy and Sarah had emptied the bottle of wine. "We'd better go," Judy said with a glance at her watch.

"Us too, actually," Barb said, and they paid the bill and said goodnight.

"It's a bit of a farce, don't you think?" Harry asked Barb as they walked down the stairs. "I mean, she's going to join me later."

"No, it's not farcical, it's civilized. After all, we do spend most of our lives doing things other than sex, and without convention, we'd have nothing to say at times like this. Either that or we'd be at each other's throats. Can you drive?"

"No," Harry answered. "But it's just a couple of blocks."

"I know," Barb said glumly.

"But you always drive, don't you?" Harry commented, unable to resist smiling. "Either your car or your moped."

"Don't be so self-righteous," grumbled Barb, latching onto Harry's arm.

"I couldn't resist," Harry laughed, steering Barb left on Duval.

"Wow, I'm bushed! Look, we'll talk about my news tomorrow," Barb mumbled.

"Fine," Harry agreed. Wine, even in its white incarnation, did not mix well with rum and Coke, and all she wanted to do was sleep. "Here we are," she told Barb, leading her up the stairs to Isadora's Hideaway.

"Home, sweet home," Barb sighed.

"Don't knock it." Harry opened the door and she and Barb tottered into the hall.

"Oh, hell, what's a woman to do?" Barb asked rhetorically.

"Oh, hell is right," Karen commented, glaring at them as she stepped out of the front office. Pearl was close behind her. "You're making enough noise to wake the dead."

"Oops," Barb said, freeing herself from Harry's grasp.

"Never mind," Karen sighed.

"What's going on?" Pearl inquired, looking from Karen to Harry.

"What were you doing in my office?" Barb asked.

"Helping Karen check someone in," Pearl replied, gesturing to an attractive, middle-aged woman hovering behind her. The woman was of medium height and had hair so black that it had obviously been dyed. "This is Alison Wheatley," Pearl added, "and she claims to know you quite well."

"Darling," Alison gushed at Barb.

"Alison!" Barb exclaimed.

"You don't have to look so pleased to see me," Alison said sarcastically, her face falling. "After all, you were the one who suggested I drop by for a visit sometime."

"So I did," Barb replied. "Let's see, when was that? When I was at that conference in Chicago a couple of years ago?"

"It was last year in Dallas," corrected Alison, her eyes venomous.

"That's right," Barb snapped her fingers. "Has everyone met Alison Wheatley, by the way? Harriet, you haven't, have you?

Alison and I had a little aff — I mean, we became acquainted in second year university."

"What?" Harry yelped involuntarily. She sneezed several times in rapid succession.

"After you and I broke up," Barb said hastily.

"Another addition to your harem?" asked Karen sarcastically.

"Don't worry, girls, I'm not here to compete with you," Alison reassured them. "Wheatley's my married name, although it didn't take. I'm bisexual, of course, but I've been into men lately, if you know what I mean."

"I hope you're aware that this is a women's guesthouse, and that most of the guests are *lesbians,*" Pearl warned, looking as if her feathers had been ruffled. It was wonderful how effectively a tall woman could use her height to intimidate others, Harry thought as she stifled another sneeze. Unfortunately, Alison Wheatley seemed to be having none of it.

"Of course I do, but I don't mind," Alison said cheerfully.

She doesn't mind! Harry thought incredulously. Realizing that she was allergic to Alison's robust perfume, she reached into her purse for a tissue and blew her nose.

"Hey, sex is sex, if you know what I mean," Alison said, oblivious to the deepening silence. "After all, we're big girls around here, aren't we?"

"It's way past *my* bedtime," Karen said, giving Barb a glacial glare just before she turned and rushed down the corridor.

"She goes to bed quite early, doesn't she?" Alison Wheatley commented to no one in particular as the door slammed at the other end of the hall.

It was funny how mistakes could come back and haunt you, Harry reflected, especially those that walked on two legs and with whom you had engaged in sex. Had Barb been so intemperate as to resurrect an affair with Alison last year in Dallas? She tried to keep a grin from lifting the corners of her mouth.

"I'll show you to your room," Barb said tersely, taking the key from Alison's hand and glancing at the number stamped on it.

"Oh, would you?" Alison gushed.

Pearl rolled her eyes at Harry and all four of them walked down the hall to the patio, Barb in the lead.

Harry locked her door behind her, switched on the light in the living room, and immediately wished she hadn't refused Pearl's offer of a drink. It wasn't yet eleven o'clock, she wasn't expecting Judy until midnight, and she suddenly felt too restless to sleep.

"It wouldn't have to be in my suite, which is just across the hall, by the way," Pearl had assured her. "The Club International is around the corner on Simonton, or we could sit on the patio under the stars and sip cognac from plastic glasses. It's a beautiful night, there's not a cloud in the sky. Or if you're tired of drinking, I could get a couple of cans of Coke from the vending machine. Best of all, I know where Barb keeps the key to the breakfast nook, so we could conduct an illicit raid and score some orange juice and a few croissants."

"I'm pretty tired," Harry had prevaricated, not meeting Pearl's eyes because it was perfectly evident that she was lying. Not that she wasn't tired, because she was; in fact, she was probably so exhausted she wouldn't be able to sleep for hours. But her weariness didn't matter — it never did. The truth was that she was afraid. No, make that petrified. On the one hand, she was attracted to Pearl. On the other hand, she had vowed not to become involved with other women until she could accept Judy's relationship with Sarah. But at times like this she wondered about the wisdom of that decision. Once she had tested negative for the HIV virus, wouldn't it have been better to go her own way and find solace wherever it was offered? And yet when she'd done that in the past, she'd felt like such a hypocrite.

Besides, Judy was coming back to her tonight.

Someone knocked on the door.

Harry rose from the sofa and went and opened it.

"I was hoping you weren't tired enough to go right to bed," Pearl said with a smile as she handed Harry a large tray.

"What on earth?" Harry laughed, putting the tray on the coffee table and sitting down on the sofa.

"Oh, it's just a few things I picked up here and there," Pearl said casually.

"A few things!"

There were several cans of soft drink, a half-bottle of champagne sitting in a bowl of crushed ice, an uncorked bottle of cognac — Remy Martin, at that — a mickey of rum, a decanter of orange juice, a plate piled high with danishes and croissants, a dish of butter, a bowl of grapes.

"Tokens of my esteem," Pearl said with a shrewd smile, sitting beside Harry.

"You shouldn't have," Harry replied foolishly.

"Shall we fence, eat, or make love?" Pearl whispered, moving closer.

"Eat," Harry maintained even though she wasn't hungry. She reached for a plastic glass.

"Fine," Pearl said and leaned over to kiss her.

Some things had this inevitable feeling about them, Harry rationalized, releasing her hold on the glass as they kissed. Pearl's fingers stroked her short hair, slid over her cheek and down her neck to the rise of her breast. But wait, Harry thought as passion welled; she wanted more time to make an important decision like this. She extricated herself from Pearl's arms.

"What's wrong?"

"This is a bit fast for me."

"It didn't *feel* fast. I thought you were attracted to me," Pearl responded, sounding disappointed.

"I am," Harry admitted, rising from the sofa in case her admission tempted Pearl to renew her embrace. "But I need more time. And my lover's arriving tonight."

"I guess that's the luck of the draw, then," Pearl sighed.

"Yes," Harry nodded, although she was perversely displeased about being dismissed in such a cavalier fashion.

"It would be a shame to let this go to waste, though," Pearl said with a gesture at the contents of the tray. "Why don't we finish it outside on the patio?"

"That would be nice." And safe, Harry thought as she led Pearl from her apartment.

Pearl balanced the tray against her chest and let the patio door swing shut behind her. "Let's sit here," she said, putting the tray down. She poured champagne and orange juice into a plastic glass and handed it to Harry.

"Thanks."

"Cheers, then," Pearl said.

What an unconventional woman, Harry reflected, touching her glass to Pearl's.

"A midnight tryst!" exclaimed Alison Wheatley, who had materialized from the building at the far end of the pool. "I do hope I'm not interrupting anything, if you know what I mean."

Harry heard Pearl snort. She turned around and glanced at Alison, her eyes widening in astonishment. Alison was stark naked except for a beach towel she had draped over her shoulder with such artistry that it hid nothing.

"We were simply engaging in a bit of debauchery involving sustenance and libations," Pearl replied dryly.

"How extraordinarily civilized!" Alison gushed.

Harry heard Pearl mutter something under her breath and then ask, "Would you like to join us? There's more than enough to go around."

"You're very thoughtful," Alison bubbled, approaching them.

"Pull up a chair and dig in," Pearl encouraged her.

"I was beginning to wonder if I was the only free spirit in residence. I mean, does everyone go to bed *this* early on Saturday night?" Alison remarked, gesturing to the dark-windowed buildings surrounding them and then moving one of the deck chairs closer to Harry and sitting down. Her flowery perfume wafted past Harry's nose and she sneezed immediately.

"This looks like a veritable feast," Alison said appreciatively, pouring herself a healthy dollop of cognac and helping herself to a croissant.

"Planning to take a little swim, were you?" Pearl asked.

Harry sneezed again and poured herself a second glass of orange juice, this time without the champagne.

"Are you catching a cold?" Alison inquired politely.

"No," Harry responded. "I'm allergic to your perfume."

"How unfortunate for you," Alison replied.

Harry glanced at Pearl and saw that she was staring openly at Alison. How could she be so brazen, Harry wondered, although she understood the temptation — Alison Wheatley was attractive, if you liked blowsy-looking women, and her breasts and tummy were firm. She had great legs, too. She didn't look like the type to work out, so Harry wondered whether she had benefited from a bit of nip-and-tuck surgery. She tried momentariiy to conduct a closer inspection but gave it up because she didn't want to be caught ogling. Besides, a casual look or two wouldn't tell her whether Alison had been under the knife, and she certainly didn't plan to get any closer.

"I wonder where Barb is?" Alison said with studied casualness, and once again Harry speculated about whether or not Barb and Alison had rekindled their affair of thirty years before.

"Maybe she had business to attend to," Pearl suggested.

"That's what she said when she showed me to my room," Alison agreed with a nod, "although she promised we'd spend some time together. Anyway, it doesn't matter. Are you girls interested in a little skinny-dipping under the stars?" She helped herself to another glass of cognac.

"No, thanks," Harry said swiftly.

"That's certainly a tempting invitation," Pearl replied slowly. "It's so hot that I've been seriously considering it."

For a moment, Harry was taken aback. Then she laughed at herself. Her reaction was absurd, especially since she had rebuffed Pearl's advances. "Go ahead."

"Really?" Pearl answered, sounding disappointed.

"Really," Harry smiled wryly. "I mean, you might as well."

"It's just for a swim," Pearl reassured her as she rose and stripped.

"Unfortunately, my boyfriend was held up or I would have been with him tonight," Alison commented casually.

"Are you planning to move out, then?" Harry asked, trying not to look at Pearl. She was magnificent, though, simply magnificent. Harry found a napkin and blew her nose.

"Yes," Alison smiled, "although I think it's rather silly to segregate people. You know what I mean, don't you? Gay, straight, male, female, what's the difference?"

Quite a bit when it came to skinny-dipping, Harry reflected acidly, and that was just among other things. She made the mistake of glancing at Pearl and her body threatened to liquify.

"And my Marty — that's Martin Culver — he's the most wonderfully liberated man I've ever met — why, he even suggested I stay here when I told him that there was a women-only guesthouse," Alison bragged.

"Isn't that a bit curious?" Harry asked, pouring herself another glass of orange juice and hoping no one would notice that her hands were shaking.

"Of course not," Alison responded scornfully.

"But why would he want you to stay here? Didn't you tell him you'd been sexually involved with women?" Pearl asked, moving closer to Harry's chair. Harry gulped orange juice and refused to look up. Or even sideways.

"Only Barb — " Alison blurted, and then, realizing that she'd been hoodwinked, she looked vexed.

"Aren't you two going swimming?" Harry asked desperately. If Pearl moved any closer, she was going to touch her, and that would be fatal.

"Yes!" Alison gave Harry a grateful look as she rushed toward the pool.

"Did it ever occur to you that she and her pal Marty are looking for a bisexual woman willing to indulge in a little fun and games?" Pearl asked bluntly as Alison dove into the water.

"No!"

Pearl looked at her and started to laugh.

"What's so funny?" Harry grumbled.

"I can't believe how innocent you are," Pearl commented.

"I wasn't thinking," Harry claimed.

"Like hell," Pearl teased.

"Really," Harry declared indignantly.

"Sure, sure," Pearl said.

"Go jump in the lake," Harry told her.

"You want me, don't you?" Pearl asked.

Harry allowed herself a long, shameless stare at Pearl's body. "Yes," she said finally, her voice husky.

"Another time, then," Pearl whispered. "And remember, this is only a swim."

And then she was gone. Shortly after, Harry heard laughter from the pool. It generated a feeling of emotional weariness she was quite unaccustomed to feeling.

"So here I am," came a voice from behind her.

"Judy!" Harry exclaimed, jumping up and spilling her orange juice.

"You were expecting me, weren't you?"

"Why of course," mumbled Harry. "You're just a little early. Would you like something? Scotch? Juice? A soft drink?"

Judy put down her suitcase and looked at the tray. She sat in the chair Pearl had vacated but didn't pour herself a drink. "Have you been having a party?"

"Sort of," Harry replied, glancing at the pool, and then she saw Judy's raised eyebrows and knew it was no good. "Pearl and Alison are in the pool, and — "

"I've met Pearl," said Judy, a perceptive look on her face.

"Have you?"

There was a shriek from the swimming pool. Alison, Harry thought, trying not to imagine who was doing what to whom.

"I'll have an orange juice," Judy said.

"Sure," Harry replied eagerly, reaching out to pour.

"If I hadn't been joining you tonight, would that be you in there?"

"No."

Eyebrows again.

"Oh, hell, I don't know."

"Maybe I should meet you in your room," suggested Judy.

"That's not necessary," Harry assured her.

"Then bring the tray with you. It would be nice to have croissants and orange juice later," Judy replied, rising from the chair and picking up her suitcase. She placed a hand on her hip and posed momentarily for Harry's inspection. Then she gave a rather breathless laugh and turned and ran for house.

Extraordinary, Harry thought as she rose slowly from the deck chair, grasped the tray and followed Judy. Her lover was actually flirting with her.

Harry woke cautiously, as was her habit when she feared she'd had too much to drink the night before. But if she was hung over this morning, she couldn't tell. There were mornings after and then there was euphoria, and she was certainly capable of distinguishing between the two. She opened her eyes and instantly closed them again; she hadn't shut the bedroom curtains and the morning sunshine was streaming across the bed. She turned over, a smile tugging at the corners of her lips when she recalled why she hadn't had time to close the drapes and why she was feeling euphoric rather than soggy.

"Judy?" she whispered.

There was no answer.

"Judy?" she inquired, raising her voice.

There was still no answer. She opened her eyes again and confirmed that the other side of the queen-sized bed was empty. "Damn," she muttered with a sigh, throwing off the covers and getting up.

Someone began knocking on her door. She grabbed her bathrobe and put it on as the tempo and intensity of the pounding increased.

"All right, all right," she shouted. "I'm coming! Who is it?" She hurried into the living room.

"Constable Lambert of the Key West Police Department," came the reply. "We'd like to talk to you."

Police? Harry opened the door an inch, wishing there was a chain or some other security device on the inside. She would have to speak to Barb about that.

Once her door was open, Harry's living room instantly filled with people. There were two burly young men in uniform, one of whom was evidently Constable Lambert, a tall, thin, older man in an expensive, cream-coloured suit; and a gaunt-looking woman in a severely tailored dress. The woman stared suspiciously at her. "What's the matter?" Harry asked.

"How did you know that there was something the matter?" the woman asked at once.

"You wouldn't be here if there wasn't," Harry responded. "Who are you, anyway?"

"Detective Dovercourt," the woman replied, flashing her badge. "And this is Detective Allan. And you are?"

"Harriet Hubbley," Harry replied uneasily. "What do you want? What's wrong?"

"Can we see some identification, please?" Detective Dovercourt asked.

"I'll get my passport," Harry replied, retreating into the bedroom to find her purse. She did not feel reassured when Detective Dovercourt followed her. "I'm not going to disappear," she said to the police officer, knotting her housecoat more tightly around her.

"You don't have to talk to them if you don't want to!" Pearl said breathlessly as she rushed into Harry's suite.

Harry saw Detective Dovercourt frown at Pearl and then glance at Detective Allan, who was rocking on his heels. "Would you mind telling me what's going on?" she said as she handed her passport to Detective Allan.

"They — " Pearl began.

"Let's talk," Detective Dovercourt insisted, grasping Pearl by the upper arm and leading her from the room. "There are a few questions I forgot to ask you. Let's go back to your suite."

Pearl looked back at Harry, her expression distressed, as Dovercourt bustled her through the doorway into the hall. The door closed behind them.

Harry felt suddenly bereft. Here she was, surrounded by three police officers with questions in their eyes. Where the hell was Judy, anyway?

"So, what do you know about Barbara Fenton?" Detective Allan inquired, returning Harry's passport.

What didn't she know about Barbara Fenton, Harry mused, glancing from the minimalist sofa to an armless upholstered chair and wondering whether she should sit down. The police officers circled unobtrusively in response to her eye movements and for a second she wondered whether they would levitate if she looked up at the ceiling. "She's a good friend of mine," Harry replied slowly. Detective Allan looked interested.

"Why do you want to know?" asked Harry. She felt suddenly anxious.

Detective Allan looked away. "She's been hurt."

"What happened to her? Where is she?"

"In the hospital," Detective Allan replied.

"I have to go there at once —"

"Later," Detective Allan interrupted. "She's still unconscious, so I'm sure they wouldn't let you in to see her yet. And there are some questions I have to ask you."

Harry's legs began to tremble. She fell into one of the upholstered chairs. Detective Allan sat down in the armchair next to her and the two men in uniform lowered themselves onto the sofa. One of them removed a notebook and pen from his pocket.

"What happened?" Harry asked again. "How did she get hurt? Is she going to be all right?"

Detective Allan raised his hand and squeezed his chin between his fingers.

"You don't want to tell me," Harry surmised.

"It may be that you already know," he replied, dropping his hand from his chin.

"Don't play games with me," Harry retorted, suddenly angry. "She's a good friend of mine, and I don't deserve to be treated like this. Either tell me what's going on or I'm going to find out for myself."

"She must have fallen and hit her head on the edge of the dresser!" Pearl said, bursting into the room again.

"Maria!" Detective Allan complained, rising swiftly from his armchair.

"Sorry," Detective Dovercourt muttered. "Come with me," she said to Pearl.

"No," Pearl responded bluntly.

"Do as she asks, Ms. Vernon," Detective Allan warned.

"Am I under arrest, then?" Pearl asked.

Detective Allan glanced at Detective Dovercourt, who shook her head. A feeling of regret emanated from the police officers.

Pearl crossed the room, stood by Harry's chair and casually rested her hand on Harry's shoulder.

"Was Barb attacked?" Harry asked.

All four police officers looked up at her with renewed interest.

"Do you know something about it, Ms. Hubbley?" Detective Dovercourt inquired immediately.

"I may not be an expert on police procedure, but it doesn't seem normal to send two detectives and two uniformed police officers to look into an accident."

Detective Allan grunted. Detective Dovercourt didn't respond, but she stared so hard at Pearl and Harry that Harry was certain she was homophobic. She couldn't imagine why anyone who disliked gay people would choose to stay in Key West. "Well?" Harry said more sharply than she had intended. She was growing impatient with how the police were treating her.

"Ms. Vernon was right," Detective Allan replied. "Barbara Fenton hit her head on the edge of her bedroom dresser. We won't know the extent of her injuries until she's undergone a more complete examination at the hospital."

Harry shivered. She tried to dismiss the image that instantly sprang to her mind, of Barb falling, falling, falling, clipping her head against sharp, unyielding wood, her neck snapping like a piece of dry kindling as she fell to the floor, flopping like a rag doll —

"Harriet? Are you all right?" Pearl asked anxiously. "Where are you going?"

"What?" Harry mumbled. She had involuntarily sprung to her feet in an attempt to catch Barb.

"Sit down, Ms. Hubbley," Detective Allan requested, his voice genuinely kind. "I realize this is quite a shock, but we've got a few more questions to ask."

The impulse to reach out and save Barb from pain and injury had been overwhelming. Harry took a deep breath and returned to her chair. "I'd like to get this over with as quickly as possible," she said to the detective, suddenly desperate to talk to Judy. She wanted to bolt from the room, find her lover, rush to her car and drive to the hospital. And what about Karen? She would need support, too. "Why do you think she was attacked?" Harry said briskly. "Couldn't it have been an accident?"

"Her bedroom was turned upside-down, so it was pretty obvious that she struggled with whoever assaulted her. There also seemed to be bruising around her neck," Detective Allan replied.

"Like someone was trying to strangle her?" Pearl interjected.

"Could be," the detective said with professional caution.

"She wasn't sexually assaulted, was she?" Pearl asked.

Harry hadn't even thought of that. She took a deep breath and stared at Detective Allan.

"We don't think so, but again, we have to wait for the report from the hospital to be certain," Detective Allan responded. "When did this happen?" Harry asked. "And who found her?" "She was attacked sometime during the night," Allan said. "But we don't know who discovered her. Someone made an anonymous phone call from the pay telephone across the street at precisely four-thirty this morning. Ms. Fenton was found lying on the floor. She was unconscious."

"What did you do last night, Ms. Hubbley?" Detective Dovercourt asked.

"I just got into town late yesterday afternoon," Harry said. She took a deep breath and retraced her steps from the time her airplane had landed at the Miami airport. One of the uniformed police officers took notes.

"So you had dinner with Ms. Fenton, went to a tea dance at La-Te-Da, where you met Mr. Peter Fenton and Mr. Ross Hunter, and later, Ms. Sarah Reid and Ms. Judy Johnson, whom you describe as your partner. Then you came back to the Hideaway and had a few drinks on the patio with Ms. Vernon. You were soon joined by Ms. Alison Wheatley, after which the two of them went swimming, and then Ms. Johnson arrived," Detective Allan summarized. "And after that?"

As if on cue, Judy walked into the room and answered, "Harry and I spent the night together."

Harry felt Pearl remove her hand from her shoulder.

"All night?" persisted Detective Dovercourt.

"We've been lovers for twelve years, so we're accustomed to spending the night together."

Harry looked up at Judy in surprise, which she immediately stifled. "Is that true, Ms. Hubbley? Was Ms. Johnson with you all night?" Allan asked.

"Yes," Harry replied, reasonably certain she was telling the truth. She and Judy had made love well into the night before falling asleep a couple of hours before dawn. It had been the best sex they'd had with each other in months. When it was over, they had been so physically relaxed that Harry didn't see how Judy could have been awake much before she was.

"And neither of you heard anything," Detective Dovercourt said sceptically.

"What do you mean?" Harry asked.

"Barbara Fenton's apartment is next to yours, and from the look of her bedroom, she put up quite a struggle. We found a lamp on the floor, its base and bulb broken, and jars of cream and other articles were knocked off the top of the dresser," Dovercourt said. "And your bedroom backs on hers."

"I didn't hear anything out of the ordinary," Harry responded.

"Me neither," Judy claimed.

Harry glanced at her lover. She had a composed look on her face although there was pallor beneath her tan.

"And you, Ms. Vernon, you claim you were with Ms. Wheatley all night in a room in building three, which is on the other side of the compound, behind the swimming pool," Detective Allan said, consulting his notes.

"That's right," Pearl responded.

Harry turned and looked up at her, but Pearl refused to meet her eyes. Just a swim, she thought scornfully, feeling curiously betrayed.

"Is there anything else?" Harry asked, directing her question at Detective Allan. She was becoming increasingly impatient to get to the hospital.

"I'd like to know more about your relationship with Barbara Fenton," the detective responded.

"We've known each other since we were in university," Harry responded.

"And you, Ms. Vernon?"

"What?" Pearl replied absently. "Oh, we're good friends. Of course, we started as lovers, but it didn't last."

"When was that?" Detective Allan inquired.

Harry had to admire his *sang froid*; it was Detective Dovercourt who was discomforted by Pearl's blatant lesbianism, although Harry would have thought that Allan, as a man, would have been more uncomfortable. But perhaps that was reverse sexism. Then again, maybe Detective Allan was gay. Not that it mattered; the attack on Barb was going to expose them — and their lesbianism — to the harsh scrutiny of a thorough police investigation.

"We had an affair in university," Pearl answered. "That was in England, of course. It was the year before Barb and Harriet were an item."

"Is that so?" Detective Allan asked, looking at Harry with a mixture of disappointment and interest.

"Oops," Pearl said. "Sorry, Harriet. Perhaps I shouldn't have mentioned it."

"That's all right," Harry responded with a glance at Judy, who was studiously examining her lap. "I should have said something about it myself."

"Actually, we're not the only ex-lovers of Barb's staying here at the moment," Pearl commented casually.

"We spoke with Karen Lipsky before she went to the hospital, so we know she lives with Barbara Fenton," Detective Dovercourt interjected.

"Of course," Pearl said. "Everybody knows that. They've been together for years and years."

"Fifteen, to be precise," Harry added. Poor Karen, she thought, hoping she wasn't alone. Would these cops never stop with their questions?

"Is there anyone else?" Detective Allan asked.

Pearl looked as if she regretted having led the conversation in this direction. "Alison Wheatley," she muttered.

"And?"

Were there others, Harry pondered, recalling how she and Barb had joked about Barb convening her ex-lovers at Isadora's Hideaway over March break and Karen's cynical comment about Barb's harem. Ex-lovers were connected to the past, prone to making demands in the present and apt to be part of one's future. Ex-lovers also maintained emotional ties, carried indelible memories, waxed nostalgic on the flimsiest of pretexts, and were capable of holding lengthy grudges.

"I'm not sure," Pearl replied, glancing at Harry.

Who was she protecting, Harry wondered. And why had she looked at her like that?

Detective Allan stared at Pearl for a long time, but Pearl didn't budge. "Perhaps you'll remember after you've had some time to think about it," he finally said. "In any case, we'll want to talk to you again."

"All of you," Detective Dovercourt added, looking from Harry to Judy. "By the way, we've asked Ms. Lipsky to close the guest-house."

"You mean we'll have to move out?" Pearl asked, sounding upset.

"No. But we've strongly recommended that new reservations not be accepted until this matter's been resolved," Detective Allan clarified.

"This was obviously an inside job," Detective Dovercourt added.

Unfortunately, Harry had come to the same conclusion. How many ex-lovers did it take to attempt murder? "Detective Allan," she said.

"What?" he asked, pausing by the open door.

"Was there any sign of forced entry to Barb's apartment?"

"No."

"So Barb let her assailant in."

"It would seem so," he said cautiously.

"Then she knew her," Harry concluded slowly.

"Or him," Pearl added.

"If you want to know the truth, it sounds to me like Barbara Fenton was acquainted to one extent or another with every woman staying at this resort and then some," Detective Allan said with a half-smile.

He was right, Harry realized; several of them, including her, knew Barb as intimately as it was possible to know another woman. And although Pearl wasn't talking, it seemed like there might be at least one other unidentified ex-lover currently staying there. In addition, Barb had told her all thirty rooms were let, so there were anywhere from thirty to sixty women staying at Isadora's Hideaway, and Barb had a roving eye and an uninhibited tongue. "What are you implying?" Harry asked slowly.

"That we've got our work cut out for us," Detective Allan said guardedly, "so we'd appreciate it if you didn't leave town for the moment."

Harry nodded her acquiesence, although she was shocked to realize that she was a suspect. But she and Barb had been lovers, although not recently, and her apartment was next to Barb's. Still, there were other women staying in the guesthouse who were just as suspect. One thing was certain, she reflected as the police left: There were more than enough suspects to go around in this particular case.

5

Judy gave Harry a fierce hug as soon as the door closed behind the police. "I'm so sorry about Barb."

Harry nodded, holding her breath to stop herself from crying.

"I feel like I'm in shock," Pearl commented.

"I think we all are," Harry sighed, disengaging herself from Judy. She felt self-conscious in front of Pearl. "I want to go the hospital."

"Yes," Judy agreed at once. "Give me the keys to your car and I'll back it out while you get dressed."

Harry searched through her purse, found her car keys and handed them to Judy, who left the room after a quick glance at Pearl.

"I'll just be a minute," Harry told Pearl as she went into the bedroom.

Pearl trailed after Harry, plopping down on the unmade bed. "I can't believe someone attacked her," she said, her voice hoarse.

"Neither can I. Look, I've got to get changed," Harry said.

"Hurry up, then," Pearl answered absently.

Harry stared at her for a moment and then turned her back and removed her housecoat. She could feel Pearl watching as she swiftly put on her bra and panties and then a pair of beige linen slacks, a dark brown tee-shirt and, over that, a matching beige short-sleeved jacket. The attraction was still there, but this was not the time to act on or even mention it, and Harry sensed that both of them knew it.

"You look ready for business," Pearl commented as Harry sat down beside her on the unmade bed and fit her feet into her sandals.

"I do," Harry said. She knew from bitter experience with friends who were dying of AIDS that it was best to be equipped to deal with stubborn and insensitive hospital personnel when someone to whom she wasn't related was seriously ill. One way of doing that was to dress well and act confident. Perhaps the Key West hospital would be different because there were so many gay people living in this city, but Harry preferred to be prepared for the worst. "So who else was Barb's lover?" she inquired casually.

"I said I wasn't certain, and I meant it," Pearl responded as she rose from the bed. "I don't want to make unnecessary trouble for anyone."

"You shouldn't have baited the police if you didn't know," Harry said.

Pearl gave an uncomfortable laugh and moved away. "Look, I want to apologize about last night. I know I said it was just going to be a swim. But then you disappeared with the tray and I ended up going back to Alison's for another cognac, and one thing led to another. You know how it is."

"It's none of my business," Harry remarked, and suddenly a weight lifted from her shoulders. It didn't matter whether Pearl had slept with Alison. She'd just met Pearl yesterday, and although she'd been interested in her, she had no business feeling a sense of ownership. Perhaps her perspective had been altered by the attack on Barb. After all, what was a little perfidy when someone had tried to kill her closest friend?

"When was the last time you slept with Barb?" Harry asked, remembering the intimacy she had sensed between Barb and Pearl when Barb had introduced them. And what had Barb wanted to tell her, she wondered suddenly. They'd never kept secrets from each other, so what could it have been? Perhaps Barb had a new lover and she hadn't mentioned her the last few times she and Harry had chatted on the phone because she'd wanted to tell Harry in person.

"You heard what I told the police — when she and I were in university together in Britain," Pearl responded.

Harry was positive that Pearl was lying. "I'm sure Karen would tell me the truth," she said. She hoped her bluff would work because she had no intention of questioning Karen about something so sensitive, at least not until Barb was well on the way to recovery.

"You're probably right," Pearl sighed. "Look, Barb and I ended up in the sack together the night before last, but for god's sake, don't tell the coppers. I'm sure Karen suspected it; lovers have a way of knowing, don't they? Especially since the two of them have been together since the dawn of creation. It didn't mean a blasted thing, of course, it was just a little erotic fun and games. You know how these things happen; one minute you're reminiscing about bygone days, the next you're trying to recreate them with bodies thirty years older. A little more flab, a lot more sag. Or vice versa, depending on genetic factors impossible to control and other imponderable personal propensities."

Harry smiled involuntarily at the image which came unbidden to her mind, although, in her opinion, Pearl's body had held up rather well to the ravages of gravity and middle-age spread. Better than hers, anyway, she admitted ruefully to herself.

"Mind you, it wasn't bad, although I suppose I shouldn't tell you that. Somehow, though, you don't quite seem like the jealous type," Pearl added.

Little did she know, Harry thought, ignoring Pearl's glib comments. It suddenly occurred to her that while she had no reason to believe that the Key West police weren't competent, as an insider, she was in a unique position to conduct her own investigation. It wouldn't be the first time she had done so, with positive results. She changed the subject and asked the question that was really on her mind. "Did you spend the whole night with Alison?"

"What, do you think I attacked Barb?" Pearl asked, trying to hide her disappointment. "Well, I didn't. I was with Alison Wheatley, and although I'm not particularly proud of that fact, it's the truth. I'd rather have been with you, of course, but there it is. Anyway, I'd better be going."

"I'm sorry — don't be offended," Harry said, exasperated with herself. Was she apologizing for not acting on her attraction to Pearl, or for suspecting Pearl of harming Barb?

"I'm not. I'll see you at the hospital," Pearl replied wearily.

"But I thought you were coming with us — "

"No, I'll go on ahead," Pearl interrupted. "I've got a few things to think about and I'm sure you and Judy would prefer to have a little time to yourselves." And with that, she left the room.

Pearl was right, of course, Harry reflected. She hurried into the bathroom, splashed lukewarm water on her face and ran a hand through her unruly hair, an act which only made it look worse. Now that she was alone, she could think only of Barb. She couldn't believe that Barb was so badly hurt — not Barb, who was so humorous, generous and spirited. Wasn't it strangers who became victims of violence, not dear friends?

"Aren't you ready yet?" Judy asked, popping into the bedroom.

"Just about," Harry replied, taking her lover in her arms, searching for comfort. "Have you seen Karen, or has she gone to the hospital?"

"I think she left a while ago," Judy responded, pulling back to look into Harry's face.

"I hope she's not alone," Harry remarked. She retrieved her purse from the sofa and they hurried from the guesthouse.

"Pearl's quite attractive, isn't she?" Judy commented as she turned the key in the ignition, put the rental car in gear and eased into traffic.

"Yes," Harry nodded, knowing there was no point in lying.

"I wish we could work things out," Judy said suddenly. "I think the only thing standing in the way is your jealousy."

"You've been known to feel that way yourself," Harry replied, opening the window and feeling hot air wash over her.

"I know," Judy admitted. "But at least I deal with it rather than letting it fester. Would you mind closing the window? I've got the air conditioning on."

"Anyway, I don't think that my jealousy is the only problem in our relationship," Harry said, pressing the button and watching the window silently roll up.

"Perhaps not, but your jealousy is incomprehensible," Judy continued. "You've been attracted to other women all along, and once I got sexually involved with someone else, so did you."

"That was more of a reaction than anything else," Harry pointed out.

"But you enjoyed it," Judy said as she swung into a street under construction, braked, made a three-point turn and headed in the opposite direction. "Why is it difficult for you to accept it? It's been over two years now and we're still together, so why do you always feel so threatened?"

"I can't help it."

"Sometimes I think you don't want things to work," Judy said, distractedly running her fingers through her long hair.

"That's not true," Harry insisted as they pulled into the hospital parking lot. "Look, two years ago you unilaterally changed the rules. You wanted the freedom to explore your feelings for other women. That was hard enough for me to deal with, but then you became involved with Sarah, which was even more difficult. But what's worse is that most of the time we don't talk anymore."

"That's not entirely my fault," Judy said, backing the car into a parking space.

"I didn't say it was," Harry said impatiently as she opened the car door. Hot air instantly rushed in and she broke out in a sweat. "I'm trying as hard as I can, but I'm not sure that you are."

"You wouldn't leave me over this, would you, Harry?"

Leave? Did Judy think things had deteriorated to that extent? The thought made Harry's mind reel. She turned and looked into her lover's brown eyes. "No. But we have a lot of work to do."

Judy's eyes dropped and they briefly hugged each other before getting out of the car.

"By the way, where were you this morning? You were gone when I woke up," Harry asked as they walked toward the emergency department.

"I was hungry so I went to the kitchen to see if I could find something to eat," Judy answered, handing the car keys to Harry.

"But we had that tray of juice and croissants," Harry persisted. She held the door open for her lover and followed her into the hospital.

"I know, but we forgot to cover them with anything or put the juice in the fridge, so the rolls were as hard as rocks and the juice was warm," Judy explained. "Why, do you think I had something to do with what happened to Barb?"

"No!" Harry protested a little too vehemently.

"Oh, Harry," Judy said, her voice sad. "I figured that you'd want to find out who tried to kill Barb, but please don't suspect me."

"Sorry," Harry muttered for the second time that morning, although she felt just as exasperated with herself as she had the first time. "But the fact is, the police are going to suspect everyone who stayed overnight at the Hideaway."

"That's their job. But I'm your partner, and I don't appreciate you suspecting me," Judy responded sharply. "I woke up starved and went to look for something to eat, that's all. Anyway, I'm sure Barb will wake up any minute now and tell the police who attacked her."

Harry saw Karen sitting at the far end of the waiting room, which was nearly filled with people, many of them half asleep. "Karen!" Harry exclaimed, rushing toward her. "How's Barb? Are you by yourself?"

"Pearl's gone to find a doctor," Karen replied lethargically, rising from the plastic chair. Harry give her a fierce hug, which wasn't returned in kind. She must still be in shock, Harry thought.

"And Barb?" Harry asked as Karen and Judy hugged.

"Not good," Karen sighed, sitting down again. She was wearing a black, paint-stained tee-shirt over black walking shorts, her hair was dishevelled and there were dark shadows under her eyes.

Pearl ushered a tall, thin woman with long, grey, fuzzy hair into the waiting room. Karen stood up again and approached the doctor, who was wearing a threadbare lab coat. A stethoscope dangled around her neck. "This is Dr. Albertini," Pearl announced.

"How is she, doctor?" Harry asked.

"As well as can be expected," the doctor said evasively.

"We're all close friends of hers," Harry said hastily, hoping to avert a pithy and likely alienating remark from Pearl.

"And I'm her partner of fifteen years," Karen announced, making heads turn in the waiting room.

"Isn't there somewhere more private we can go to discuss this?" Judy asked.

"We don't really want to involve our lawyer," Pearl added softly.

Dr. Albertini looked at them. "Fine," she finally said. "Ms. Fenton has what is commonly known as a broken neck."

"But she will be okay, won't she?" Harry asked.

"We're not certain," the doctor said cautiously. "She's in a coma."

Karen made a noise low in her throat and sat down.

"But there's no permanent damage, is there?" Pearl inquired swiftly.

"We don't know yet."

"You mean she might be paralysed?" Judy wanted to know.

"It's going to take time to discover these things," the doctor answered.

"But when's she going to wake up?" Harry asked.

The doctor's expression made it clear that she didn't know that, either.

"Shit," Pearl muttered.

"She wasn't sexually assaulted, though," the doctor reported.

It was the only good news Harry had heard all day. "We'd like to see her," she said firmly.

The doctor hesitated and then said, "She's in intensive care. You can go in, one at a time, for five minutes only."

They all looked at Karen.

"I don't want to be alone," Karen murmured. Her eyes shifted from Pearl to Judy and finally settled on Harry, although the expression on her face indicated that Harry was the best of a bad lot. "I'll go with you," Harry said. "Where's intensive care?"

"I said one —"

"I know what you said, but Ms. Lipsky doesn't feel up to going in by herself. I'm sure it isn't the first time something like this has happened, either," Harry said firmly. "Now, where's Barb?"

Dr. Albertini pursed her lips, but led them from the waiting room to the elevator. She pressed one of the buttons and the door closed with a nearly silent burp. Harry stared at the shiny metal walls and breathed slowly, trying to ignore the distinctive hospital smells.

"This way," the doctor said. She took them down a long corridor and pushed open a heavy door, gesturing for Harry and Karen to follow. Harry grasped Karen's arm and then entered intensive care. The pungent odour of disinfectant couldn't completely mask the smell of illness, bodily functions gone awry, death. "Five minutes," the doctor warned, leading them into a cubicle which contained a narrow hospital bed, banks of flickering monitors and several IV poles from which various tubes dangled.

A police officer — a woman — was seated in the corner where she could see both Barb and the door leading to the hall as well as a second door which Harry assumed led to other rooms in intensive care. "Don't touch her," the police officer warned.

"How inhumane," Karen remarked harshly as she and Harry approached the bed.

"Someone attacked her once and they may try again," Harry said, relieved that the police had taken security measures.

"Oh, god," Karen whispered, staring down at her lover.

Barb was so still that at first Harry thought she was dead, but then she saw the slow, regular rise and fall of her chest. There was a breathing tube inserted in Barb's mouth and IV lines snaked under the sheet on both sides of the bed. Her skin was pale, almost translucent, and her eyes were closed. Salve had been rubbed on her open lips to prevent them from cracking, and on her eyelids, too. She looked insubstantial, strangely reduced.

"Hello," a nurse said.

"Hi," Harry replied, her voice hoarse. Nothing had prepared her for the sight of someone she loved lying there like that.

"Are you members of her family?"

"Yes," Harry replied. "Sisters."

"I wish we could touch her," Karen said.

"I wish you could, too," the nurse responded. "But the police have requested that no one but medical personnel touch her for the moment. But you can talk to her, and that's important."

"Wake up," Karen said suddenly, bending over Barb, grasping her shoulder through the sheet and giving it a violent shake. "Wake up, goddammit!"

"Karen!" Harry exclaimed, rushing to stop her, but the police officer was faster. She pulled Karen away from the bed.

"You heard me. Touch her again, and I'll eject you," the officer said firmly.

"I won't," Karen promised.

The police officer released her and went back to her chair, but she didn't sit down.

"That kind of behaviour won't help at all," the nurse said gently. "Even if she can hear you, she might not be able to respond."

"But when's she going to wake up?" Karen groaned as she collapsed against the wall.

Harry looked helplessly at the nurse.

"Her lover?" the nurse asked in a low voice as she smoothed the sheet covering Barb's body.

"Yes," Harry admitted warily. She reached out and clasped Karen to her side, feeling her body tremble.

"It doesn't matter to me," the nurse murmured.

Harry glanced at her name tag. Amy Lomans. "That's good, because they've been together for fifteen years."

"It's been well over five minutes," said Dr. Albertini as she came back into the room.

"But — "

"I know you want to stay, but she's still critical," the doctor interrupted Harry. "Critical but stable," she added when she saw the stricken look on their faces. "Look, you can visit often if you like, but you mustn't stay long. And only family members and close friends. It's for her own good, you know."

Harry nodded, bit her lip and stared at Barb, wondering where she was. What did it mean to be in a coma, anyway? "Thank you," she said, more to Amy Lomans than to Dr. Albertini, but the doctor didn't appear to notice. "We'd better leave now," Harry said to Karen.

"She's going to be all right, isn't she?" Karen said with a backward glance.

"Yes," Harry replied with more certainty than she felt. "I'll be right along," she said. She watched until the door closed behind Karen and then approached the doctor. "Can I speak to you for a moment?"

"What is it?" the doctor asked. "Look, I know it seems like we might be holding back, but you have to realize that in cases like this, we all have to wait — "

"It's not that, doctor," Harry interrupted. "Someone tried to kill her, and I'm worried about them trying again. I mean, she wouldn't be able to protect herself, would she?"

Dr. Albertini put her file down on the wheeled table. "No. Obviously not. That's why they put a guard in the room with her."

"Twenty-four hours a day?"

"That's what I was told," Dr. Albertini answered.

Relieved, Harry rejoined Judy, Karen and Pearl and waited while Pearl and then Judy visited Barb. Each of them offered to stay at the hospital with Karen, but Karen was adamant about returning to Isadora's, at least temporarily. "What's the point in staying here if I can't be with Barb all the time? I can feel just as miserable at the guesthouse as I can at the hospital. Besides, it's not that far to come. I'll drive over in an hour or two and see her again."

And so they returned to the Hideaway.

"Would you mind if I go see how Sarah's doing?" Judy asked Harry once they had parked the car.

"You're still planning to stay with me, though, aren't you?" Harry queried somewhat hesitantly.

"Of course. It's just that I don't think I should leave Sarah completely alone."

But Harry didn't want to have to fend for herself, not even for a minute. All she had ever wanted in life was to find a woman to love. Sharing time and affection had never been part of her concept of what a long-term relationship was all about.

"I'll be back soon," Judy assured her.

"Fine," Harry responded. She would not beg. It didn't work, anyway. She had tried it a couple of times and all it did was leave her with a bad taste in her mouth and the feeling that she had compromised her dignity.

"I love you," Judy said.

"I know," Harry said, but, privately, she wondered whether that was still enough.

As soon as the door closed, she went into the bathroom, stripped, and took a shower. Nothing moderate ever happened in Key West, she thought as hot water streamed over her shoulders. Everything was intense, erotic and torrid, including the weather, the food, the music, the women, the sex. No wonder Barb had felt comfortable enough to settle here after years of roaming the world. Key West had a soul as expansive as hers.

Harry stepped out of the shower, towel-dried her short, blond hair and combed it into submission. Then she returned to the bedroom, dressed in shorts and a white tee-shirt and left her apartment before she had the opportunity to think. She knew that if she stopped to reflect on Barb in her coma or ponder her problems with Judy, she'd hole up like a hermit when what she really wanted to do was to ferret out Barb's assailant.

Several women were seated in the breakfast nook, but Harry wasn't hungry. It wasn't quite noon, but it was already hot and the humidity was high. There wasn't a cloud in the sky. She sat on a deck chair and tried to collect her thoughts, but they wouldn't come together. She was too upset. Some people insisted that adversity gave meaning to life, but Harry believed that was a rationalization. What meaning would there be in spending the rest of your life in a coma, or in being paralysed? Or in being attacked, having your neck broken, hanging on to life by a thread for a certain amount of time and then finally dying?

Both the AIDS and breast cancer epidemics had made death a personal enemy of Harry's. She hated it with a passion, especially when it robbed her of someone she cared about. Perhaps it was ironic, then, that in the past few years she had investigated two cases of suspicious death. But maybe it wasn't ironic at all; murder was intolerable precisely because it deprived the victim of life.

"Harry?"

"Karen," Harry said with a start. "I thought you'd be resting."

"I tried, but I can't seem to settle down," Karen said, alighting on another deck chair. "I keep thinking of Barb lying there not able to move or say anything and it drives me nuts. The police won't let me into her apartment or the office."

"I suppose they're not finished with them yet," Harry responded. The midday sun was directly overhead, and she was sweating.

"I told them I needed to get into the office as soon as possible, and anyway, what do they expect to find there?"

"I guess they're searching her files in the hopes of coming up with something."

"They said they'd be finished later this morning," Karen said. "And they did agree to let me turn on the answering machine once they'd listened to the messages which were already on the tape. They want me to close the guesthouse, too, except for the people who are already here. I suppose it'll be simpler that way, but I've got so much to do."

"Things will work out," Harry said, wondering for the second time that day why Karen had chosen to turn to her for help. Karen didn't even like her.

"God, but it's hard to believe she's in the hospital in a coma. It hasn't sunk in yet. I guess that's because we weren't together every minute of the day and night. Sometimes she had something going with another woman and sometimes I did, and days could go by when I'd only see her in the office or we'd wave to each other across the patio. Or I'd go off on a painting jag and not want to see another living soul until I'd worked it out of my system, which could take days. I feel like that now, you know. She could just be preoccupied with a new lover and be back in a couple of days, a week at the most. But I don't know why I'm telling you all this."

Harry wiped the sweat from her forehead and sighed. It was a mystery to her, too.

"Maybe she'll never be back again, though," Karen murmured, rocking back and forth. "Maybe she'll be in a coma for years and die without waking up."

Harry opened her mouth and closed it again. "I'm sure she'll be all right," she said eventually. "I bet she'll wake today or tomorrow and tell the police who did this to her," she added with false cheerfulness. But what if she didn't? What would happen then? "Did Barb leave a will?"

"Yes," Karen answered. "We both prepared wills, powers of attorney and living wills. But I don't have a copy of hers. I never did, actually. The police haven't found one among her things yet, but that's not surprising. Barb wasn't the type to leave important documents lying around the guesthouse. They're trying to track down her lawyer, but it's Sunday and apparently he's not answering his messages. Oh, god, what a mess," she moaned, tears spilling from her eyes and running down her cheeks. "I have to close the Hideaway, but it's high season and all the other guesthouses are full, so where am I going to send all the women who've made reservations? Even if they have empty rooms, the regular motels and hotels are a lot more expensive. Most people will probably be quite understanding, but some of them might sue."

"Oh, I rather doubt that," Harry said automatically.

"I can't run the place all by myself or get in touch with everyone who's made reservations," Karen sniffed. "Would you help until I get things sorted out?"

Harry was taken aback by this sudden request from someone who usually acted as if she didn't exist. "But I don't know anything about running a guesthouse."

"I'll teach you what you need to know, and anyway, it's just until Barb gets back. Look, I realize that we've never been close, and you probably know I'm not all that fond of you. You've always been just another one of Barb's hangers-on, after all."

"That's not true," Harry said vehemently. "Barb and I are good friends."

"And lovers," Karen added.

"In the old days."

"Now."

"No we're not," Harry insisted, but it didn't do any good. She could tell that Karen didn't believe her. The whole thing was untenable; Karen would never trust her enough to leave her in charge of the guesthouse, so why was she bothering to ask?

"It doesn't make any difference. The thing is, there isn't anybody else I can ask," Karen replied. "Pearl and I don't get along."

"So I noticed," Harry said. Pearl had this way of being in your face. Just like Barb, actually. They must have been quite a pair in their day.

"I don't think Barb and Pearl ever really broke up," Karen continued. "Whenever Pearl came to visit, it took about twenty-four hours for them to hop in the sack together."

"Really," Harry said. So what had happened on this visit hadn't been an aberration even though Pearl had tried to make it seem that way.

"Didn't Barb ever tell you?"

"No," Harry answered, feeling more surprised than she let on. She'd believed that she and Barb hadn't kept secrets from each other but apparently she'd been wrong. And not only that, Pearl had lied to her. "How often did they see each other?"

"Pearl came down to visit at least twice a year," Karen responded.

"Where does she live?"

"New York," Karen answered. "They were too much alike to stay together for long, though."

"I can see that," Harry said. Both of them were opinionated, assertive, idiosyncratic and incredibly sensual. Constantly having to bargain with a mirror image must have been as aggravating as hell. A woman with charisma would never willingly choose to cohabit with her counterpart. It would have driven both of them crazy. "I wonder where Pearl went?" Harry asked.

"I don't know, and frankly, I don't care," Karen responded bitterly. "As far as I'm concerned, she can go to hell."

Harry had no response to that. Death was too close for her to wish hell on anyone.

"You think I'm overreacting, don't you?" Karen asked.

"You're upset," Harry said. How could she criticize Karen when she had sometimes experienced the same sentiments about Sarah?

"I'll bet she attacked Barb," Karen muttered.

"What?" Harry exclaimed with shock although she had had the same thought herself.

Just at that moment, Judy and Sarah approached them from the main building.

"Karen, I'm so sorry," Sarah said.

Karen rose from the deck chair and the two women embraced, and then, to Harry's surprise, kissed full on the lips.

"Hi," Judy greeted Harry.

"Harry's going to help me run the guesthouse," Karen told Sarah.

"You're what?" Judy said.

"Don't sound so surprised," Harry said, slightly irritated by Judy's incredulity. She led Judy away from Karen and Sarah and added, "I know that, basically, she hates my guts, but she's desperate and I didn't know how to refuse. Anyway, it's just until they find Barb's lawyer and sort out her power of attorney and all that."

"I suppose Karen's the beneficiary of Barb's will, so I guess she'll be named to manage her affairs," Judy commented.

"I would imagine so," Harry replied.

"Harry, the police seem to be finished with the office, at least for the time being. Do you think you could give me a hand right now?" Karen asked.

"Sure," Harry replied, glancing at Judy.

"Sarah and I are going for lunch. We just dropped by to see if you wanted to join us," Judy said. "I'll be back later."

Harry nodded and followed Karen from the patio into the main building to the office, wishing she'd been able to leave with Judy but relieved that she hadn't had to have lunch with the two of them. She'd promised to help Karen, so help her she would, leaving her ambivalence intact for another day.

"Dammit, Karen, why did Peter have to learn that Barb was at death's door from the police instead of you?" Ross Hunter raged.

"I tried to call you — "

"Apparently not hard or often enough," Ross interrupted, his voice icy.

Why did men take up so much more space than women, especially when they were angry, Harry wondered. She could almost smell his rage as he leaned over Karen, who was seated at Barb's desk in the small office.

"It's been rather hectic around here," Harry told him, pondering whether men were normally permitted to enter Isadora's Hideaway and then deciding to leave that decision to Karen.

"Hectic? His sister's been brutally attacked and you're talking about things being hectic?" Ross roared at her.

"Now, Ross, they've had to deal with the police, and all that — " Peter began uncertainly.

"Do you think I give a shit?" Ross retorted.

"*Enough!*" Harry shouted firmly, using the tone of voice she employed with her students when the moon was full and they were on a rampage or when one of them had decided that physical education classes were the pits and was threatening to stop participating in them ever again. That kind of adolescent hysteria was only a state of mind, but it could spread in seconds and result in revolts of the most embarrassing dimensions.

Ross Hunter shut up, a startled look momentarily crossing his face. "How dare you talk to us like that," he protested after a pause. "Peter's only sister is in a coma!"

"His only sister also happens to be Karen's partner of fifteen years," Harry retorted, rising from the chair behind the desk where Karen had been showing her how to use the computer's reservation software to check guests in and out.

"Never you mind," Ross said haughtily. "We'll see what's what after the power of attorney's been activated."

"What are you talking about?" Karen asked sharply.

"What do you think?" Ross said. "Peter is Barb's only living relative."

"I'm not going to sit here and listen to this crap," Karen said angrily.

"There's no point to all this hostility," Harry remarked evenly as Karen pushed past Peter and Ross and left the office.

"She started it," Ross replied petulantly.

"Everyone's under a lot of stress," Harry pointed out. "And it didn't help for you to speak to her the way you did."

"I'm certain Peter will be in charge," Ross said arrogantly, "so she might as well get used to him being the boss. I told the police as much, and it's only a matter of time until they find Barb's lawyer."

"We don't know that for sure, Ross," Peter said tersely. "Besides, Barb could wake up any minute."

Privately, Harry thought Ross was living in another dimension if he truly believed that Barb planned to leave everything to her brother, especially power of attorney during her temporary incapacitation. She recalled how annoyed Barb had been about his habit of sponging off her, and said, "I think you're presuming too much."

"Unfortunately, Barb never has been all that crazy about me," Peter said forlornly.

"What, do you think she wants Karen to have everything?" Ross asked incredulously.

"Maybe," Peter admitted, looking down at the floor.

"Perhaps not everything, but a major share," Harry said.

"Like hell," Ross said scornfully.

"But we don't really know, do we, sweetie?" Peter replied softly.

"I'll wait for you outside," Ross said.

Peter made a face, sat down in the chair Karen had vacated and took a pack of cigarettes from his shirt pocket.

"I'm afraid there's no smoking in here," Harry said, her voice not entirely unsympathetic as she pointed to the sign affixed to the wall. She was an ex-smoker herself, and knew how strong the urge to smoke could be in stressful situations.

"Never mind — there aren't that many places where you can smoke, even down here," Peter sighed, pushing his cigarette pack into his pocket.

"How true," Harry replied. "Smoking today is like sex in the fifties."

"I guess," he said. Only then did Harry realize that he was quite a few years younger than she was, and, by extension, than Barb.

"I can't believe she's really in a coma," he said.

"I feel the same way," Harry replied. "Have you been to see her?"

"Not yet. I've grown rather allergic to hospitals over the years," Peter said with a wistful smile. "Besides, we've never been close," he continued, rubbing his cigarette lighter with his thumb. "She's ten years older than me, so by the time I reached my teens, she had already left home."

"I didn't know that."

"But everyone was always telling me about her," he said with a cheerless chuckle. "Holding her up to me when I flunked courses or goofed off or got into trouble, which happened frequently. I was a pretty wild kid. I suppose they thought comparing me to Barb was for my own good, but eventually, I came to dislike her intensely. It was like she'd been put on this earth to make me look bad. Do you know what I mean?"

Harry smiled and nodded. She'd never had any personal experience with this sort of ordeal, but she'd taught many students who had lived through similar personal hells. They were rigid, competitive and aggressive, although they crumbled the minute they were challenged. Poor kids, she thought, thinking of the dozens of students who'd stood up on their hind legs and confronted her because they were angry about never being the best, at least in their own minds.

"I got in touch with her once I was out on my own, but we didn't see each other all that often," he said. "Not in the beginning, anyway. She was always living in out-of-the-way places that I couldn't afford to visit."

"I know," Harry replied. "I didn't see her often in those days, either. I remember when she moved to Paris and lived in a garret on bread and cheese and red wine for two years and before she'd been back in Montreal for more than a month, she suddenly got in her car, drove down to Mexico and rented a shack on the outskirts of a small town and proceeded to stay there for nearly a year."

"I wonder why she could never settle down in one place for any length of time?"

"Wanderlust, I suppose. She once told me that she relished the excitement of waking up in the morning and knowing she was going to learn something new that day, or meet a character she had only read about in a book, or eat exotic dishes and learn how to cook them or see spectacular scenery. When she no longer woke up feeling excited, she knew it was time to move on," Harry replied.

"That sounds just like her," he commented.

"And she never got homesick or lonely or felt any discomfort about being in strange places," Harry added, wishing she could be more like Barb. Harry preferred to be at home in the cosy, second floor walk-up she and Judy rented in downtown Montreal than on a crammed, bacteria-filled plane on its way somewhere exotic where she couldn't speak the language or drink the water and where she wouldn't be able to relax because everything was different and she felt just a little bit scared.

"She's been here for over eight years, though," Peter said.

"She's always loved Key West," Harry responded. "She said it was the only place she'd ever been where you could sit on the beach or in a bar and wait for the world to come to you. Especially people. She loves meeting new people and finding out what makes them tick."

"That would be mostly women, I suppose," he said with a restless laugh, tossing his cigarette lighter in the air and catching it on the way down. "Look, would you mind stepping outside so I can have a cigarette?"

Harry wondered whether she was responsible for answering the telephone should it ring, or being in the office to answer guests' questions. Karen hadn't actually told her she was on duty before she'd gone to her room. "Sure. Why not?" she responded, deciding it was important not to pass up the opportunity to spend time with Peter Fenton. After all, as Barb's brother and a possible heir, he was a prime suspect. She had to interrogate all the suspects, and as swiftly as possible, for Barb was lying in a coma in a hospital bed, vulnerable to another attempt on her life if the police officer protecting her let up her guard or was outwitted by an assailant desperate to silence Barb before she woke up.

"Good," he said, getting up from his chair. "I'm about to have a nicotine fit." As they sat outside on the steps, he remarked, "You know, I used to think that the fact that both Barb and I were both gay would make a difference, but it didn't, even when our parents died and she and I were the only ones left."

It was a beautiful afternoon. The sun was beating down and wisps of clouds floated lazily across the tropical sky. How could the sun shine like this when Barb was lying in a sterile hospital room halfway across town with tubes pouring various liquids into her veins, Harry wondered, sneezing from the cigarette smoke. "Sometimes I think gay people develop different definitions of family because our blood relatives frequently disown us," she commented.

"But I don't think Barb ever liked me much, and she always despised Ross," Peter said without so much as a tinge of regret in his voice. "It was hate at first sight when I introduced them."

"How long have the two of you been together?" Harry asked.

"Nearly five years," Peter said, his voice atypically devoid of pride, which surprised Harry, since gay and lesbian couples were usually pleased about the length of their relationships.

"Frankly, we've had a lot of ups and downs. He's a bit prickly, as I'm sure you can tell. But he's had a rough time in life," Peter explained. "He's also fifteen years older than me, and that makes him feel a little insecure."

Who was Peter trying to fool, Harry wondered. Ross seemed like a first-class jerk as well as a misogynist, although misogyny might not be a problem for Peter. She found Ross to be an unsavoury character, much like one of those oily villains in silent movies, and she wouldn't put it past him to attack someone who got in his way or who annoyed him just a little too much. Peter was another matter; he seemed caught between his sister and his lover's dislike for each other and more bemused about his role in life than anything else. Harry surmised that he wandered passively through life, taking whatever was given him and protesting only mildly when things went wrong. "What do you do for a living?" she asked.

Peter chuckled and tossed his cigarette butt in the gutter. "Do you mean my sister didn't tell you?"

Nothing she wanted to repeat, Harry thought, shaking her head negatively.

"I'm in sales," Peter said, glancing at her as he lit another cigarette.

"What kind?"

"Actually, I'm not working at the moment," he admitted. "There are a couple of possibilities, but nothing firm. I'll know in a few weeks, though."

"And Ross?"

"Ross rather old-fashionedly calls himself a man of independent means," Peter replied, "although the income he gets from an old family trust doesn't permit us to maintain the lifestyle to which we've become accustomed. In fact, we'd starve if one of us didn't get a job now and then."

Or sponge off Barb, Harry thought as the phone in the office rang. "I'll be right back," she told Peter as she rushed inside, answering it on the third ring. It was a woman calling from Fort Lauderdale to see if they had any rooms available for next week. "Hold on," Harry requested, stumped by that question. How long did the police want the guesthouse to remained closed? As long as it took them to find out who had attacked Barb, she thought. She made an executive decision and told the caller that they were fully booked.

When she got back outside, Ross had joined Peter on the stairs. They were sitting off to the side, both of them smoking. "So what did you two do last night, anyway?" Harry asked casually as she smiled at two young women running up the stairs. "If you need anything, just ask — I'm taking a little break," she called to them.

"We're just fine, thanks," one of them answered.

Harry's question had obviously annoyed Ross, who jumped to his feet. "Are you accusing Peter of — "

"I was being sociable, that's all," Harry said firmly. "We met at the tea dance, and I just wondered whether you went off to the bars after."

"We didn't leave the La-Te-Da until the dance ended around nine," Ross responded. "And then we went back to our motel and went to bed."

"Together?" Harry couldn't resist inquiring, looking at Peter.

"What the hell do you think?" Ross asked testily.

"Come on, Ross, lighten up," Peter cajoled. "She was just teasing."

"That's right," Harry reassured him. Still, they didn't really have an alibi, she thought as she looked more closely at them. They were handsome, Ross traditionally so, Peter in a more effete way. They were dressed in white trousers and shirts with rolled up sleeves. They were both fashionably muscular, as if they worked out regularly, something which so many gay men had done since the advent of AIDS, as if crosstraining and looking healthy could stop the virus. Sort of a modern day garlic necklace or rabbit's foot, Harry mused.

"Are you two still here," Karen commented, letting the door slam behind her as she walked out on the steps.

"Let's go," Ross said, reaching down for his lover's hand. "There's no point in hanging around where we aren't wanted."

"Where are you staying?" Harry asked Peter as they both rose to their feet.

"At the Atlantic Shores Motel," Peter replied. "It's just around the corner on South Street."

"Come on," Ross said impatiently, tugging on his arm.

"I'll see you later," Harry said, waving as the two men jaywalked across Catherine Street.

"I hate that bastard," Karen muttered as she watched them leave.

"Ross?"

"Yes. He's been such a bad influence on Peter," Karen replied. "He used to be a nice, sweet boy who was a little in awe of Barb, but once Ross sank his teeth into him, he decided that the world owed him a living."

"Specifically Barb," Harry remarked.

"You got it," Karen said.

"Someone called to see if there was a room available for the middle of next week," Harry said, "and I told them there wasn't."

"Fine. I was a bit worried that we'd have a mass exodus because of what happened to Barb. So I went back to the patio to chat with some of the guests to reassure them that everything was okay, I don't think anyone's planning to check out, but there are a few nervous nellies around," Karen said.

"There always are. But you should get some rest," Harry suggested.

"I don't think I could sleep," Karen said. "Do you mind if I go back to the hospital?"

"Of course not," Harry hastened to reply. "I'll mind the office."

"Thanks," Karen mumbled. "Maybe you could cancel some reservations. All the information is on the computer."

"Perhaps someone should go with you — "

"I actually prefer to go by myself," Karen interrupted. "There isn't anyone I want around."

How dismal, Harry thought as Karen walked away. But who would she want to comfort her if something happened to Judy?

The afternoon passed rapidly. Harry became proficient in checking out women who had come to the end of their vacation in Key West as well as the few nervous nellies Karen had mentioned and in fielding numerous phone calls from women all over North America as well as a couple from Europe. She liked chatting with departing guests, who were invariably appreciative of the efficient and friendly service they had received at Isadora's Hideaway and pleased with the good times they had had in Key West. A few of them asked Harry about what had happened to Barbara Fenton, as most of them had met her at some point during their stay at the guesthouse, and Harry chose to be honest rather than to attempt to hide the fact that she had been attacked.

Harry also had time to call women and cancel reservations for the next two weeks. Again she told them the truth and gave them the toll-free telephone number of the Gay West Business Guild, a gay business people's organization which could help them find another place to stay.

A few guests who had chosen to remain came by the office. Their main concern seemed to be whether the police would make an effort to be unobtrusive or whether they would be clumping through the hallways and the patio at odd hours of the day and night when women might be socializing or skinny-dipping. Harry tried to reassure them that, to her knowledge, the police were being understanding, but she couldn't guarantee that this situation would continue forever. "Who could?" one woman had responded with a rather laconic nod.

"If things change and you want to leave, we'll provide you with a full refund and help you find another place to stay," Harry reassured her. She hoped that Karen wouldn't mind her promise of a full refund, but it felt right to her. Anyway, lesbians were fairly calm souls, and she didn't expect anyone to run screaming from the guesthouse should a cop or two appear.

By early evening, the majority of guests planning to check out had done so, and Harry settled into a relaxed routine of answering the phone and making conversation with guests who were on their way out for the evening. She discussed the pros and cons of countless restaurants listed in various guides to the city, wishing she had more information on each of them and wondering whether Barb and Karen had made a point of dining out regularly so they could reply with authority when guests inquired. She gave directions to the main tourist attractions and gay bars, relieved that she had visited Key West before and was thus familiar with the layout of the city. And sometimes she just stood in the doorway of the office and chatted with someone who seemed a bit lonely, suggesting that they rent a VCR and video if they didn't feel like going out or that they charter a moped and take a drive around town.

"Who's in charge here?" a voice interrupted her during a momentary lull.

Harry turned and saw Alison Wheatley push through the front door and stride toward her, followed closely by a portly, middle-aged man. Great, she thought, stifling a sigh of resignation. "Hi, Alison. Karen's still at the hospital with Barb."

"Do you know that I went all the way over there and they wouldn't let me in to see her? The gall," Alison raged.

"She's seriously ill," Harry rebuked her mildly.

"I realize that, but she and I were close," Alison insisted. "In any case, I need to see someone in charge right this very minute."

"Well, here I am," Harry replied as her nose began to twitch from Alison's perfume. What did she do, take a bath in it?

"But you've nothing to do with this place, you're a guest just like me," Alison protested.

"Karen asked me to help," Harry said patiently.

"What's the problem?" asked Alison's companion, a tanned man who appeared to be in his late fifties. He was dressed in tight shorts and a golf shirt which revealed a slice of protruding belly. Although he wore a baseball cap, his face, arms and legs were so deeply tanned that if his skin hadn't been smeared with an oily lotion, it likely would have cracked like water-starved soil.

"Karen's not here," Alison complained.

"And meanwhile, I'm taking care of things," Harry offered reluctantly as she sneezed again, wondering for the second time that day whether it was permissable for a man to be in the Hideaway. Karen hadn't protested Ross and Peter's presence, so perhaps they were allowed as far as the office. "Why don't you come in and we'll talk about it?" she suggested, gesturing to the office.

"She's invited us into the inner sanctum," the man said in a stage whisper to Alison, who tittered, much to Harry's disgust. Her own personal feelings aside, how could Pearl have stooped so low?

"This is my Martin," Alison announced as Harry sat behind the desk, pushing a pile of papers to the side. Several files fell to the floor, but she didn't retrieve them. She hated messy desks, and if Barb was going to be in the hospital for more than a few days, she intended to ask Karen if she could do a bit of filing and otherwise bring some order to the office.

"Nice to meet you, Martin," Harry said politely, extending her hand.

"Martin Culver, actually," Martin said, giving Harry's hand a brisk shake.

"So, what can I do for you?" Harry said, resisting the urge to wipe her oily fingers on her clothes. She rubbed her hands together under the desk, spreading what she hoped was suntan lotion until it sank into her skin, and then searched through her purse for a tissue.

"Well, you see, I feel quite nervous about staying here now that Barb's been attacked. It's much too dangerous, if you know what I mean, especially since I'm by myself," Alison explained as she sat down. The smell of her perfume settled over Harry like a shroud and her eyes immediately began to sting and her sinuses to ache.

"It would be different if we were together, because then I'd be able to protect her," Martin interjected, sitting beside Alison.

"And?" Harry asked more sharply than she'd intended as she recalled Pearl's speculation about Alison and her boyfriend looking for a willing bisexual woman with whom to have some sexual fun and games. She also marvelled momentarily at the size of Martin Culver's ego, wondering how he intended to ensure his lover's safety by the simple fact of his presence. She glanced ostentatiously at her watch in the hope that they would take the hint and leave before she developed a full-fledged sinus headache.

"I'm going to check out, but I need help finding somewhere to stay for the next two nights," Alison implored, leaning forward in her chair. "You see, Marty has an apartment a couple blocks away, but the plan was for me to stay here for three nights and then move in with him for the rest of my vacation."

"Why can't you move in with him now?" Harry asked with an audible sniff, absently opening the top desk drawer. It was so crammed with papers and unopened envelopes that she could barely close it again. Poor Karen, she thought; she was going to have her work cut out for her.

"She can't," Martin said impatiently. "Look, I don't think you understand."

So now they were even, Harry thought, opening the second drawer, which was full of files.

"Marty's girlfriend isn't going on vacation until Tuesday," Alison confided.

"I see," Harry said, stifling an urge to grin. "I'll check you out right now, then, and give you the address and phone number of the Chamber of Commerce. I'm sure they'll be able to help you find a place to stay, especially if it's just for two nights."

"Can't you do it for me?"

"Actually, it would be better if you drove over there and consulted their lists," Harry suggested. "They might also be able to give you some pointers."

"With everything we have in common, I thought you'd be much more sympathetic," Alison said plaintively.

"What?"

"Well, both of us were once intimate with poor, dear Barbara," Alison reminded her. "And you and Pearl certainly looked chummy enough last night until I came along."

Martin smirked until he saw the expression on Harry's face. "I'll wait outside so you gals can have a little chat and work things out," he said hastily, rising from his chair and leaving the building.

"You don't like men, do you?" Alison said suddenly.

Not that particular specimen, that was for certain, Harry thought sharply as she blew her nose. "That has nothing to do with this, although it certainly isn't true," she responded tiredly, locating Alison's file in the computer and noting that she had paid by credit card for three nights. "I'll ask Karen to reverse the charges on your credit card for two nights," she added.

"Thank you," Alison said. "The police — stupid dolts that they are — told me not to leave town, otherwise I'd run over to Marathon and stay there for the next few days. I knew cops were dumb, but this takes the cake. I mean, why should they suspect me when I've only seen Barbara Fenton once since that year in university in Montreal? Actually, Marty's more upset than I am, but I think that's because I slept with Pearl."

That made more sense to Harry than anything Alison had said yet. Now that they were alone, Harry decided to take the opportunity to question Alison; after all, she was one of Barb's ex-lover's and she'd been at the Hideaway last night, so she'd had the opportunity to attack Barb. "Perhaps the police think it's too much of a coincidence that you decided to stay in the guesthouse owned by your former lover," Harry commented, playing devil's advocate.

"*What*? But when I saw her in Dallas last year, she said to hunt her up if I ever came to Key West," Alison protested.

"Quite a coincidence, actually," Harry continued, pretending that she hadn't heard what Alison said.

"No it's not," Alison protested. "Martin winters here every year and we've been lovers for a long time, now."

"But you have to admit that your choice of Isadora's Hideaway is curious, to say the least," Harry insisted.

"What are you implying?" Alison asked haughtily.

"Oh, nothing. I was just thinking out loud. Are you certain that you and Barb weren't involved in any hanky-panky in Dallas?" Harry asked.

"You're nuts!" Alison exclaimed, rising from her chair. "And I don't have to sit here and listen to this insulting crap for one second longer."

"Of course you don't," Harry said with a smile. "But I'm sure the police would be interested in knowing that you and Barb resumed your affair just last year. And then what happened? Did you come here thinking everything would be like it was in Dallas and that you could get a little on the side while you were waiting for Martin's girlfriend to clear out? It must have been quite a shock when you discovered that Barb wasn't interested because she had other fish to fry. Did you have a little spat last night in her room and try to strangle her?"

"How dare you!" Alison sputtered, her face reddening. "All right, so Barb and I had a little fling in Dallas, but it didn't mean a thing. I've always thought of myself as bisexual, although I haven't had much experience with women. Barb brought those feelings back, and I didn't hesitate to act on them. But I didn't come down here to get reinvolved with her, I came to see Marty. Now, if you'll excuse me, I've wasted quite enough time on this," Alison added as she turned to leave.

"Here's the address and phone number of the Chamber of Commerce," Harry said, holding out a piece of paper.

"Stuff it," Alison said succinctly.

The door slammed hard enough to rattle the glass in the window. Harry grinned, tossed the piece of paper into the garbage can and answered the ringing telephone.

"I'm looking for a Ms. Harriet Hubbley," a man said.

"That's me. How can I help you?" Harry asked guardedly.

"I'm Porter Ambrose, Barbara Fenton's lawyer," he said. "I wonder if you'd mind coming by my office?"

Harry shifted the receiver and leaned back in the chair. "What for?"

"There are a few things I'd like to talk to you about, but I'd rather not discuss them over the phone," he replied.

Harry was curious but reticent. "I don't know. I've got to look after the guesthouse — "

"It's important, Ms. Hubbley," he interrupted.

Harry stewed in that for a moment, and then said, "All right."

"Good," Porter Ambrose said. Before hanging up, he gave Harry his address.

His office was just down the street, so Harry decided to walk. She gathered up her purse and locked the office door, wondering why Barb's lawyer wanted to see her. Hadn't the police been looking for him to discover who had Barb's power of attorney? Porter's office was located over a trendy boutique which sold native art. The side door was open. She climbed a flight of stairs and walked along a hallway painted a chalky white until she reached a door that had the name "Porter Ambrose" written on it in ornate gold script.

"Thank you for coming," Porter said, shaking her hand. He led her through a tiny office with no windows. It was empty at the moment but Harry assumed it was normally occupied by his secretary. He ushered her into a much larger office which was obviously his. The walls in both offices were painted the same colour as the hall, although the stark expanse of chalky white was alleviated by several large abstract paintings on the wall, all of them bright with primary colours. The furniture, including a leather sofa tucked in one corner and two leather armchairs facing Porter's desk, was black, as was the desk itself. A white leather chair was posed behind the desk. It was all very dramatic.

"Have a seat," Porter said, sitting in the white leather chair and fussing over a pile of papers. He was a short, plump man in light brown pants and a white shirt open at the collar and he was obviously agitated.

Harry sat in one of the black leather chairs and waited.

"This is all very unusual," he declared, finally having chosen the documents he wanted.

"Perhaps you should tell me about it," Harry suggested.

"Perhaps I should," he agreed with a worried smile. "In the first place, I'm pissed as hell that someone attacked Barb."

"You and me both," Harry said, suddenly feeling all choked up.

He studied her for a moment and then consulted his files. "Well. Where shall I begin? And don't say at the beginning," he added swiftly, "because it would be bloody facetious."

Harry realized then how angry he really was. "I have no intention of saying anything of the sort," she asserted. "All I want to know is why you asked me to come here."

"Do you love her?" he asked suddenly.

"Yes," she said without hesitation.

"Me, too," he said gruffly, putting down his papers. If he'd worn spectacles, this would have been the moment he'd have taken them off and laid them on his desk.

"I take it there's a problem," Harry said gently, hoping to spur him on.

"It's like this," Porter began. "Barb has a living will, a document stipulating power of attorney and a will, as do most sane gay people these days. Her living will contains all the usual things, such as what should be done under certain circumstances and not done under others, but it also contains a rather unusual clause, which I argued with her to drop, but to no avail."

Harry waited for him to tell her what that unusual stipulation was, but he didn't.

"But before we go into that, there's her power of attorney," he said, "and that involves you."

"I don't understand," Harry said, growing alarmed.

"She's given you power of attorney," Porter said, sounding almost apologetic.

"What?"

"It's true, Ms. Hubbley," Porter said earnestly. "I've got the documents right here."

Harry didn't bother look at them.

"I take it you didn't expect this," Porter commented.

"Hell, no," Harry replied emphatically. "I must be the only ex-lover Barb hasn't gone to bed with since the old days."

"Perhaps that's why," Porter said pointedly. "But back to her living will."

Harry nodded, although she wasn't sure why one followed from the other.

"The unusual proviso in Barb's living will states that her will must be read if she's incapacitated in a manner which leaves her incapable of managing her own affairs," Porter explained. "And again, that implicates you."

"What on earth are you talking about?" Harry asked.

Porter sighed. "She's leaving you a fifty percent share in the guesthouse and the bulk of her estate, which is worth about three hundred thousand dollars. Because they're interested in finding out how all the principals will react, the police are insisting that the conditions of Barb's living will be fulfilled to the letter, which means that her will be read publicly, or at least in front of her relatives and friends."

"I don't believe it," Harry sputtered. "Three hundred thousand dollars?" She'd earned a teacher's salary for years, but in spite of her best intentions, she had never managed to put much away. Money slipped through her fingers as if they were greased. As well as having to pay the customary credit card and utility bills, she seemed to incur unexpected expenses on a regular basis. She took vacations during which she invariably spent more than she had budgeted for, her deteriorating car habitually ate more than its fair share of her earnings, and there was always another invoice lurking somewhere on her desk for an item she had purchased through the mail or bought on impulse but didn't really need. She was a typical middle-aged, middle class lesbian, no different from most of her friends. Some of them had even less than she, but a disturbing number had managed to scrounge up enough cash for a down payment on an inner-city condo or a house in the suburbs. Equity, they called it. Planning for the future. Sometimes it bothered Harry that she and Judy were nearly fifty and had hardly anything in reserve. All Harry possessed was a small retirement savings plan which she thought about once a year, when her accountant berated her for making such puny contributions. And here Barb was planning to leave her nearly everything, Harry thought, impatiently wiping the tears from her eyes before they cascaded down her cheeks.

"I hadn't realized that you didn't know anything about any of this."

"Well, I didn't," Harry responded. She searched through her purse for a tissue and blew her nose.

"This must come as quite a shock," he replied, sitting back and looking at her. "But I'm afraid you'll have to deal with it rather swiftly. Look, what I'm really quite perturbed about is the police wanting Barb's will read to all and sundry. After all, she's still alive."

"What about the provision in her living will?"

"There is that," he agreed. "But it goes against my instincts as a lawyer to have the contents of one of my client's wills read before that client dies."

Although Harry didn't know much about legal matters, she'd never heard of a will being read while the person was still alive. "I don't want to sound uninterested, but what does this legal conundrum have to do with me?"

"Barb entrusted you with power of attorney and her will makes you her main beneficiary," Porter responded. "I therefore decided that I should consult you before I got back to the police about whether or not I was willing to participate in the reading of the will or whether I'd inform them that I'd require a court order."

"What do you think I should do?" Harry asked. "I mean, if I say I don't want the provisions of the will made public, won't the police think I've got something to hide?"

"I hesitate to advise you about this, as you're not my client and I don't want to say anything which might prejudice your decision," Porter said as he shuffled papers.

"I'd like to engage you, then," Harry said at once.

"Did you attack Barb Fenton?" he asked.

"No," she said emphatically. "I most certainly did not."

He looked at her for quite a long time and then nodded. "Fine. As you are my client, I feel bound to tell you that whether you agree to let them read the will or not, you're a prime suspect in this case. And even if we inform the police that we don't think it would be appropriate for the will to be read, they could probably get a court order to proceed anyway."

"Because Barb wanted it to be read if she was incapacitated," Harry said.

"That's right," Porter answered.

"They might as well go ahead, then," Harry decided.

"I agree, but I don't like it," Porter grumbled. "Exceptional circumstances or not, it's just plain irregular."

Harry was having trouble taking in the enormity of what Porter had just told her. Power of attorney ... the main beneficiary of Barb's will ... the leading suspect — the only mitigating factor was that while the will was being read, she'd be able to watch the other suspects and see their reactions. She could search for clues, she thought, as Porter picked up the telephone, dialled a local number and mumbled into the receiver. If she was ever going to discover who assaulted Barb, she was going to have to find out who had the most opportunity and the strongest motive. "Who else stands to inherit if Barb dies?"

"Karen Lipsky gets a half share in the guesthouse plus twenty thousand dollars. Her brother Peter Fenton and Pearl Vernon — have you met her?" Porter paused to ask, and then continued when she nodded. "Well, they both get twenty thousand."

No wonder the police considered her their main suspect, Harry thought with no little bemusement.

"How about a coffee? We've got half an hour before we have to head down to the police station," Porter said.

"Coffee would be fine," Harry replied. "But why are we going to the police station?"

"Oh, didn't I tell you? That's where the will's going to be read."

This way, Ms. Hubbley," Detective Allan said as he hovered in the doorway.

"Detective Allan," Harry greeted him as she squeezed past. They were on the second floor of the police station, which was air conditioned to the point of being too cold. She was alone, having left Porter downstairs with Detective Dovercourt.

"I was wondering when you'd show up," Alison said, slumping in her chair. Martin Culver was sitting next to her, trying to look haughty and detached but failing so abysmally that he resembled a trapped weasel more than anything else. Perfume wafted in Harry's direction, making her sneeze. She took a packet of tissues from her purse, selected one, and blew her nose. Then she sat on the chair furthest away from Alison, although the room was so small that it didn't help much.

"It's getting rather crowded in here," Alison commented as a rather pale looking Peter Fenton and an exceedingly irritated Ross Hunter were ushered into the office by a uniformed police officer.

"They found Barb's lawyer," Peter said. "I think they're planning to read the will."

"They can't do that," Martin said, jumping up and hopping around like an agitated bantam rooster. "I might not be a lawyer, but I know damn well that a person's got to be dead before the will can be read."

"Everyone just relax," Detective Allan said.

"But what the hell are we doing here?" Martin asked plaintively, switching tactics. "I never even met Barbara Fenton and Alison's got nothing to do with any of this — she's straight, and I'll swear to that in court."

"Don't listen to him, detective. I've got it from a good source that she's screwed every second dyke in town," Ross Hunter interjected.

"Christ!" Martin Culver exclaimed, balling his fists at Ross. Ross gazed disdainfully at him.

Harry stifled a laugh, sneezed and then stood up. "I think I'll wait outside," she said to Detective Allan.

"I'd rather you stay here," the detective responded.

"I'm violently allergic to her perfume," Harry said, gesturing to Alison just before she sneezed three times in rapid succession.

"All right," Detective Allan agreed reluctantly.

Harry opened the door and went out.

"It's the goddamn day of reckoning," Pearl commented as she walked unsteadily down the hall.

"What's the matter with you?" Harry asked.

"Oh, hi darling," Pearl responded, draping her arms around Harry's neck.

"You've been drinking," Harry said, unable to hide the reproach in her voice.

"I readily confess," Pearl responded, backing off. "I had a few in my room. Is that a problem?"

"I don't know," Harry answered equitably. "Is it?"

"I normally enjoy riddles, but I'm not into solving them today, not even with you, special as you are," Pearl rejoined cheerlessly.

"Sorry," Harry muttered. Pearl was old enough to make her own decisions. And she wouldn't be the first woman with a drinking problem to whom Harry had been attracted. Then again, perhaps Pearl had simply been letting off steam.

"That's all right," Pearl whispered, bending over to kiss her.

"Jeez, Pearl, we're in a police station!" Harry exclaimed, pulling away.

"But there's nobody around," Pearl said with a laugh.

Harry could hear people coming up the stairs, and she tried to compose herself.

"And I thought we were late!" Judy commented as she spotted Harry and Pearl. Sarah followed closely on Judy's heels.

"I'm surprised they asked you to come," Harry remarked, managing to give them both a smile.

"I was in the guesthouse overnight, so I guess I'm just as much of a suspect as the two of you," Judy responded with a glance at Pearl.

Before Harry could respond, Karen rushed up the stairs. "Damn," she said as she approached them. "I hate police stations."

The door opened and Detective Dovercourt's head appeared. "It's time, ladies."

The five of them filed into the room. Harry leaned against the wall a few feet from the door so that she could see everyone's face. She crossed her arms and tried to look casual, hoping Detective Allan wouldn't make her go sit with the rest of them.

"Thank you all for coming," Detective Allan said, looking around the room.

Harry felt his gaze linger on her and resisted the urge to avert her eyes. Fortunately, he didn't say a word.

The door opened and Detective Dovercourt led Porter Ambrose into the room. Porter was carrying a fashionably worn leather briefcase in one hand and an unlit cigar in the other.

"Mr. Porter Ambrose is Barbara Fenton's lawyer," Detective Allan announced. "He has graciously agreed to come here today to impart to us the details of Ms. Fenton's power of attorney even though it's on very short notice."

"See?" Martin hissed at Alison. "I told you he couldn't read her will unless she was dead."

Detective Dovercourt glanced at Martin but refrained from saying anything.

Porter Ambrose cleared his throat. "I'd like to extend my sympathies to Ms. Fenton's extended family and friends and to say that I'm sorry to be here under these circumstances," he said solemnly.

Harry looked up, saw that he really meant it and warmed to him again.

"I'm sure we're all wishing for Barb's speedy recovery and for her return to active life," Porter continued. "Meanwhile, she wisely made provisions so that there would be continuity in her business affairs should she be incapacitated."

He paused and Detective Allan interjected formally, "I have just returned from the hospital, and we have in our possession a letter signed by Dr. Anna Albertini which states that, in her professional opinion, Barbara Fenton is not currently capable of making reasonable or rational decisions about her own affairs because she's in a coma of indeterminate length."

"Thank you, Detective. I met Barb Fenton shortly after she moved to Key West and we've been good friends every since," Porter continued. "Although I'm personally reluctant to tell you this, as Barb's lawyer I believe that it's time to activate Barb's power of attorney."

There was an almost imperceptible rustle of anticipation in the room as he unfolded several pieces of paper. "As you may know, power of attorney simply gives one or more people the legal right to act on someone's behalf. In this case, Barbara Fenton has indicated that power of attorney be vested in one person, and that person is Ms. Harriet Hubbley." He paused again.

Alison Wheatley gasped in disbelief. Karen looked stunned. Pearl glanced at Harry with a half-smile on her face, while Judy and Sarah appeared distracted. A self-deprecatory grin curled Peter's lips.

"As for the provisions in Barb's living will, it's quite clear that she didn't want any extraordinary measures used to keep her alive if she was suffering from a terminal illness or had been the victim of an incapacitating accident," Porter continued as he refolded the document.

"But she's on life support right now," Pearl protested. "It's not going to be turned off, is it?"

"Of course not. According to Dr. Albertini, there's potential for recovery, and they're going to attempt to remove the respirator tomorrow," Porter explained. "She's not brain dead, which is one of the legal definitions which comes into play in cases like this."

Harry's stomach sank. What if Barb never woke up? Would she eventually be called upon to decide whether Barb lived or died?

"Ms. Hubbley, are you willing to accept the responsibility Barb has entrusted in you?" Porter asked.

"I am," Harry replied apprehensively.

"Fine," Detective Allan said. "And now there's the matter of Ms. Fenton's will."

Everyone began to talk at the same time.

"But you can't read her will while she's still alive," Karen protested.

"Yes, as Barb's only living relative, I strongly protest," Peter added.

"Enough," Detective Allan barked. "Mr. Ambrose, would you explain the situation?"

"I'd rather you do it, sir," Porter answered, his expression impassive.

Detective Allan glanced at the lawyer and scowled. "Ms. Fenton's living well contained an extremely unusual clause stipulating that, in the event that she was massively incapacitated, either through accident or illness, her will was to be read."

"Jesus!" Ross exclaimed. "Why'd she do something stupid like that?"

"More to the point, why'd you let her?" Pearl asked Porter, who raised his arms and lowered them again.

"Did any of you ever succeed in stopping Barb from doing something she was determined to do?" Porter asked. This question effectively silenced them.

"Mr. Ambrose has already voiced his grave reservations, and we've taken them into account," Detective Allan said. "But we believe that Ms. Fenton's instructions should be followed."

"Do you think it'll help you find Barb's assailant?" Judy asked.

"It might," Detective Allan replied warily.

"And what do you think?" Karen asked Porter.

"They could be right," Porter answered evenly. "If financial gain was the motive for the assault, that is. But I still think it's highly irregular."

"Then why aren't you challenging it?" Ross asked.

"For two reasons: first, Barb was adamant about having that clause in her living will, and secondly, Ms. Hubbley, who holds power of attorney, agreed in an earlier meeting that Barb's wishes should be respected and that the will should be read," Porter responded.

"You've known about this all along?" Karen asked, her eyes narrow with anger.

"I informed her of the situation just before this meeting," Porter interjected smoothly.

"Perhaps she might like some time to reconsider," Karen said.

"That's not necessary," Harry replied.

"Fine," Karen said with a shrug.

"We have your permission, then," Detective Allan verified.

"Yes," Harry responded.

"Do it," Karen said harshly.

"Why not just invite the whole town?" Pearl said sarcastically.

"Does that mean you're for or against it?" Porter asked, a twinkle in his eye.

"Guess," Pearl rebutted dryly.

"Could we proceed, please?" Detective Allan requested, sounding impatient for the first time.

"Splendid," Porter said. "I assume my objections have been duly noted?"

"Yes," Detective Dovercourt responded curtly.

"Good," Porter said. "Look, I'm not going to read all the sound body and sane mind clauses, if you don't mind. It's sufficient to say that while they're rather wordy, they're quite standard and legally correct. I'd rather get to the salient points, and I suspect you'd prefer me to as well."

"Fine, fine," Karen said hoarsely.

"I want to remind you that this is all quite hypothetical, since Barb is still alive," Porter said, his voice thin.

"Get on with it, man," Ross urged.

"Don't," Peter uttered.

"'To my close friend Pearl Vernon, I leave the sum of twenty thousand dollars,'" Porter Ambrose read.

"You've got to be kidding!" Martin Culver squawked as if he had been nipped in the heel by a sharp-toothed terrier. Alison poked him in the ribs with her elbow, everyone else pretended that they hadn't noticed his outburst.

"'To my only surviving blood relative, my dear brother Peter Fenton, whom I have supported liberally during my lifetime, I leave the sum of twenty thousand dollars,'" Porter continued, his voice reedy.

"That's *it*?" Ross said, astounded.

"That would be fine," Peter said swiftly.

"It most certainly would not," Ross insisted.

"We'll discuss it later," Peter cajoled, although he sounded disappointed.

"Well, boys, don't mind us," Pearl commented caustically. "We're just along for the ride."

Ross glared at her.

"Mr. Ambrose?" Detective Allan prodded.

"Yes, yes," the lawyer said. "The next clause reads, 'To my long-time companion, Karen Lipsky, I leave the sum of twenty thousand dollars and a fifty percent share in the guesthouse located in Key West and known as Isadora's Hideaway, deed and other identifying documents attached, etcetera, etcetera.'"

"Fifty percent?" Karen exclaimed, gazing around the room. "I don't understand."

"Don't look at me," Peter commented bitterly.

"Or her, thank god," Ross added, gesturing to Pearl, who opted for dignity by ignoring him.

"But what about the other fifty percent?" Karen asked, directing her question at the lawyer. "Who does Barb plan to leave that to?"

"I'm just coming to that," Porter responded. "It's right here at the end, and it reads, 'To my dear friend Harriet Hubbley, I leave a fifty percent share in the guesthouse located in Key West and known as Isadora's Hideaway, deed and other identifying documents attached, and the bulk of my estate.'"

9

"I don't believe it," Karen said, her voice faltering as she turned and looked at Harry. "And you knew about this."

"Only since earlier today," Harry replied.

"What about me?" Alison wailed. "I can't believe that Barb isn't planning to leave me anything."

"I'm afraid she isn't, Ms. Wheatley," Detective Allan responded blandly.

"Then why did you make her sit through this?" Martin complained.

"Because of Ms. Wheatley's relationship with Ms. Fenton," the detective replied.

"But why her and not me?" Alison protested, gesturing at Harry.

"Precisely my question," Ross trumpeted, rising from the sofa. "From what I understood, Barb was planning to leave Peter more than twenty thousand dollars, and we'll be discussing this with her as soon as she wakes up. Come on, Peter, let's get out of here."

"Wait a minute," Peter cautioned, grasping Ross's arm. "Barb hasn't cut me out of her will altogether, you know. And she never really said exactly how much she was planning to leave me."

"You've just seen the future, Peter, and you've been royally shafted. Are you telling me that you're going to accept it?" Ross asked, turning his anger on his dumbstruck lover. "I'm going to give Barb such a piece of my mind — "

"Stop it!" Harry exclaimed bitterly, outrage energizing her. "Barb's lying in a coma in the hospital and all you can do is argue about who's going to get what if she dies."

"Hear, hear," Alison commented sarcastically.

"Oh, fine," Ross sniped. "It's all right for you to say that, but what about us?"

Harry opened her mouth but remained silent when she saw the rest of them staring at her.

"Well, detective, I don't think you have to look much further to discover who assaulted Barbara Fenton," Alison said as she moved toward the door.

"Just hold on a minute, here," Harry said, feeling so shocked that she broke out in goose bumps. "I didn't know Barb was planning to leave me anything until Porter told me less than an hour ago."

"Oh, sure," Ross scoffed.

"Fat chance," Martin added sourly.

"I certainly don't have to put up with insults like this," Harry asserted, walking toward Judy and putting her arm through hers.

"You really didn't know?" Judy faltered.

"Of course not," Harry said impatiently. Judy was staring at Sarah, who was with Pearl. Both of them were fussing over Karen. Oh, great, Harry thought; if Barb died, she would be the usurper while the rest of them would *deserve* what they inherited. Well *bullshit*! If Barb meant for her to have half of Isadora's Hideaway, then so be it.

"I for one will *not* be visiting you in jail," Ross declared dramatically.

"How can I express my appreciation for that fact?" Harry retorted.

"Oh, christ," Ross said. He punched open the door and strode through it, followed by Peter, who gazed hesitantly behind him, obviously uncomfortable with his partner's belligerent attitude. He established eye contact with Harry for a second, shrugged sheepishly and left.

Harry watched the lemmings follow Peter and Ross from the office. Alison Wheatley and Martin Culver left without a backward glance, their shoulders stiff with anger.

"I'll be back," Judy said, freeing herself from Harry and walking over to Karen, Sarah and Pearl. Pearl detached herself from the group and approached Harry.

"I suppose you intend to desert me, too," Harry said angrily as Pearl drew near. "Oh, lord, I don't really mean that," she sighed. "I'm just overwhelmed."

"I know," Pearl sympathized. "That's why you're being confrontational."

"What?"

"It's quite understandable that you feel defensive," Pearl said soothingly.

Harry was not consoled. "I don't feel defensive."

"Of course you do," Pearl replied sedately. "I certainly would in your situation."

"What are you talking about?" Harry sputtered.

"Whether you really knew what was in Barb's will," Pearl replied, her expression unfathomable.

"Well, I didn't," Harry retorted angrily. Did everyone distrust her?

"Stop sulking," Pearl scolded. "You can't blame people for being resentful, after all. Barb led Peter to believe he'd get something substantial if she died before him, and Karen feels that she's been betrayed. She needs a shoulder to cry on, so I've offered mine."

How was Karen ever going to be able to choose from all those shoulders, Harry wondered cynically? "I'm out of here," Harry said to Porter, who was hovering near the door.

"I'd like to speak with you," Detective Allan said.

"Of course," Harry responded, watching Pearl return to Karen's side, where Judy and Sarah already hovered. All she wanted was to get out of there. "Later."

"No, now," he insisted.

Detective Dovercourt went over to the group of women clustered around Karen, but before she could say anything to them, they began to move toward the door.

"We're going for coffee with Karen," Judy told Harry gently as the others left the room. "I'd like to invite you along, Harry, but under the circumstances — "

"It's all right," Harry interrupted. "The police want to talk to me anyway."

"Maybe I should stay, then," Judy said, looking at detectives Allan and Dovercourt.

"Mr. Ambrose, I don't think we require your services any longer," Detective Allan said politely.

"I've engaged Mr. Ambrose," Harry interjected as she reached out and squeezed Judy's arm. "I'll see you later, okay?"

Judy looked worried, but she nodded and left.

"You thought it necessary to consult a lawyer?" Detective Dovercourt asked.

"Barb entrusted me with her affairs until she's recovered, and I'm not particularly well-versed in legal or financial matters, especially here in Florida," Harry replied. "So this is for her good as well as my own."

"Shall we sit down?" Detective Allan asked.

Harry and Porter sat facing the two detectives.

"Did you know about the contents of Barbara Fenton's will before Mr. Ambrose told you?" Detective Allan asked.

"Or about the power of attorney or her living will?" Detective Dovercourt added.

"Of course I didn't," Harry replied.

"That's rather difficult to believe," Detective Dovercourt responded.

"But it's the truth," Harry insisted.

"Barbara Fenton drew up a new will just last month," Detective Allan said. "Before that, the bulk of her estate had been divided equally between Peter Fenton and Karen Lipsky, with Fenton inheriting her investments and Lipsky the guesthouse and cash, and twenty thousand to Pearl Vernon and to you. As you can see, her new will drastically changed that, so it seems peculiar that she didn't tell you anything. Or call to ask if you wanted to run a guesthouse or let you know that she planned on leaving you a significant amount of money."

"Well, she didn't," Harry responded, clasping her hands together to stop them from shaking when she realized how strong her motive must seem to the police.

"She didn't call or write to tell you that she'd amended her will in your favour?" Detective Allan persisted.

"No."

"Don't you think that's rather strange?" he asked.

"Perhaps she planned to discuss it with me during my current visit," Harry suggested reasonably. "Or maybe, like most people, she made her will without really thinking that it was going to be read soon. Anyway, Barb is quite capable of acting in an arbitrary fashion. But then, you don't know her," Harry replied with the ghost of a smile.

"No we don't, so perhaps you'll explain what you mean," Detective Allan requested.

Harry wondered how she could describe a lesbian who was gifted with a *joie de vivre* and a wicked sense of humour not to mention a well-developed sexuality and a penchant for complex relationships. "She's independent, determined, involved," she began, and then stopped because she couldn't find the right words. "Look, this is extremely frustrating for me. As I told you before, Barb and I were lovers in university, but that was only for a year. And although we didn't see each other often after we graduated, we remained close friends." Kindred spirits would be a better description, but Harry supposed the police would have no understanding of what that could mean between two women. Barb had been her first lover, and even now Harry could remember the intensity of their relationship. First loves should be exceptional and Harry had been fortunate that hers was. She closed her eyes momentarily as a wave of sorrow washed through her. Would she ever again pick up the phone and feel that particular warmth when she realized Barb was on the other end of the line? Or walk into a room after months of separation and be enveloped in Barb's welcoming arms? If Barb remained in a coma or, heaven forbid, died, an enormous chunk of her past would be amputated.

"You mean that you're in touch on a regular basis," Detective Allan said.

"Yes."

"Often?"

Harry thought back. "We usually call each other on special occasions. Birthdays, holidays or when something significant happens in our lives. I don't know how many times, I never kept track."

"We can check your phone bills," Detective Dovercourt said evenly.

"As for writing letters, I'm better at it than Barb is," Harry continued, refusing to be provoked by the police officer. She wondered whether the police in Montreal would soon be asking Bell Canada for a record of phone calls she and Judy had made. It didn't matter, she decided; she had nothing to hide. Still, she didn't like the idea of the police poking into her private affairs. "Barb's more likely to pick up the phone and talk for a couple of hours."

"Did you speak with her in the last month?" Detective Dovercourt inquired as she turned the page in her notebook.

"Several times," Harry confirmed. "Judy and I were planning our trip down here, you see."

"And Ms. Fenton didn't mention that she'd changed her will," Detective Dovercourt said with obvious scepticism.

"No," Harry said emphatically.

"What did you talk about, then?"

"I told you — we were planning our trip," Harry repeated. "Look, it was all very ordinary; we spoke early in the new year about whether March break was a good time for us to visit, and then I suppose I called her again once we had made our reservations to let her know exactly when we were coming."

"What do you mean, you suppose you called her?" Detective Dovercourt asked.

"I didn't keep a log of how many times I called and what each call was about," Harry replied impatiently. "I mean, sometimes one of us would just pick up the phone and call for no particular reason. Isn't that what friends generally do?" she added peevishly, directing her question at Detective Dovercourt, who chose not to reply. "Do you have any other questions?"

"You said this morning that you spent the night with your partner, Judy Johnson," Detective Allan said.

"That's right," Harry replied.

"The whole night?"

"Yes," she affirmed.

"Did you spend any time sleeping?"

"Well, yes," she admitted. When Porter Ambrose took a deep breath, she realized that she had given the police an important piece of evidence they could use against her or Judy. They'd just lost their alibis. But it was the truth, she thought; she and Judy hadn't made love all night long. Ninety-nine out of a hundred couples who claimed they did would be lying. Besides, why should she hide that fact from the police? She hadn't done anything wrong and she most certainly hadn't attacked Barb.

"So Ms. Johnson slept, too?"

"I suppose so, but you'll have to ask her. I couldn't watch her while I was sleeping, could I?" she asked in an attempt at levity which fell flat on its face.

"Then either of you could have left your suite," Detective Allan surmised.

"But we didn't," Harry replied. Or at least *she* hadn't, Harry thought guiltily, although she was still reluctant to tell the detectives that Judy hadn't been there when she woke up this morning. She could and did suspect Pearl Vernon, Peter Fenton and Ross Hunter, Alison Wheatley and even Karen Lipsky, but not her lover Judy, whom she had known and loved for twelve years. Under no circumstances could she entertain the thought that Judy was capable of hurting anyone. It was too painful. "Now, is there anything else?"

"Not at the moment," Detective Allan responded.

All four of them rose from their chairs and left the room. Detective Dovercourt guided them down the stairs to the front door, and turned away with a curt nod.

"The feeling is mutual," Harry muttered at the detective's receding back. She turned to Porter. "I don't know about you, but I could really use a drink."

"That's quite understandable," he replied, glancing at his watch. "It's nearly seven o'clock. Did you have lunch before you came over to my office?"

"No," Harry said. "But I'm not really hungry."

"You have to keep your strength up," Porter admonished her. "Why don't you join me for dinner? My boyfriend's on duty tonight and I hate eating alone."

"Where would you like to eat?" Harry asked as they left the police station. It was still hot and sunny outside.

"If you don't mind somewhere informal, we could just drive over to the restaurant at the Atlantic Shores Motel," he suggested, lighting his cigar.

"Fine," Harry replied. "Could you take me back to the Hideaway so I can change?"

"No problem," Porter smiled. He extinguished his cigar when they got into his car.

"Would it be a problem if Judy came along?" Harry asked. "If she's back from having coffee with Karen, that is."

"Of course not," Porter assured her as he pulled up in front of the guesthouse. He waved his cigar in her direction and said, "I'm dying for a good, long smoke, and that's not meant as an joke. I'll wait for you out here."

Harry hurried to her suite, disappointed to find it empty. Judy, Pearl, Karen and Sarah could have decided to have dinner together, she thought, or they could have realized their basic incompatibility and split up after coffee. She scribbled a note for Judy on a piece of paper she tore from her address book and left it propped up against the mirror on the dresser. Then she changed, wondering as she shed her shorts and slid into black jeans whether she should be minding the office. She went into the bathroom and combed her rebellious hair, startled by the dark circles under her eyes. The hell with it, she thought as she left her suite. The guesthouse would have to fend for itself until she and Karen sorted things out.

This is just what I needed," Harry said with a sigh as she pushed away her plate of chicken wing bones and licked her fingers. They were seated at a patio table adjacent to the sidewalk, and in spite of her anxiety about Barb and her fatigue, she couldn't help but be amazed at the gay scene happening in front of her. Gay and lesbians couples sauntered hand-in-hand, singles cruised on skateboards or on in-line skates, while others loitered under the tropical sun as it moved slowly toward the horizon. It was wonderful, Harry thought as she took a sip of white wine which had been perfectly chilled before being served.

"Well, I always say that there's nothing like food to make you feel better," Porter commented as he forked the last few ketchup-drenched French fries from his plate into his mouth. "Although my lover Jock certainly doesn't agree with me. He's a doctor, by the way."

"So he makes you eat leafy things and lots of dark vegetables the rest of the time, does he?" Harry queried with a half-smile.

"What do you think?" Porter responded as he finished his beer.

"I think that you're a very nice man and Barb's lucky to have you as a friend," Harry said softly, picking up her wine glass and draining it.

"She obviously thinks a lot of you, too," he said, blinking back tears. "And I can see why."

"But didn't she tell you why she changed her will?" Harry asked. "And why didn't she get in touch with me?"

Porter gestured at the waiter and once he had his attention, pointed at their empty glasses. "She didn't say a darn thing," he replied, shrugging in apology. "I was sort of surprised, because you know what she's like. She'd call periodically and rant with reckless abandon about something, usually that she and Karen weren't talking yet again and that she wanted to write her out of her will. I'd convince her to think it over for a day or two and of course she'd calm down and I wouldn't hear another word about it until the next time. The same thing would happen on a regular basis with her brother, who would have sucked up her money faster than she made it if his lover had any say in the matter. Peter is sweet, but he's weak, and Ross is such a despicable character," Porter said with a shudder as the waiter served their drinks.

"But you talked her out of that, too," Harry commented.

"I didn't try to talk her out of anything," he answered. "When she was angry, I just took everything she said with a grain of salt, which gave her the opportunity to let things settle a bit before she finally made up her mind. Actually, most of the time I don't think she had any intention of changing her will. She was just using me as a safety valve to blow off steam. It's a good thing, too. Otherwise I'd have been rewriting it every other month."

"But that still doesn't answer my question about why she changed her mind and decided to leave me half the guesthouse," Harry said, running her fingers up and down the stem of her wine glass.

"I know," he sighed. "Unfortunately, that was the one time she wasn't particularly forthcoming. She simply asked me to make the changes without giving any reasons for them and then came in a few days later and signed it. The only thing I can tell you is that she didn't seem upset. In fact, it was just the opposite. I don't think I'd seen her in such a good mood for ages."

Harry frowned.

"I'm sorry I can't be more helpful than that," he said.

"That's all right," Harry replied. "I wonder who knew she'd changed her will."

"The police were interested in the answer to that question, too," Porter added.

"The police are interested in everything," Harry said calmly. What a cosmic joke. Barb would think her status as a suspect was hilarious.

"Since you've been given power of attorney, you're soon going to know more about Barb's affairs than I ever did," Porter commented.

"But I've never done anything like this before," Harry protested. "And I don't know a thing about Florida law."

"Don't worry — I've got lots of written documentation about your duties and responsibilities, and as I said before, you can rely on me for help if you need it," he reassured her. "Anyway, all you have to do right now is make sure that the bills are paid and the deposits made. If this goes on for a long time, there'll be other things to do and certain decisions to make about her investments, of course. But nothing too complicated. It might seem surprising, but Barb was quite a conservative investor. I don't think she ever touched the capital or used much of the interest except in exceptional circumstances. I believe she was saving for her retirement, actually. She was always talking about wanting to have a supremely comfortable old age, otherwise what's the point of living through it?"

"It hard for me to believe she did something which would have such an impact on my life without telling me," Harry said, unable to get past this fact.

"She did instruct me to give you this if something happened to her," Porter said, holding out a white, legal-sized envelope. "I'm sure she meant in the event of her death, but since the doctors have no idea how long she's going to be in a coma or whether there's going to be permanent damage, and since the police insisted that the will be read, I though I'd better give it to you now. She'll probably give me shit when she wakes up, but I don't care."

Harry's mouth grew dry. "What is it?"

"I don't know," he replied. "I didn't open it."

Harry reached out, took it from him and dropped it on her lap.

"Aren't you going to see what it is?"

"Yes," Harry replied, looking down at the envelope.

"Good, because I didn't think you were a coward, and besides, I'm curious as hell," he said, rising from his chair. "Meanwhile, all this beer has gone right through me, so I think I'll pay a little visit to the men's room."

"Porter, did Barb leave an envelope for anyone else?" Harry asked.

"I'm not supposed to tell you things like that," he replied.

"Sorry."

"But if she did, she didn't give it to me," he said with a lopsided smile.

"Thanks." Harry watched him walk slowly to the back of the restaurant, where he stopped briefly to talk with several men seated at the bar. She plucked the envelope from her lap, tore it open and took out two sheets of paper which were covered with Barb's distinctive scrawl. The letter was dated a month ago, although the scent of Barb's perfume radiated from it as if its half-life was nearly as long as Harry's memory.

Harriet, my sweet,

If you're reading this then I'm probably dead, which is a damn shame as I hadn't planned on departing from this life for a long, long time — perhaps never if I could have figured out how to bribe the angels. But that's another story, and we'll have plenty of time to discuss their unreasonable intractability when you join me in the great beyond (or not). If it's the latter, then it won't make any difference, will it? Or perhaps it's that we won't be around to care what difference it makes. What a shame. But then again, that's from the perspective of the living. Who knows what the dead think, after all? Or if at all. Well. I can never quite figure it out, not that I've thought about it a lot. It's like whether the chicken comes before the egg or whether a tree that falls in the forest makes a noise if there's no one around to hear it. Those were student-day — or more truthfully, daze — conundrums we quite conveniently forgot as soon as it was decently possible precisely because there were no answers.

Tant pis, as they say. Too bloody bad, as Pearl would say. And what would you say? You can tell me when we meet again.

But if I'm really dead, I'm mad as hell because I'm not nearly finished living yet.

Oh god, listen to how narcissistic I'm being. You'd think I was expecting an audience of millions instead of one. Well, sweetheart, I'll never change, and that's the one constant in my life these days. If you ever write or commission a book about me, I will thank you not to include this in it.

But on to the serious stuff. My decision to leave you half of Isadora's Hideaway and whatever's left of my estate once Karen, Peter and Pearl have had their share was taken only after a lot of thought. I had planned to leave my brother the bulk of my investments simply because he was my brother, but then I changed my mind. I've basically supported Peter for most of his adult life and I suppose I could have set up some sort of unbreakable trust which would had provided him with a monthly income for the rest of his life. But then I asked myself if I'd worked hard all these years simply to do the conventional thing with my savings, and the answer was no. Peter will have to fend for himself after I'm gone. And who knows? Perhaps I'm doing him a favour. Maybe he'll finally grow up.

As for Karen, I once cared deeply for her, but sad to say, we've grown inexorably apart. I no longer love her and she no longer loves me, although I couldn't tell you precisely when either of us came to this realization. It remains unstated, of course, and we go through the motions, but it's over. If one of us fell in love with someone else, there would likely be movement to dissolve our union, which remains in place more out of habit than anything else. But I'm afraid that before too long, we'll end up hating each other. Karen blames me because her art suffers here in Key West. There's too much work to do in the guesthouse, although I try to do most of it to give her time to devote to her painting. But to no avail. I think she'd be happier if I sold the Hideaway and we moved back up north, or to New York or San Francisco or Paris, but I love it here. For the first time in my life I don't wake up every morning with the urge to pack my bags and move on.

But I digress. For a long time I thought I owed Karen something the same way I thought I owed Peter something, but I've changed my mind. Should I die, the Hideaway will need a firm hand on the tiller, and you've always been so organized that it frightens me. Who else could crawl out of bed at seven in the morning after a night of making love and not only get to class on time but actually manage to colour coordinate her clothes and to find the right textbook to take with her? You're a wonderful manager and yet you can also soar like an eagle — although in my opinion, you've forced yourself to remain earth-bound for far too long. I think in our society this is called growing up — also known as becoming an adult — but I'm of the firm opinion that it's entirely over-rated. The object of life should be to find a way to do something you like doing while making enough money to live a decent life. This is probably subversive, but so be it. It has always suited me fine.

Why am I saying this? Because if I die young — and oh, how subjective that is now that I've passed the mid-century mark — I want someone who has dreams like mine to carry on. Do what you will with your share in Isadora's Hideaway and the rest of my estate, but remember, I'll be mad as hell and come back and haunt you forever if you don't take full advantage of this second lease on life.

Eternal love (and that's not a joke),

Barb

PS: Any self-respecting Key West innkeeper should insist on being called Harriet. (What she's called in the gym in Montreal is another matter. Should she choose to return there, that is.)

Harry carefully refolded the letter and held it tightly against her chest, as if that would help to bring Barb out of her coma or at least stop her own heart from aching so much. She felt wetness on her cheeks and reached up with her fingers, surprised to find that she was crying. "Damn," she muttered, searching under the table for her purse.

"Here," Porter said kindly, handing her an absurdly white handkerchief.

"Lurking in the wings, were you?" she replied with an unsteady laugh as she wiped away the tears and blew her nose.

"You may not know this, but aspiring attorneys are required to take a course in hanky laundering and folding," he replied swiftly. "Fail that and you're toast."

"Law schools clearly grasp what's important," Harry smiled.

"Quite. Look, is there anything I should know about what's in that envelope?" Porter asked as he sat down.

"Here," Harry said, handing it to him.

"Are you sure?"

She nodded and drank some wine as she watched him gingerly unfold Barb's letter.

"Yes, well, that's clear," he muttered when he'd finished reading it, obviously touched.

"But it's not something the police would necessarily understand," Harry commented. "Especially Detective Dovercourt."

"You should consider sharing it with them anyway," he said. "However, as your lawyer, I want you to realize the position you're in. To date, you've been honest with the police even though it's put you under suspicion. But no matter what you told them, you'd still be the main suspect because of what's in her will."

"I didn't do it," Harry protested.

"Of course you didn't," Porter replied. "Finish your wine and then we'll go to the tea dance."

"Where?"

"Here at the Atlantic Shores," Porter responded. "Just around the corner on the dock."

"I don't know," Harry said hesitantly. She should go back to the hospital and sit with Barb. Or return to the guesthouse and mind the office. There were so many things she had to think about, including uncovering whoever had attacked Barb. And then there was her relationship with Judy, which seemed to be unravelling with frightening speed despite their twelve years together. What had happened to their ability to communicate, to cut through extraneous clutter and overcome anger, exasperation and sporadic alienation?

"Why don't you give Judy a call and invite her to the dance?" Porter suggested.

"That's a wonderful idea," Harry said. She made her way to the back of the restaurant and called the Hideaway.

Judy picked up the telephone on the first ring. "Harry? Where are you? I saw your note, but I was starting to get worried."

"I'm still at the restaurant at the Atlantic Shores with Porter," Harry answered. "Listen, I'm going to the tea dance with him. Want to come?"

"But I'm already undressed."

"Well, put your clothes back on."

"Where is it?"

"Here at the Atlantic Shores. On the dock."

"I'll be there in a couple of minutes," Judy said, hanging up.

"Did you find her?" Porter asked when she returned to their table.

"Yes, and she's coming right over," responded Harry.

"Let's be off, then," Porter said, leading her from the restaurant.

As they walked around the side of brightly painted building, Harry could hear dance music coming from the pier. They passed through a courtyard with motel units on either side. Cars and mopeds were parked in front of the rooms, and some of the doors were open, presumably to provide a cross-breeze. Not everyone preferred air conditioning, even when the tropical heat was stultifying. Still, sometimes any respite from the humidity and the heat was welcome, Harry thought as sweat dripped down her sides. Scantily dressed gay men and lesbians were sitting on stoops or deck chairs, chatting back and forth. Others were strolling toward the dock. It was nearly dark and the sky was mottled with clouds. The predominant colour tonight was an uncommon shade of violet.

"Do you want to go over by the pool or see if we can find a table near the bar?" Porter asked, raising his voice to be heard over the throbbing music.

Harry stuffed her hands in her jean pockets and looked around. There were three docks, two of which were wide and flanked a wharf so narrow that two people side-by-side constituted a crowd. There were so many gay men and women swarming over them that it was hard to tell where one dock ended and the next began. "What's the difference?" she shouted as several tall, tanned and muscular women sauntered by, looking as if they owned the night and knew it.

"The dock behind the pool is mostly used for dancing," he bellowed in explanation, and when Harry stood on tip-toes, she could see a multitude of heads bobbing. "Gosh, they look so packed together. Does anyone ever fall into the pool?"

"I would imagine so, although I'm sure it's all in good fun, if not precisely in good taste," Porter responded. "Mind you, on a night like this, the water would probably feel wonderful. Now, let's see if we can find a place to sit. Unless you feel like dancing, that is."

"Not really," Harry told him, glancing regretfully toward the bobbing heads. The unremitting music had fugued from "What is Love," a recent hit by Haddaway that invariably set Harry's feet to tapping, to the historic and respected "YMCA" by the Village People. This had elicited ragged cheers from all corners of the dock, presumably because it was a gay anthem that evoked memories of pre-AIDS days, when gay sex in Key West, at least among men, was a promise and not just a dangerous aspiration.

Harry and Porter made their way through the crowd, climbed a short flight of stairs past the bar and arrived at a table on the edge of the dock just as several men dressed in jean shorts and singlets were leaving.

"What luck," Harry remarked, leaning over the railing. The pier had been built several feet out over the Atlantic Ocean. It was low tide, and the pungent odours of salt flats and tar pinched her nostrils. She had been born and raised on the South Shore of Nova Scotia, and, although she hadn't lived there for over thirty years, the smell was so familiar that she abruptly felt homesick.

"I'll get us something to drink," Porter said, leaving his briefcase on his chair.

"Fine," Harry replied, glad to be alone for a moment. She sat down and stared out to sea. The sun had fully set, although the sky wasn't completely dark and she could just make out boats proceeding toward shore. Some of them were fishing vessels while others likely plied the tourist trade. Harry was prone to sea-sickness and had never been overly enthusiastic about trusting her equilibrium to the treacherous ocean waves. Perhaps it was time to give it another try, she mused as she stared at the water, watching it swirl restlessly around the thick posts of the dock. Maybe it was time to stop procrastinating and to really *live*.

She recalled how, when she had thought there was even the slightest possibility that she might be infected with the HIV virus, she had made that same resolution about living life to the fullest. But her resolve had gradually slipped away. It wasn't that she had been afraid, it wasn't even that she had stopped thinking about death. No, it was even dumber than that: She had become bogged down in the mundane details of everyday life. Who could she blame then? The frenzy of modern living? Herself?

"Here we are," Porter said, placing a bottle and three long-stemmed glasses on the table.

"Champagne? Isn't that rather extravagant?"

"I thought it was appropriate. Besides, I'll put it on your account," he joked as he removed the foil from the bottle and then firmly grasped it under his arm and pulled out the cork. Champagne spilled onto the table until Harry swiftly placed a glass under it.

"What's the occasion?" Judy asked, sliding into the seat beside Harry.

"Must there be one?" Porter asked.

"I like this man," Judy said, gesturing to Porter.

"So do I," Harry said.

"Flattery will get you everywhere," Porter said with a grin. He poured champagne into Judy's glass.

"Doesn't it always?" Judy retorted. "You know, I can't believe that Barb decided to leave you all that money."

"I know," Harry admitted. "I was shocked, too."

"The police thought reading the will was going to break the case, but a fat lot of good it did," Porter said glumly.

"If I'd had time to think about it, I could have told them that," Harry commented. "I mean, people simply got upset once they learned the bulk of Barb's estate was going to come to me. But be that as it may, someone wanted Barb to die."

"Harry, is there something about your relationship with Barb that you've always meant to tell me?" Judy asked suddenly.

"I hope that was a joke," Harry responded slowly. She took Barb's letter out of her purse and handed it to Judy, watching as her lover read it. Judy's face grew pale as she turned the pages.

"I never would have imagined," Judy said as she handed Barb's letter back to Harry.

"Me neither," Harry said, her voice hoarse. "But she's not going to die, and she's not going to stay in a coma. Not Barb."

"I'll drink to that," Porter said solemnly, touching his glass to Harry's.

"Me, too," Judy said quietly.

Harry watched Porter drain his glass. She raised hers to her lips and did the same, feeling the bubbly warm her stomach. She felt like tossing her glass over her shoulder, wanting to hear it fragment into a thousand pieces. Only the fact that she was in a crowded, outdoor bar prevented her from giving in to her impulses.

It was after eleven when Harry and Judy returned to the guest-house. They had finished their bottle of champagne, and Harry had stopped Porter from ordering a second. All of them were a bit tipsy, and Harry had greater respect for the hangover inducing ability of champagne than he did.

"Call me," he said after they had strolled back to Catherine Street and paused beside his parked car.

"I will," Harry responded, leaning against Judy.

"If you don't, I'll call you," Porter warned, pointing his remote control at his car to open the door.

"That's reassuring," Judy commented.

"It's meant to be," he said with an irrepressible grin.

They kissed on the cheek and Porter got into his car and drove away. Harry led Judy past the front door to the guesthouse gate, relieved that it was still open so they could slip unseen into her suite. She closed the gate, standing in the shadows until her eyes grew accustomed to the subdued light emanating from the outdoor lamps placed strategically throughout the grounds. The patio was de-serted, but deck chairs and recliners were lying helter-skelter, wine glasses and coffee cups were sitting on tables and in the garden, and the pool and hot tub were uncovered.

"What a mess," she said to Judy.

"Isn't it," Judy responded.

"But I can't do anything about it now," Harry said with a glance at her watch. It was too late and she was too weary to search for the pool covers, arrange chairs in a neat row or even gather up the cups and glasses and take them to the breakfast nook. She would have to meet with Karen in the morning to divide up the work before the quality of services in the guesthouse deteriorated. "There's so much I don't know," she said disconsolately as they went into her building.

"You mean about the guesthouse," Judy said as they walked down the hall to their suite.

"And about the attack on Barb," Harry responded, taking a deep breath of cool, dehumidified air. "She's given me power of attorney, but how on earth am I going to cope with these new responsibilities when I have to go back to Montreal in eight days and start teaching again?"

"You have to talk with Karen," Judy said, following Harry as she trudged into the bedroom.

"That I know, but I'm too exhausted to deal with it right now," Harry sighed as she dropped her purse on a chair, undressed and tossed her clothes on top of it. "Aren't you coming to bed?" she asked Judy as she got into her nightgown and slid under the covers.

"Do you mind if I sit up and read for a bit? I'm too wide awake to sleep," Judy replied.

"Not at all," Harry said as Judy bent to kiss her and then went in to the adjoining room. She was exhausted, too weary to think. Besides, sleep was the best escape. She breathed deeply, waiting for consciousness to fade. It didn't. She squinted and realized that she hadn't shut the curtains. She got up and closed them and padded into the bathroom, poured herself a glass of water and drank it. She refilled her glass, stood it on the bedside table and got back into bed, but not before she noticed that there was no light on in the living room. Had Judy gone out or was she sitting in the dark? "Hon, are you there?"

"Yes," Judy responded. Seconds later a light came on.

This was a fine kettle of fish, Harry decided indignantly after she had tossed and turned and dishevelled the sheets. She switched on her own lamp and sat up. If she couldn't sleep, then she might as well get up and face her problems. The first dilemma, though, was to decide which one to tackle first.

At the root of the problem was Harry's pain over the visceral fact that Barb was in a coma and that no one knew when — or if — she would come out of it. There were so many conversations the two of them hadn't finished, so many things they hadn't done together, so many secrets they hadn't shared. They'd only been lovers for a year, but late at night, when the dorm had been silent and traffic on the streets of Montreal had been light and their youthful sexuality had finally been sated, they'd stretched out on the damp sheets and talked, creating a wonderful future for themselves. They were going to get great jobs which would pay huge salaries and provide intellectual stimulation and they would have amicable co-workers and appreciative bosses. They would live in a house with high ceilings and hardwood floors and there would be a stereo with speakers in every room, even the bath. The rest of the furniture would be tasteful and of necessity expensive and modern in design, construction and colour. They would be intrepid vacationers and travel to daringly remote tropical locales that took two days to reach by air and sea and sometimes foot and that required a multitude of inoculations, some of which were sickeningly painful. And they would grow old together and sit in adjacent rocking chairs on the veranda of the old-age home, where they would regale each other with tales of past conquests and exploits. They had been so innocent then, assuming that they'd find jobs they'd enjoy doing and that there would always be enough money to live in affluence and vacation in stylish discomfort. The most naive presumption was to imagine that it would be possible to be out lesbians in a residence for seniors. Even today that wasn't possible. What had perhaps been more ingenuous was the belief that they would be together for life — although there was nothing wrong with dreaming, Harry reflected. For her, finding Barb had been the culmination of years of fantasy, so everything had seemed attainable. Later, when she thought back, she wondered whether Barb had simply been indulging her fantasies.

But enough of that. Barb had been attacked. She hadn't been shot or stabbed, so there was a chance it hadn't been premeditated. Still, from what the police had said, there had been signs of a struggle. And from the bruises on Barb's neck it seemed that someone had tried to strangle her, and Barb had broken free and then fallen and hit her head. Or perhaps she had been pushed.

But by whom? And why?

Harry got out of bed, went into the bathroom and poured another glass of water, resisting the temptation to go into the living room. She didn't want Judy to think she was checking up on her.

There was no lack of possible suspects, that was certain. Porter thought that she, herself, was number one on the police list; she had both opportunity and motive. Well, at least she was one up on the police, she thought ruefully; she knew she hadn't done it. So while they investigated her, she would investigate the others, keeping in mind that the already complex web of motives had become even more complicated once the will had been read and its surprises revealed.

She would start with Peter Fenton and the odious Ross Hunter, who, Harry thought, was fully capable of murdering someone if he could benefit financially. Both before and during the reading of the will, he had insisted that Peter was going to inherit his sister's estate. Harry had privately thought he was out of touch with reality, but it turned out that he actually hadn't been, for Barb's old will had amply provided for Peter. What if they'd known about Barb's old will but not her new one? Would Peter have attacked his sister for financial gain? He was so influenced by Ross that it was a possibility, especially if he and Barb had been arguing. Barb had mentioned that Peter and Ross only visited when they needed money, so Peter had likely been making continuous requests for financial help, and Ross would have made these pleas sound like self-righteous harangues. Either one of them could have arranged to meet with Barb in her apartment after the tea dance last night. Barb would have been irritable, annoyed and impatient. An altercation could have developed, particularly if both Peter and Ross were there, Harry thought excitedly.

Then she frowned and reluctantly put aside her growing sense of satisfaction. It would be all too easy to blame it on the boys — and especially on Ross, simply because she was unable to find any socially redeeming qualities in his personality. But the timing seemed a bit off if they'd come by right after the tea dance. Still, the gate had been open late tonight, so perhaps it wasn't normally locked early, if at all. She'd have to ask Karen about that.

But Peter and Ross weren't the only suspects. What about Alison Wheatley? She and Barb had been lovers in university and then they'd resumed their affair when Barb had gone to Dallas last year. Why on earth had Barb been in Dallas? Perhaps it had been a business trip. Harry couldn't imagine that she'd gone just to visit Alison. Alison herself maintained that their affair hadn't been serious. But why had Alison insisted on staying at the Hideaway when she came to Key West? After all, she couldn't invite Martin over for the night when she was staying at a woman-only guesthouse. In fact, she couldn't even invite him in for a drink or for a dip in the pool. There were too many coincidences in Alison's relationship with Barb for Harry's liking; she would have to find a way to get Alison alone and ask her a few pointed questions without making her run home to daddy.

And then there was Karen. From what she had seen of Barb and Karen's relationship, there had obviously been trouble in paradise, and this impression had been reinforced by Barb's letter. Harry had always thought that Barb had short-changed herself by settling down with Karen, although she'd never told Barb that. People made important decisions for reasons which were sometimes apparent, sometimes bewildering. Karen was a jealous, petty and vindictive egoist, but that hadn't seemed to bother Barb, who had always claimed to like feisty women. Harry didn't have much use for someone so mean-spirited. Perhaps she wasn't being fair, though. But as much as she loved Barb, Harry wasn't ignorant of her faults. She just knew that, under all the bluster and camp and eccentricity, Barb had been a gentle, thoughtful soul. Had Karen known this too?

The one thing Barb hadn't mentioned in her letter was whether she had become serious about another woman. But if she had been deeply involved with someone other than Karen, wouldn't she have written that particular woman into her will rather than Harry? Perhaps that meant that Barb wasn't in love with anyone else; it was quite conceivable that she could have fallen out of love with one woman without falling in love with another, especially if her disenchantment with Karen had been growing over a lengthy period of time.

Harry sighed, slid down in bed and then sat up again when she heard Judy's voice. She opened her mouth to ask her lover to speak louder and then realized that she must be talking on the phone. Had she called Sarah to wish her goodnight, Harry wondered. But never mind. She had work to do, she decided, getting tough with herself and forcing her thoughts back to Barb's attacker.

When Porter had read the will, Karen had professed shock that Harry was to receive the bulk of Barb's estate. Of course, Karen could have been as ignorant about the conditions of Barb's will as Harry. Still, Karen lived with Barb; wouldn't she have noticed that something in their relationship had changed? Why hadn't Barb said anything about the will? Didn't she owe her lover an explanation about why she had altered it? Had she been biding her time or waiting until something happened? Harry retrieved her purse from under her clothes and took Barb's letter from it, but it was maddeningly silent on that particular topic. Only then did it occur to Harry that Barb might have been planning to tell her about her new will over dinner last night. Maybe that had been the big surprise she'd talked about. Perhaps she'd changed her mind because she had realized she should inform Karen first. If Barb had chosen last evening to tell Karen, Karen might have become angry enough to attack Barb. But once Karen discovered that she wasn't going to inherit Barb's estate, she wouldn't have wanted her dead, would she? Wouldn't it make more sense for Karen to spend some time courting Barb in an attempt to talk her into changing her mind? Or would Karen have simply lost her temper?

And then there was Pearl Vernon, Harry reflected listlessly. She leaned back on her pillows and reflected on the difficulty of suspecting that someone to whom she was attracted was capable of violence. And yet she knew so little about Pearl. She lived in New York and, according to Karen, she was one of Barb's long-term lovers. She was physically stunning and well aware of it. She was smart and used it to her advantage. And that was all Harry had to go on. For all she knew, Pearl might even have a live-in lover; Harry hadn't thought to ask.

Pearl's motives weren't as compelling as Karen's, but they were basically the same: jealousy or greed. Karen wasn't the only one who might have been upset about so many of Barb's ex-lovers descending on the Hideaway — Pearl might have felt the same way. Harry would have to find out how long Pearl had been in Key West and whether she and Barb had been together most of that time, thus displacing Karen from Barb's affections and possibly her bed. She would also have to discover two other things: whether Pearl had still been in love with Barb, and whether she was in desperate need of cash. Had Pearl known that Barb was planning to leave her money?

Matters were further complicated, Harry thought with a sigh, because many of the suspects' motives shifted depending on whether or not they had known the contents of Barb's new will. Under the terms of the old will, Karen and Peter — and by extension, Ross — had the strongest motives to want Barb out of the way; under the new will, Harry herself was the big winner. Pearl's share stayed the same under both wills. But in a way, that reasoning was simplistic, Harry reflected, because it didn't take into consideration the anger that Karen, Peter and Ross may have felt if they had discovered they'd been stripped of much of Barb's estate. Had any of them had known about Barb's new will before Porter had read it earlier today at the police station? If so, they were darn good actors.

"Harry, are you awake?" Judy called from the living room.

"Yes," Harry responded. "Aren't you ever coming to bed?"

"Can I talk with you?"

"What?" Harry asked cautiously, padding into the living room on bare feet.

"I've got insomnia," Judy answered. "I guess you do, too."

"It looks like it," Harry responded, sitting down on the sofa beside her lover. She knew that Judy would get to the point in her own good time. "What are you drinking?"

"Scotch on the rocks," Judy said.

Harry hadn't spent enough time in her suite to realize that it contained a wet bar. She rose from the sofa, walked to the cabinet in the corner, spread the top doors and uncovered an enormous television set with a built-in VCR. She closed them and opened the bottom ones. "Nice," she commented when she saw the fridge.

"And quite well stocked," Judy remarked.

She was right. The fridge was crammed with small bottles of rum, vodka, scotch, rye and gin as well as mixers, beer, wine and cognac. There was even a half-bottle of champagne and a freezer just large enough to hold a tray of ice cubes. Harry removed a bottle of rum and a can of Coke. "Are you ready for another?"

"Yes," Judy replied.

There was a shelf above the fridge that contained glasses, a cork screw, a bottle opener and several ceramic mugs. Harry took a glass, tossed in two ice cubes and then emptied the miniature bottle of rum and half the can of Coke into it, making silent supplication to her body to forgive her such an indulgence after wine and champagne. Then she extracted a bottle of scotch from the fridge and carried the drinks back to the sofa.

"So what's keeping you awake?" she asked Judy as she handed her the bottle of scotch.

"The same thing that's bothering you," Judy responded.

Harry glanced at her and then looked away. "I was lying there trying to figure out who attacked Barb."

"So what did you decide?"

"Nothing," Harry said glumly.

"I wish we could get out of here," Judy said vehemently. "Drive up to Miami Beach or Fort Lauderdale for a decent vacation or even fly back home to Montreal."

"Do you think the police would stop you if you really wanted to go?" Harry asked.

"Yes," Judy replied.

"Because of me," Harry surmised.

"In part," Judy replied, frowning as she finished her drink. "Could I have another?" she asked, holding up her glass.

"Certainly," Harry replied, feeling perplexed. She glanced at her lover, but Judy's face wasn't giving anything away. She got up and retrieved another bottle of scotch from the fridge. "What do you mean, in part?" she asked hesitantly. She sat down beside Judy and handed her the bottle.

Judy broke open the seal and refilled her glass.

"Judy?" Harry asked uncertainly. She glanced at her partner of twelve years and, not for the first time recently, wondered how well she knew her.

"Sarah and Karen used to be lovers," Judy said in a flat voice.

"You never told me that," Harry asserted, flinching when Judy glared at her. She was fortunate Judy hadn't retorted that it was none of her business. Which it wasn't, of course. Still, she knew it would do nothing for her state of mind if Judy actually had said that to her. "It's all so incestuous," Harry muttered, mostly to herself.

"Yes, quite, isn't it?" Judy remarked with bitter flippancy.

She wondered then whether Judy had known; if she hadn't, that would explain why she was so perturbed. "But I suppose you didn't know," she ventured.

"Of course I didn't," Judy said with a caustic laugh, "although it shouldn't really matter."

"But it did," Harry surmised, "and you weren't pleased."

"How right you are," Judy sighed. "But you always were good at figuring things out. I suppose it's like when we went to Nova Scotia to attend your reunion and one of your classmates was killed. You couldn't rest until you found out who did it. You feel the same way about finding Barb's attacker, don't you?"

"Even more so," Harry said, sipping her drink.

Judy got up, walked over to the cabinet and searched noisily through the fridge. "I seemed to have finished my quota of scotch," she said finally.

"I could check in the kitchen," Harry said. She noticed for the first time how tipsy Judy was.

"Never mind. I've found something else," Judy responded, returning with a couple of bottles of cognac.

"Are you sure you want to do that?" Harry asked with amusement as her lover emptied one of them into a crystal brandy snifter.

"Absolutely."

Harry watched her sip cognac as if it was water. She felt a momentary and guilty elation that Judy was estranged from Sarah because of Sarah's relationship with Karen, but delight swiftly turned to dismay when she realized how hurt Judy was. She didn't want Judy to love Sarah nearly that much. "So Sarah and Karen were lovers way back when," she commented, mentally adding Sarah to her list of suspects.

"They lived together for a couple of years before Karen and Barb met."

That still didn't explain why Judy was so upset, Harry reflected. After all, Sarah was in her late thirties and had likely been involved in quite a few relationships before her friendship with Judy had become romantic. Judy never drank obsessively like this, either. Something else was wrong. "Are they still involved?" Harry speculated, thinking of Barb and Pearl's long-term, long distance affair.

"Yes," Judy replied. "But how did you know?"

"It wouldn't be like you to be upset about something which ended years ago," Harry replied.

"It's a hell of a mess, isn't it?" Judy commented with a shaky laugh.

Harry reached out and held Judy's hand. Despite the fact that the air conditioning was on, her palm was sweaty.

"Hold me," Judy said urgently.

Harry put her rum and Coke on the coffee table and took Judy in her arms. Breathing in her lover's familiar scent was like coming home.

"Sarah didn't try to kill Barb," Judy murmured.

Who was she trying to reassure, Harry wondered as she ran her fingers through Judy's silky hair. Not that long ago they had been in their apartment on Ste-Famille Street in Montreal, sharing the same bed, eating breakfast across the kitchen table, planning their vacation, making love. Now Harry felt like they barely knew each other. "What are you trying to tell me?"

"That you don't know everything," Judy said cryptically, sitting up and then pouring the last few drops of cognac into her glass.

"Of that I'm certain," Harry responded, watching her partner finish her drink.

"You don't know, for example, that the last time we were down here, Barb and I jumped in the sack together," Judy said in a rush.

Harry's heart stopped.

Of course she hadn't known. But it was logical in a way, she thought wearily — coming full circle. Harry herself had been with Judy and Barb. And Pearl had been with Barb and Alison, while Karen had been with Barb and Sarah, and Alison had been with Barb and Pearl. And Judy had been with her, with Sarah and ... with Barb. Was Judy the ex-lover of Barb's whom Pearl had refused to identify?

"I see," she said softly. The last time she and Judy had visited Key West, they'd still been in a monogamous relationship — or so Harry had believed. She rose from the sofa, tossed some ice cubes in her rum and coke and sat down on one of the easy chairs. "Why?"

"You were off doing something or other, I don't remember what," Judy began. "Barb and I were having a few drinks and watching erotic films on the VCR and then suddenly we were making love."

Even during the monogamous years of their relationship, Harry had been no stranger to lascivious feelings about other women, although she hadn't acted on them. The combination of her first lover and her long-term lover was lethal, and they both must have known it. What had Judy been thinking about when she'd made love with Barb? Hadn't she realized how she was betraying Harry? And what about Barb? Harry closed her eyes and cursed under her breath because she already knew the answer. Barb would have known how devious her actions were. She wasn't the type to dupe herself. Oh, god. Had Barb changed her will in Harry's favour because she felt guilty about sleeping with Judy?

"You're awfully quiet," Judy commented, carefully placing her brandy snifter on the coffee table and attempting not to upset the empty bottles already sitting there.

"And you're drunk," Harry replied. "I think you should sleep it off and then we'll talk."

"This isn't like you."

"Perhaps not," Harry responded, "but I can't deal with this now."

"Let's go to bed, then," Judy said, rising from the sofa and moving unsteadily toward her.

"Yes," Harry sighed. She rose and met Judy half-way, grasped her arm to steady her, and then turned her toward the bedroom.

"Not here," Judy said, pulling away.

"What do you mean, not here?"

"I called the Southernmost Motel and rented a room while you were trying to sleep," Judy told her.

"Whatever for?" Harry asked, feeling stunned.

"Because I didn't think you'd want me here after you heard the truth," Judy responded. "And yet you had to know, especially now."

"But — "

"And don't try to tell me that you'll always want me, because it isn't true," Judy said drunkenly.

"Oh yes it is," Harry replied. "Of course I feel hurt, especially because you kept it a secret all this time, but let's not get carried away."

"I'm not staying here tonight," Judy said, and Harry knew her well enough to recognize the intractable stubbornness in her voice.

"Fine," she sighed. "Let me get dressed and I'll walk you to the motel." She went into the bedroom and dressed hurriedly, grabbing her purse and verifying that her keys were in it. Then she returned to the living room and said, "Let's go," with the kind of tenderness she used with a sick child.

"Wait — I've still got a bottle of cognac left," Judy objected.

"Come on," Harry cajoled, reaching out and then dropping her hand when she saw that Judy was emptying the contents of the cognac bottle into her glass.

"I'll just take this with me," Judy said, giving Harry a bleary smile. "You can bring the glass back with you after."

"Fine." Harry grasped Judy by the upper arm, eased her from her suite and then led her to the patio.

"I'll come back soon," Judy said suddenly.

"I hope so," Harry answered. "But I don't see why you're doing this in the first place."

"I thought you'd need some time to think it over," Judy mumbled, cognac spilling on the front steps.

"Not really," Harry assured her as they walked to the corner and turned left on Duval. She couldn't afford to think, not about Barb and Judy, not when there was a risk that her imagination would take over and make it real. It was late and relatively quiet, but so hot and humid that Harry was surprised there wasn't ground fog swirling around their legs. There were cars moving slowly along the street and they passed a few other couples out strolling and several men walking swiftly as if they knew precisely where they were going. No one even took a second look at Judy although she was staggering slightly and carrying a dripping brandy snifter in her hand.

"What floor are you on?" Harry asked as they walked onto the grounds of the Southernmost Motel.

"The second one," Judy responded, raising her glass. "Hey! It's empty!"

"I think you spilled it on the way over here," Harry explained, trying not to laugh.

"Oh, well. There's probably a bottle in my room," Judy muttered, handing the glass to Harry. The brandy snifter was coated with sweet, sticky liqueur so Harry stood it under a bush. She left Judy weaving unsteadily on the lawn for a minute and quickly found the front office, where an unflappable night clerk gave her Judy's room key.

"I'm not sure you should drink any more," Harry told Judy when she returned.

"You're right," Judy admitted as she turned towards the stairs and nearly fell flat on her face. "I'm going to regret this in the morning, aren't I?"

"Probably. Look, I'd better go with you," Harry responded. She put her arm around Judy and helped her up the stairs.

"This way," Judy burped, staggering along the walkway.

Harry grasped her arm to steady her. They sounded like a herd of buffalos and she was worried that they would wake the other guests. "Here's your key."

"Thank you," Judy said regally as she turned abruptly and nearly fell into the door of room 222.

"The object is to unlock it, not to knock it down," Harry couldn't help but comment as she removed the key from Judy's hand and opened the door.

"Stop laughing at me," Judy retorted as she turned on the light.

"It's just that I've never seen you like this before," Harry said by way of apology. She looked curiously around the room. It was quite large. A queen-sized bed faced a dresser with a cabinet perched on top. At the far end of the room, near the balcony door, there was a sofa and a small table with two chairs. On the table was a solitary brandy snifter and a bottle of cognac. The walls were painted a subdued shade of coral, which was also the dominant colour in the bedspread, the upholstery covering the sofa and chair seats and the two bamboo-framed paintings on the walls. "This is nice," she commented.

"There's even a small balcony overlooking the pool," Judy said. "Want to see?"

"Sure," Harry said, crossing the room.

Judy slid open the patio door and they both went out.

"Why don't you sit down," Harry suggested, helping Judy into one of the lawn chairs. Then she moved to the railing and leaned against it, staring down at the deserted compound. There was a large pool surrounded by a double row of deck chairs. At the far end was a thatched cabana with a shuttered bar. The courtyard was well lit but deserted.

She turned and leaned her behind against the railing. "I still don't understand what we're doing here."

"Do you want the long story or the somewhat abbreviated one?" Judy asked. "I mean, shall I start with Adam and Eve or Harriet and Judy or — "

"How about with your reasons for renting a room when we've already got one," Harry interrupted, her voice dry.

"Spoil sport," Judy responded, reaching out and stroking Harry's thigh.

"Don't change the subject," Harry said, although she didn't move away.

"Don't you care that I slept with Barb?" Judy asked suddenly, her hand tightening for a moment.

"Of course I do," Harry responded with measured intensity. "I care so much that I ache inside."

Judy's hand fluttered away.

"But it happened, and nothing I can do or say can change that," Harry said, not adding that what made it worse was the fact that Barb was inaccessible to a dressing down or show of temper or a good, old-fashioned telling off.

"I'm sorry," Judy muttered, her head dropping on her chest.

This simple statement shocked Harry. Judy never said she was sorry as she claimed not to believe in apologizing. She maintained that actions and words sprang from one's inner character, not from intent to wound, so pain was the result of the incompatibility of two people in a relationship and not due to aggression or spite or the desire to offend. Harry thought Judy was mistaken. Women wouldn't intentionally hurt each other in a perfect world, but this was not a perfect world. Still, the fact that Judy had said she was sorry shook to the core Harry's faith in the durability of their relationship. She bent over and pulled Judy into her arms. There were so many unanswered questions, she thought as they hugged. Judy and Barb, her lover and her best friend. If she wasn't already numb from trying to deal with what had happened to Barb, she would be devastated.

"Why don't you stay?" Judy asked.

"Here?"

"I don't think I could walk all the way back to the Hideaway," Judy laughed shakily, her hands gathering at the back of Harry's head, drawing her down until their mouths met. Judy's lips were open and she tasted strongly of cognac. Harry felt passion permeate her body, a desire born of the need to reclaim her lover. This had always been the most jaded of desires, but she was unable to deny its strength. Nothing was ever simple or innocent any more, she reflected even as her hunger grew. "Dammit," Harry muttered.

They fell back into the motel room and tumbled onto the bed, and as Harry divested herself of her clothes and climbed over her lover, she heard Judy whisper, "I love you."

"I love you, too," she whispered back, and suddenly it was simple and innocent again.

And then sensory overload made her wince in a most gratifying manner.

Morning.

Harry wasn't quite ready for it, but it came anyway. "Judy?" she said, her mouth dry from champagne and rum and Coke.

"Oh, god," Judy moaned, thrashing from one side of the bed to the other.

Harry got out of bed and walked carefully to the bathroom, poured herself a glass of water and drank deeply. Then she refilled the glass and took it in to Judy. "Here," she said, leaning over her prostrate lover.

"I'll never drink again," Judy vowed. She gingerly took the glass of water and sipped.

"Of course not," Harry said with a smile. "Listen, why don't you sleep for a bit longer? I want to go to the hospital and see Barb."

"I should come with you," Judy said, her head falling back on the pillow.

"Later," Harry replied, arranging the sheet loosely around her. "I'll pick you up and we'll have brunch, okay?"

"Okay," Judy sighed, her eyes closing.

Harry walked through the motel grounds until she reached United Street. She saw an irregularly shaped stone on the sidewalk and gave it a glancing blow. Instead of falling into the gutter, it shot out straight in front of her. She caught up with it and whacked it harder, yelping when it bounced off her big toe instead of the edge of her sandal, ricocheted off a tree and rolled into the street. Why did she feel on the outside looking in? And how had everyone else involved in this case managed to sleep with Barb recently?

There was something left between her and Judy, but they'd have to work at it, she concluded as she arrived back at the guesthouse parking lot. She rummaged through her purse for her car keys. No one had ever said life would be easy, but they hadn't said it would be this hard, either. She retrieved her keys and drove to the hospital. Once there, she steeled herself against the hospital smells and made her way to the intensive care unit. "How's she doing today?" she asked the nurse on duty, glancing at the police officer sitting in the corner behind Barb's hospital bed. The woman who had been there the day before had been replaced by a middle-aged, uniformed man who had bags under his eyes and badly needed a shave.

"Are you her sister?" the nurse inquired.

"Yes," Harry lied as the police officer stood up and approached the bed.

"She sure has a lot of sisters," the nurse commented as she scrutinized Harry.

"And the goddess said to the lesbian, 'Go forth and multiply,'" Harry muttered under her breath.

"What?"

"Nothing," Harry said as Dr. Albertini walked into the room. "How is she?"

"Stable," the doctor responded, "and breathing on her own. We took the respirator off this morning."

"You mean she's not going to die?" Harry asked, staring down at Barb's still figure. She looked as if she'd lost weight. Was that possible? It hadn't even been two days since she'd been attacked.

"Her condition has stabilized," the doctor confirmed. "But she's still in a coma."

"What can we do?" Harry asked despairingly.

"Wait," Dr. Albertini said simply. "We're making sure she gets the nutrients she needs and we're trying to keep her muscles from degenerating from lack of use. As well, we're monitoring her vital signs. We'll be moving her from intensive care in a couple of days, and then you'll be able to spend more time with her."

"Can I touch her?" Harry asked.

"I wish," the doctor said, glancing at the police officer. "Touching generally plays an important part in the recovery of people in comas. But at least you can talk to her. That will certainly help until the police decide that not everyone who visits is a threat." She gave Harry a fleeting smile and turned and walked into another cubicle. The nurse scribbled something in her chart and then followed the doctor, leaving Harry alone with Barb and the vigilant police officer.

Harry approached the bed, leaned her elbows against the top rail, and stared at her friend.

"Where are you?" she whispered timidly, trying to ignore the cop standing on the other side of the bed. "Where have you gone? Listen, I'd hold your hand but the police suspect me of attacking you. I suppose you find that amusing. Actually, it's all your fault, and I expect you to come back and take complete responsibility for it, not to mention telling us who did this to you."

Barb didn't react. Harry licked her dry lips and ran her fingers back and forth over the metal rail. "Okay, I'm not very good at this. But listen, we really need you here in the world, so hurry up and finish whatever you're doing and come back to us. You can tell us who hurt you as soon as you wake up. The police suspect all of us, even me. Or maybe I should say especially me, now that they've had a good look at your will. Why didn't you ever tell me you were planning to leave me nearly everything?"

"So you're still claiming that you really didn't know," Karen said.

Harry jumped and the railing on the hospital bed jangled. "It's not a claim, it's the truth."

"I find that impossible to believe," Karen retorted, and then she turned to Barb. "Good morning, sweetie. How was your night? Did you have pleasant dreams?"

"Just as I find it hard to believe that you didn't know she'd changed her will only a month ago," Harry commented.

As the police officer hovered in the background, they exchanged cool stares, neither of them willing to back down. This wasn't what she'd had in mind when she'd planned to arrange a meeting with Karen, Harry thought wryly.

"Perhaps she meant to tell me the night before last but then changed her mind because she hadn't said anything to you," Harry suggested.

"Oh, what difference does it make," Karen said with a sudden lack of interest. She bent over Barb until she was so close that she might as well have been touching her. The police officer edged closer to the bed, his expression annoyed. Harry had the feeling that if neither she nor the police officer had been there, Karen would have crooned to her comatose lover.

"I'd like to be alone with Barb," Karen said abruptly.

"Karen, we have to make arrangements about the guesthouse," Harry reminded her.

"What arrangements? It's clear that Barb wants you to have it," Karen replied bitterly.

"That's not true," Harry protested, glancing at Barb and hoping that their argument wouldn't push her further into a coma. Could something like that happen? She didn't know, although for Barb's sake, it would be prudent to err on the side of caution. And besides, she wasn't exactly pleased that the police officer was openly listening to every word they said. She was surprised he wasn't writing everything down. "Why don't we step outside to discuss it? We've been here for five minutes, and you can come back later."

Karen grudgingly followed Harry from the room.

"Look, whatever her reasoning, Barb obviously wanted us to share the Hideaway," Harry said, hoping to start off on an even keel.

"Whatever her reasoning," Karen said scornfully. "You don't know the half of it."

"So tell me about it."

"She changed her will just to punish me," Karen continued.

"What for?"

"You didn't really know Barb," Karen said, staring at her with such hostility that Harry shivered. "Everybody thought she was this wonderful, liberated woman whose main philosophy was to live and let live, but she wasn't like that at all, at least not with me. She could be incredibly jealous, believe you me. And if she didn't like something I did, she had her own way of getting back at me."

"And you think that's why she changed her will."

"Yes. She was mad at me for screwing around."

Harry didn't believe it, not for one second, especially after she'd read Barb's letter. Karen was dreaming if she thought that Barb had one jealous bone in her body. But it would be to her disadvantage if she antagonized Karen, so she responded carefully. "Look, I'm not to blame for Barb's decisions. However, she did give me power of attorney, and I have certain responsibilities to fulfill, one of which is to make sure that the guesthouse doesn't go all to hell with itself."

Karen stubbornly resisted this appeal to her better nature. Actually, Harry was beginning to doubt whether she had one. "You do stand to inherit a half interest in the Hideaway," Harry reminded her. "But I suggest we put all of that aside and think about Barb for a minute."

"What the hell do you think I've been doing?" Karen responded.

Harry continued doggedly. "Her condition is stable and Dr. Albertini told me they're going to move her to an ordinary room in a day or two. She's bound to come out of this coma sooner or later, and when she does, she's going to expect the Hideaway to be running smoothly. So I suggest we cooperate and share the work."

"What do you intend to do once your vacation's over?" Karen asked, crossing her arms across her chest and staring at Harry like a cheshire cat.

"I don't know yet," Harry admitted. "But I'm working on it."

"I suppose you think I should run the guesthouse in your absence," Karen said, her voice reeking with resentment.

"We can always hire someone to run it if it comes down to that," Harry responded evenly.

"That would suit me just fine," Karen asserted.

One of the nurses came out into the hall, spotted them, and said, "I thought I heard voices. Look, I'll be giving Ms. Fenton a sponge bath and turning her in a couple of minutes, so if you want to pay another quick visit, now's your chance. Otherwise you'll have to wait at least a half hour to come back in."

"Perhaps we can talk about this again later," Harry suggested to Karen.

"There's nothing to talk about," Karen replied. She turned on her heel and re-entered Barb's room.

Even the sunshine couldn't lift Harry's spirits as she drove back to Isadora's Hideaway. To make matters worse, she had to park on the street because the guesthouse's parking lot was so full of mopeds and bicycles that there was no space for her rental car. She decided to take a shower and change before she went back to see Judy in the Southernmost Motel. She felt soiled from her conversation with Karen and her skin and clothes smelled foreign, antiseptic. This case was impossible, she thought as she got out of the car. There were too many suspects, and every single one of them had more than one motive for wanting Barb out of the way. She had to clarify the situation, she just had to. Otherwise Barb's assailant would go unpunished and Barb would continue to be in danger. She had to find an excuse for getting all of the suspects together rather than attempting to corner and question them one at a time. As she made sure the car was locked and walked across Catherine Street, it occurred to her that Porter might be able to help.

"You're under arrest for jaywalking!" Pearl's husky voice boomed from behind her.

Harry stopped abruptly in the middle of the street and wheeled around.

"You look wrecked! What on earth have you been up to?" Pearl asked as she walked up to Harry, took her in her arms and kissed her firmly on the lips.

"How can you do that?" Harry sputtered.

"Easily," Pearl replied complacently, kissing her again. "See?"

"You know what I mean," Harry retorted, pulling away and looking around.

"And what if someone saw?" Pearl asked, amused. "Would they give us a ticket for jaywalking or kissing in a public place or what?"

"I'm too tired to play this game," Harry said, crossing to the sidewalk in front of the Hideaway.

"Have you been to see Barb?" asked Pearl, turning serious.

"Yes." Harry brought Pearl up to date on Barb's condition.

"I'm going to see her later," said Pearl, her arm circling Harry's waist.

"You should," Harry told her. They walked down the hall, opened the door, and went into the patio. Several women were lounging on patio chairs, but the pool and hot tub were empty.

"Feel like having a swim?" Pearl asked.

"I'm having lunch with Judy."

"But it's not even ten thirty yet."

Harry considered possible excuses: She could say that she was tired, that she was confused, that she needed some time to be by herself. All of them were true, but it was hot and, besides, she was too weary to make excuses. She walked toward the swimming pool and plunged her hand into the water. It was barely cooler than the surrounding air.

"What's the matter?" Pearl asked apprehensively.

Harry turned and looked at her and then removed her hand from the water.

"Is it something I did?" Pearl queried, flustered.

"No. I'm just worried about Barb," Harry responded. And her relationship with Judy, and Karen's anger, and the fact that she had to return to Montreal soon. And the knowledge that someone had tried to kill Barb and she didn't know who it was. Maybe it had even been Pearl, who had just kissed her like she meant it. Harry mounted the stairs to the deck. It was made of pressure-treated two-by-fours — built to last forever. She shucked her sandals, stripped out of her clothes and climbed down the ladder into the pool, letting go as the silky water enveloped her. She closed her eyes and sank slowly until her feet touched bottom, then pushed off and burst through the surface, opening her mouth to suck in air. She breathed deeply and settled on her back, her eyes shut.

"Are you all right?" Pearl asked.

"What do you want me to say?"

Harry heard a nervous tinkle and realized that Pearl was laughing. "That was a dumb question. Of course you're not all right," Pearl said. "None of us are."

Harry drifted on top of the water, wishing she was floating on the slow-moving current of a mountain-fed, fresh-water stream through a forest of pine and spruce and moss and fields of wildflowers somewhere in the Canadian wilderness. The air would be fragrant with the smells of summer and there would be fish all around her, their gills puffing as they drew oxygen from the water. There would be water-polished stones beneath her, slowly sinking in the silt. And there would be silence.

"Do you want me to go away?"

"No," Harry replied finally. She didn't want to be alone. "You can stay." She heard the creek of wood and then a subdued splash. Gentle waves rocked her body and she knew that someone else was in the pool. "I don't feel like being touched," she warned Pearl.

"I understand," Pearl answered from a distance.

The water stopped rolling. She opened her eyes and looked up at the cloudless sky, where she could see the faint outline of the moon.

"Are you all right?" Pearl asked again. Her voice sounded nearer this time and somewhat fatigued.

"Yes," Harry replied. "Don't worry."

"I'm not," Pearl answered. It was obvious she was lying.

"You don't have to stay," Harry told her.

"But I want to."

How easy it would be to swim to the ladder, climb from the pool and wave her little finger at Pearl, who would rapidly follow. Harry shivered and momentarily lost her buoyancy.

"Do you think I attacked Barb? Is that why you don't want anything to do with me?" Pearl said, suddenly materializing right beside her.

"Don't be an ass," came Alison Wheatley's brittle voice from outside the pool. "She obviously did it herself."

"What the hell?" Pearl sputtered.

"I'm sick and tired of you accusing me of having assaulted Barb," Harry said indignantly.

"Don't be such a bitch," Alison replied complacently. "I think I'll join you."

"I'd rather swim in acid than share this pool with you," Harry declared.

"Oh, calm down," Alison replied. "You're just jealous about me and Pearl."

Harry heard Pearl burst into laughter.

"Or me and Barb last year in Dallas," Alison added, stripping to her bra and panties.

"What?" Pearl interjected.

"You didn't know about that?" Harry asked, turning to face Pearl.

"I don't believe it," Pearl muttered, a chagrined look on her face. "Why didn't we all just jump into bed together?"

"It's still not too late," Alison responded. She tossed her bra and panties aside.

"I'm out of here," Harry told Pearl, breaking away and swimming toward the ladder. "And don't even think about it," she said through clenched teeth when she saw Alison looking at her.

Alison laughed and dove into the pool. Seconds later, Pearl started up the ladder.

"Hey, where do you think you're going?" Alison shouted from the pool.

"Sorry, but my skin was getting wrinkled," Pearl said as she reached the top of the ladder, water dripping from her body.

"You know, I bet you were in it with Harriet, that the two of you tried to kill Barb — "

"SHUT UP!" Pearl roared.

She was magnificent, Harry thought, not for the first time.

"Have lunch with me, will you?" Pearl asked suddenly, her eyes burning into Harry's.

"I'm supposed to meet Judy," Harry said hesitantly. Her regret was palpable.

Pearl sighed. "Never mind. I just had some things I wanted to talk to you about, but they can wait."

"Judy was feeling a little under the weather this morning," Harry said slowly. It would really be a shame to pass up this opportunity to question Pearl. Not that her motives were entirely altruistic, of course. "Why don't I see how she feels and give you a call?"

"Fine," Pearl said. She gave Harry a smile warm enough to melt snow.

Are you awake, hon?" Harry asked, closing the door to Judy's room and not moving until her eyes grew accustomed to the darkness.

"I feel like a truck ran over my head," Judy moaned as Harry sat down on the bed.

"It's a little after eleven," Harry told her. "I came back to see if you want to go to lunch."

"Are you kidding?" Judy grunted.

"Would you mind if I went with Pearl, then?"

Judy struggled to one elbow and stared at Harry with red-rimmed eyes. "Would it matter if I said I did?"

"Of course it would," Harry replied, the image of Pearl's naked, water-beaded body flitting into her mind and out again.

"You're such a lousy liar," Judy sighed, falling back on the bed.

"I won't go if you don't want me to," Harry insisted.

"Oh no, I'm not going to tell you what to do," Judy replied, sensible even when hungover in extremis.

"I'll bring you back something to eat, then," Harry said, giving her a kiss on the cheek and standing up. She felt guilty, but she was still going.

"Thanks," Judy muttered. "Have a good time."

Right, stick it in a little further. She let herself out, an inane smile on her face which she was thankful no one could see, and hurried back to Isadora's Hideaway. Once in her suite, she called Pearl and arranged to meet her in the patio in twenty minutes. Then she turned on the shower, adjusted the water temperature and stepped in. She washed and rinsed her hair and stood under the sharp-needled spray until her skin tingled. Why was life so bloody difficult? Even after twelve years of living with Judy, Harry was still attracted to her like a moth drawn to light. Perhaps that was a large part of the problem, she mused. How could she share someone she never wanted to be parted from?

It had been hard enough to maintain equanimity with Sarah in the wings, constantly having to negotiate who got to spend nights, long weekends and vacations with Judy. Now that Judy had confessed her affair with Barb, all kinds of doubts had crept into Harry's mind, partly because Judy had kept her affair with Barb concealed when they had agreed long ago not to keep important secrets from each other. And Judy had been in Key West for a week before Harry had arrived. What if she and Barb had become intimate again? What if they had argued about whether to reveal their relationship to Harry? Perhaps tempers had flared. No, she told herself as she turned off the shower. Judy had a temper, but she had never touched Harry in anger, and it was illogical to assume that she would suddenly become abusive in a relationship with someone else. On the other hand, Barb had this not so subtle way of letting you know that you were making a fool of yourself. But she was also an excellent judge of character and generally wouldn't taunt people past their capacity to maintain some sort of self-control and thus retain a modicum of self-respect. Still, Judy had broken more than one plate and several glasses over the years.

No. It was impossible, Harry decided as she stepped from the shower and dried her hair. She knew on an intellectual level and from previous experience that her taste in women was not infallible and that she could fall in love with someone capable of violence. But she just couldn't suspect Judy. If she'd been there when Barb had been hurt, it must have been an accident. Maybe they'd argued and Barb had lost her balance, fallen and hit her head. The police were bound to understand that it hadn't been attempted murder. Yeah, right, Harry thought. Even she wasn't deluded enough to believe that. After all, there were those bruises around Barb's neck, as if someone had been trying to strangle her.

"So what would you like to eat?" Pearl asked when they met in the patio.

Harry shrugged.

Pearl lifted Harry's sunglasses. "Let's see: we could use some carbohydrate loading and lots of vitamins, and — "

"Never mind," Harry muttered, pulling her sunglasses back down.

"Hey, I've got it. I know just the place," Pearl said, leading her through the main building. "Pier House does a great brunch."

"But that's at the other end of the island," Harry exclaimed.

"Yes, I know," Pearl replied. "But I've got a moped and you can use Barb's."

"I haven't got the key," Harry said, reluctant to tell Pearl she had never driven one.

"It's probably in the office somewhere," Pearl replied.

"Oh," Harry responded. Pride cometh before a fall, she thought desperately, resigned to being maimed, if not slaughtered, because vanity prevented her from admitting that she'd never mounted the saddle of that unfamiliar, motorized beast. She unlocked the door to the office, sat in the chair behind Barb's desk and opened the top drawer. She rummaged in it for a moment, and then said, "Well, it's not here. I guess we'll have to take my car. Or a cab."

"Try the next one," Pearl suggested with the hint of a grin in her voice.

Harry opened the second drawer.

"Well?" Pearl asked.

Harry plucked a key chain from the drawer, held it up and closed the drawer. "Is this it, do you think?"

"Why don't we find out?" Pearl responded.

Harry followed her down the steps to the parking lot beside the guesthouse, glancing longingly at her full-sized, gas-guzzling rental car parked across the street.

"That's Barb's," Pearl said, pointing to a metallic red moped, "and that black one over there is mine. I taped my name to the licence plate so I could distinguish it from half a million other black ones."

"So what do I do next?" Harry asked once she was astride the moped.

"You mean you've never ridden one before?" Pearl responded, sounding as dumbfounded as Barb had been.

"Well, you know what winters are like in Montreal. These things aren't much good in the snow," Harry responded.

"First you put the key in the ignition," Pearl instructed, using her feet to roll her scooter closer to Harry's. "Then you turn it like this," she continued.

Harry turned the key and felt the moped roar into life. "Woah!" she exclaimed as it vibrated threateningly under her.

"You advance by doing this, stop by doing that, and reverse like so," Pearl demonstrated.

"I'll never remember all that," Harry protested.

"Of course you will. Just watch me," Pearl said patiently. She slowly repeated the basics several times until Harry could follow her instructions without making a mistake. "Is that better?"

Harry nodded dubiously.

"Let's go, then," Pearl exhorted. "I'm starving."

Pearl gunned her moped and roared from the parking lot. "Come on," she shouted.

Harry moved this, pressed that, and suddenly found herself in motion. "Holy shit," she muttered anxiously, her mouth dry as she swerved right and then right again onto Duval and remembered how to apply the brakes just before she went through a red light.

"See how easy it is?" Pearl crowed.

Harry nodded as the light changed and Pearl shot through the intersection. She gulped and, ignoring the horns blaring behind her, went through Pearl's instructions until the moped finally moved. It was really quite simple, she reassured herself as she trailed behind a long line of cars, one of which turned without signalling while another ran a red light and a third stopped early on the orange. All she had to do was stay well behind cars and vans so she could stop before she rear-ended one of them. Pearl was quickly out of sight.

"Where on earth have you *been*?" Pearl asked as Harry steered her moped into a parking space not far from where the Conch Tour Train began its slow circuit of the island.

"I was unavoidably detained," Harry replied solemnly.

"By what?" Pearl asked.

"Gross inexperience," said Harry succinctly.

Pearl grinned. "Have you been to Pier House before?"

"Yes, actually," Harry replied as they walked to the end of Duval and turned into the finely manicured Pier House grounds. Pier House was on the Gulf of Mexico end of Duval Street while its counterpart, the Casa Marina, was on the Atlantic side of the city. These two hotels and the much newer townhouses in the Truman Annex were among the most exclusive — and expensive — addresses in Key West. "Judy and I once ventured to Pier House to have drinks and chili on the deck at sunset. It was a great place to watch the sun go down, although we ended up walking over to Mallory Square for the grande finale."

"I've done the sunset, too," Pearl said, "but with Barb."

"This time around?"

"No, last year," Pearl responded as they arrived at the restaurant on the dock. "Isn't this pleasant. You know, I've always enjoyed eating by the water. There's something so civilized about it."

"Do you come down here for a visit every year?" Harry asked.

"A table for two?" a waiter interrupted.

"Yes," Pearl responded.

"Do you have a reservation?" he asked, consulting his list.

"No," Pearl replied with an ostentatious glance around the restaurant, which had several empty tables.

"Follow me, please," he said, leading them to a table overlooking the Gulf.

"This is impressive," Harry commented. The harbour was filled with sailboats of every size and description.

"Isn't it, though?" Pearl said with a smile. "Bring us a number twelve, if you please," she said to the waiter.

"Certainly, madam," he responded.

"What's a number twelve?"

"Wait and see," Pearl said mysteriously.

"I suppose I'll have to."

"Shall I order for you?"

"If it makes you feel good," Harry retorted.

"Honestly," Pearl chortled.

The waiter returned with two long-stemmed, crystal goblets and a bottle of champagne.

"You didn't," Harry said in an accusatory tone.

"Yes, I did," said Pearl. The waiter expertly extracted the cork and poured.

"Are you ready to order, madam?" he asked politely.

"We'll start with caesar salad," Pearl said thoughtfully, "and then we'll have eggs benedict followed by strawberries and cream. And coffee."

"Very good, madam," the waiter nodded.

"To you," Pearl said.

Harry raised her glass and drank.

"Something's bothering you."

"I'm not sure why you're doing this," Harry said.

"Why shouldn't I?" Pearl asked with a melancholic smile.

"I don't know," Harry responded. "I mean, it's not that I don't appreciate it."

Pearl smiled and refilled their glasses.

"Who are you, anyway?" Harry asked.

"Your salad, madam," the waiter said.

"Why do you persist in asking impossible questions?" Pearl responded as soon as he left.

"Because I don't know anything about you," Harry said, buttering a piece of roll. It was the first thing she'd had to eat that day and she was starving.

"What would you like to know?" Pearl asked quietly, as she poised a fork over her salad. When Harry didn't respond immediately, she began to eat. Harry followed suit and there was contented silence for a few minutes.

"Are you with someone? I mean, do you have a lover in New York?" Harry asked finally, and then she felt like kicking herself. Of all the dumb questions to put to a suspect in an assault case!

The waiter chose that precise moment to swoop down and remove the remains of their salads and to serve their eggs benedict.

"There's no one special," Pearl answered. "That's not to say that I haven't had a lot of lovers, however."

Harry realized that Pearl was exaggerating, which made her smile. "Have you and Barb been lovers ever since you were in university?"

"Do you have a problem with the concept of non-monogamous fidelity?" Pearl asked with mock horror. "What kind of latter-day dyke are you?"

Harry nearly choked.

"I know, you want me to be serious," Pearl sighed. "It sounds inadequate to say that Barb and I are friends. Unfortunately, we don't have an appropriate word for our relationship. It's part sexual and part something which neither of us is introspective enough to want to define."

Harry wondered what it would be like if she and Barb were still lovers. The thought that she was likely the only one who hadn't remained an active sexual partner of Barb's brought unexpected tears to her eyes.

"Eat," Pearl commanded grimly, turning to her eggs benedict.

"But you do love her," Harry said when she could speak again.

"Don't you?" came the astute rejoinder.

Harry picked up her champagne glass and drained it. "Do you come down here every year?"

"Twice a year. Or at least I did," Pearl added, making a face. "Who knows what will happen now."

"Was that the only time you and Barb saw each other?" Harry asked curiously.

"Nearly," Pearl smiled regretfully. "Once in a while she'd visit me in New York."

This time Harry wasn't surprised when the waiter imposed himself between them, replacing their empty plates with bowls piled high with strawberries and whipped cream.

"Judy and I have been together for twelve years," Harry said abruptly. "But you knew they were lovers, didn't you?"

"Barb and Judy?" Pearl asked. "Yes. Barb told me. She was afraid she'd made a mistake."

"She never said anything to me."

"She was worried that you wouldn't understand."

"She was right," Harry sighed. "But it doesn't matter now. Were you referring to Judy when you told the police there might be another of Barb's lovers staying at the Hideaway?"

"Yes," Pearl nodded. "I stopped myself from blurting out her name at the last second when I realized that you didn't know."

"Have you ever lived with someone for a long time?"

"No, it never came up," Pearl said as she finished her champagne and gestured to the waiter. "There were women in my life, but no one I wanted to be with on a long-term basis. Bring us another bottle of champagne," she told the waiter.

"I think we've already had enough," Harry remonstrated as the waiter hurried off.

"Speak for yourself," Pearl commented. "This little heart-to-heart is obviously difficult for both of us. Meanwhile, I'm off to the ladies' room. Why don't you order more coffee when the waiter comes back? Rumour has it that it will keep us sober."

Harry sat back and basked in the heat. Moments later the waiter returned with their second bottle of champagne and she ordered another pot of coffee. Then Pearl slipped into her chair and picked up her champagne glass.

"Tell me more about yourself," Harry pressed.

"I wish I felt confident that you're asking that question for all the right reasons," Pearl said casually, as if they were discussing the weather instead of trust and dishonesty, love and betrayal, life and death. "But life's a bitch, isn't it?" she continued without waiting for Harry's response. "Nothing is straightforward any more, not like it used to be in the old days. Of course that was probably the ignorance of youth, although I'd rather go blithely through life and not wonder whether someone's preparing to stab me in the back or, for that matter, in the front."

"I know what you mean," Harry replied.

"Do you," Pearl commented, sitting back with a contemplative look on her face.

"Yes," Harry confirmed. The fact that she required more information if she was going to discover who had attacked Barb was something Pearl didn't have to know.

"Well, I was born a little over fifty years ago in a exceedingly small town in England, after which my parents moved to London, where my father worked as a barrister in a rather obscure government department and my mother tended house and raised me and a pack of other considerably less distinguished siblings who came along sporadically," Pearl said with a slightly wicked expression on her face.

Pearl had guessed what she was up to, Harry realized uneasily, staring down into her champagne glass and watching the bubbles rise to the surface. She wondered if she would feel a wet, fuzzy touch on her face if she lifted her glass and held it against her cheek.

"My mother was a rather vague sort of woman. Everything about her was pale. Skin, emotions, affect. So I grew up without much supervision or discipline, which was quite enjoyable for me, less so for my parents and teachers. I became a communist at quite a young age, but then swiftly switched to anarchism when I discovered, much to my fascination, that the only rule was that there were no rules. Of course that's not precisely true, but it was good enough for me," Pearl said, pouring herself another glass of champagne. "You're not drinking."

"I've had enough," Harry said.

"You should never say that," Pearl scolded.

Harry sipped some coffee. "So you met Barb, and then what?"

"Tell me, is it just plain old lust which fuels your curiosity or have you an ulterior motive?" Pearl asked, tilting her head to one side.

"That's not a fair question," Harry protested.

"I wish you'd trust me enough to tell me the truth," Pearl said suddenly.

That was likely the first genuine thing Pearl had said to her that morning, and it made her feel guilty. "It's not that I don't trust you—"

"Yeah, I know," Pearl interrupted wearily. "It's just that you don't trust me enough. But that's all right. It happens all the time."

Harry's stomach felt sour from the combination of champagne and coffee and she pushed her half-empty coffee cup away. "Sorry," she muttered. She wondered how she could find out about Pearl's financial situation without coming right out and asking. Why was it easier to pose questions about someone's love life than about the state of their bank account?

"You know, the content of Barb's new will astounded me, especially the fact that she left her brother twenty thousand dollars," Pearl commented suddenly.

"Why, did you think she'd cut him out of her will altogether?"

"It could have gone either way," Pearl responded. "Sometimes I thought she wouldn't leave him a dime, other times she seemed to feel responsible for him. Barb's always been frustrated that Peter couldn't make anything of himself. Of course she's too emotionally involved to realize that he's really passive. Barb thinks that if she can do it, then so can he. Poor guy. She's forever berating him about not being able to hold down a job for more than a couple of months. But then, he wasn't trained to do anything in particular, and these days, unless you've got a fabulous track record or you've had the opportunity to learn about computers or the know-how and financial resources to open your own business, it's terribly difficult to get a decent job."

"That's true," Harry responded, surprised at Pearl's long-winded speech.

"That's why Barb always planned to leave me twenty thousand dollars if she passed on to the big orgy in the sky before me," Pearl said, pouring the last of the champagne into her glass. "However, that's another story, and we haven't finished talking about Peter yet. I suppose you know there's absolutely no love lost between Barb and Ross. She thought he was a first-class leech."

"What would you do with the twenty thousand? Open a business?" Harry asked.

"Maybe," Pearl responded reluctantly. "Actually, I haven't thought about it because Barb is still alive." She glanced at her watch. "My, isn't it strange how time flies when you're having fun," she said briskly. "I've got to be going."

"Really," Harry said, knowing she'd been told to mind her own business.

"Yes. But you could stay and order another pot of coffee."

"I promised Judy I'd bring her something to eat," Harry said. "But I'll see you back at the guesthouse."

"Sure," Pearl responded as she waved at the waiter.

"Perhaps we can continue our conversation later," Harry added, thinking of all the questions she wanted to ask but hadn't.

"Perhaps," Pearl replied with studied ambiguity. "Actually, there a few other things besides conversation I wouldn't mind continuing."

Harry picked up her purse and pretended to search for her wallet.

"You're too ambivalent for your own good," Pearl muttered.

"Madam would like the check?" the waiter asked.

"Yes. This should cover my share," Pearl said, tossing several bills on the table.

"Pearl — "

"It's all right, Harriet," Pearl interrupted, rising from the table.

Harry knew very well that it wasn't, but Pearl left before she could say another word.

"Sorry I'm so late," Harry apologized as she rushed into Judy's room.

"It doesn't matter," Judy replied. "I just woke up."

"I'll open the curtains," Harry said, placing a brown paper bag on the table by the patio doors. She wiped the sweat from her forehead and sat down, feeling breathless and dishevelled. After leaving Pier House, she had rather unsteadily driven the moped to the hospital and visited Barb until one of the nurses had tossed her out after fifteen minutes. No one else had come in when she'd been there, so she'd tried to ignore the hovering police officer and talk softly about anything that came to mind. She'd rambled about the past, mainly — how they'd met and become lovers, some of the silly things they'd done together, the people they both knew. As she'd talked, the police officer had returned to her chair, her attention often wandering to the steady stream of nurses, interns and residents hurrying in and out. There'd been times when the officer hadn't seemed to be paying attention even though Harry had been leaning over Barb, which made Harry begin to worry about security again. What if her intentions had been murderous? What if she'd hidden a needle in her pocket, intending to inject Barb with an overdose as soon as an occasion presented itself? How long would it have taken?

"Excuse me," she had finally said to the startled police officer. "I think you should be watching me more closely."

"What?"

"I noticed that your concentration wandered a couple of times," Harry had continued, feeling stupid saying this to a cop. "What if I had a needle hidden on me? I actually think I'd have had time to inject her without you noticing."

The police officer's face had reddened and she'd asked Harry for her name, which she'd then written in her notebook. Harry had wondered whether the officer was planning to search her, but seconds later a nurse had banished her from Barb's cubicle. She'd gone willingly at that point, wondering how long it would take for her name to get back to detectives Allan and Dovercourt. She'd made her way to the hospital cafeteria, bought some lunch for Judy and then driven back to the motel.

"Are you all right, Judy?" Harry asked.

"As well as can be expected," Judy replied. She got up and walked slowly to the table as Harry opened the paper bag and removed a large cup of soup, an egg sandwich and a bottle of orange juice. "Why didn't you stop me from drinking so much?"

"I tried, but it was an impossible task," Harry laughed, twisting the cap from the orange juice.

"You're right," admitted Judy, brushing her hair off her face. "I must be a real mess."

"You'll feel better when you eat something."

"How was your lunch?" Judy asked, taking the top off the soup. "God, this is just what I needed."

"Lunch was fine." Harry got up and looked out the patio door. The compound, deserted the night before, was now crowded with svelte sunbathers, and the pool was full of swimmers.

"Have you slept with her yet?"

"No!" Harry turned around and stared at her lover.

"I'm surprised," Judy said without looking up. She was too busy demolishing her egg sandwich. "I hope you don't mind, but I called Sarah and asked her to come over. I hate being that upset about anything."

"No, I don't mind," Harry replied, not wanting to think about a possible reconciliation between Judy and Sarah. "I've got a lot of things to do. I want to visit Barb again later today, and Karen's refused to cooperate with me about running the guesthouse, so I have to do something about that. And I'm worried about hospital security."

"What on earth do you mean?"

"As you know, there's round-the-clock surveillance, but the police officer on duty this afternoon was half asleep and easily distracted. I could have killed Barb several times over if I'd had a mind to."

"But surely you don't think someone would be dumb enough to try to attack her while she's in intensive care," Judy said with characteristic logic. "They'd be bound to be caught, wouldn't they?"

"Perhaps," Harry conceded reluctantly. "But what if someone was desperate? After all, the person who assaulted her must be afraid that Barb's going to wake up and identify them."

"There is that," Judy admitted. "You shouldn't worry so much, though. The police know what they're doing."

"You're probably right," Harry said, although she wasn't convinced. She'd already decided to discuss her concerns with the police, although she didn't tell Judy that. "Anyway, I'll be leaving now."

"Thanks for lunch," Judy smiled up at her. "I almost feel human again."

"No problem." Harry leaned down and kissed Judy on the forehead. "Are you coming back to the Hideaway?"

"Would you mind awfully if I spend another night here?" Judy asked, stroking Harry's cheek with her fingertips.

So. Judy wanted to spend the night with Sarah. "Must you?" Harry queried softly.

"I think so," Judy responded just as there was a knock on the door. "You know that my relationship with Sarah means a lot to me, and I don't want to jeopardize it because of a momentary fit of jealousy."

"But we're supposed to be together this week," Harry protested.

"Look, Sarah's basically spending all of her time with Karen because Karen's so distraught. But I convinced her that we had to talk, and I need this opportunity to be with her," Judy insisted. "Why don't we meet for brunch tomorrow?"

"Fine," Harry capitulated, knowing that nothing she could say would deflect Judy's determination. She walked over to the door, opened it, and then stood aside to let Sarah in. "I'm just on my way out," she said, grabbing her purse and leaving. She closed the door and leaned against it for a moment. Pearl was right. Nothing was ever simple. She hurried down the stairs to the motel office and found the number of the Key West police department in the telephone book.

"Is Detective Allan there?" she asked, giving her name.

Ten minutes later, Detective Dovercourt arrived at the motel office. She was dressed in a cream-coloured pantsuit with matching earrings. "What do you mean, there's a problem with security in Ms.

Fenton's room?" she asked, staring at Harry as if to say, "stop wasting my time and confess."

"Why don't we go for a walk?" Harry suggested, looking around the crowded room.

Detective Dovercourt was evidently allergic to exercise, because she led Harry outside to her black, late model, four-door car, which was sitting in a no parking zone in front of the office. "Get in." Harry opened the door and slid in. The seats were leather and the interior was cool and smelled of car deodorizer. She buckled her seat belt as Detective Dovercourt pulled out of the parking lot. "I heard about what you said to the police officer on duty in Ms. Fenton's room," Detective Dovercourt said as she gunned the car around the corner. "She called in to report that you seemed to be threatening to inject Ms. Fenton with something."

"I said no such thing," Harry replied, holding on as the detective made another turn. "I simply suggested that the officer's attention was wandering a little too much, and that if someone was bent on killing Barb, they'd have the opportunity to do just that if she wasn't more vigilant."

"Do you think we're stupid?" Detective Dovercourt asked scornfully as she drove swiftly along South Roosevelt. "She was watching you like a hawk, whether you realized it or not."

The officer's head had been bobbing up and down like a pigeon's, but Harry abstained from mentioning that. She should have known that Detective Dovercourt would react badly. She stared out the window, watching the waves break lazily over the boulders dotting the coast. She was tempted to open the window and let the muggy air and the salt spray into the car, but the air conditioning was on full blast. "I wasn't making a judgement about police competency, I was simply expressing my concerns," she responded carefully, wishing she hadn't bothered to call the police. How likely was it that they would believe that one of their major suspects was worried about Barb's safety?

"Considering that you had both motive and opportunity to attack Barbara Fenton, it was rather outrageous of you to say what you did to the officer on duty in Ms. Fenton's room," Detective Dovercourt commented as she pulled off the road. "I was planning to question you again, but your remarks reconfirmed my belief that you might be ready to cooperate with us and tell us about your own involvement in this case."

Before Harry could protest, Detective Dovercourt had left the car. "Damm," Harry muttered to herself. "But I'm not involved," she shouted as she scrambled from the front seat and followed the detective.

"You were Barbara Fenton's lover and you stand to inherit a good part of her estate," Detective Dovercourt pointed out as Harry caught up to her.

"I don't deny that," Harry responded. "But I didn't attack her."

"We'll see," Detective Dovercourt said with an enigmatic smile.

What the hell was going on, Harry wondered, watching Detective Dovercourt move sure-footedly from boulder to boulder until she reached a large, flat stone at the edge of the water. Harry removed her sandals and followed her.

"There are fields of wildflowers, of daffodils, of wild grass," Detective Dovercourt commented as Harry joined her. "Well, I always think of this as a field of boulders."

Harry tried this on for size and found it a hard fit. She stared out to sea. The whitecaps foamed irregularly, some of them pounding the seemingly immovable boulders, others dissipating before they reached the shore as if there was a storm far out to sea which raged and abated according to some primal rhythm of its own.

"You think I don't like gay people, don't you?" Detective Dovercourt said suddenly.

Harry closed her eyes as a rogue wave ran up the rocks and splashed forcefully against the boulder on which they were sitting. The shockingly cold water splashed her clothes and took her breath away.

"I'm not homophobic, Ms. Hubbley," Detective Dovercourt continued, ignoring the wave. "But I've been a member of this police force for years, and I've had more than enough firsthand experience with the carefree and sometimes dangerous ways of the gay community."

Harry looked sharply at her and then glanced at the ocean as another wave crested. "I think we'd better move."

"Yes," Detective Dovercourt agreed. "It wouldn't do if one of the investigating officers and the main suspect got swept out to sea, would it?"

Harry pursed her lips and stepped carefully from boulder to boulder. "I didn't attack Barb," she said to Detective Dovercourt as they got back into her car.

"I don't believe you," Detective Dovercourt replied candidly.

They made the return drive to Isadora's Hideaway in silence.

"Thanks," Harry said as she got out.

"I did hear what you said, Ms. Hubbley," Detective Dovercourt remarked before turning away.

Harry nodded, although she wasn't particularly reassured. She hurried up the stairs, went into the office and slumped down in the chair behind Barb's desk. She was tired of Detective Dovercourt with her suspicious eyes and her intimidating scowl. But there wasn't a damn thing she could do to deter the police from suspecting her — not unless she could find out who had attacked Barb. And she had to admit to herself that she was no closer today to discovering Barb's assailant than she had been yesterday. The whole thing was enough to try the soul of a saint, Harry thought as she absently shifted a dusty file from one stack to another.

Three hours later, the top of the desk was devoid of papers. Harry hadn't planned to begin housecleaning, but the phone had started to ring and before long she'd been up to her elbows in work. When the phone had stopped ringing and she'd had a moment to take stock, she'd decided that she couldn't possibly function efficiently in such a messy environment, especially if Karen wasn't going to help. So she'd inspected the contents of the filing cabinet and then turned her attention to the desk.

Harry had sorted message slips, letters, files and anything that looked financial. Once she'd done that, she'd taken all the files from the drawers and added them to her piles. Then she'd leafed through the files to make sure they were properly labelled and placed them in the appropriate hanging file in the cabinet. She'd stopped to open several new master files, using the tabs she'd discovered in the bottom drawer and empty hanging files she'd found at the back of the bottom drawer of the filing cabinet, and she had soon tucked all of them away precisely where they belonged. She'd then tackled the letters, dividing them into two piles consisting of those which could be filed immediately and those which needed further attention. That accomplished, she'd spent a further twenty minutes filing them, after which she'd created a separate file for those that still had to be answered and put it in the top drawer. She'd spent considerably more time browsing through financial documents, relieved to see that things seemed to be in order. She'd assumed that there was accounting software on the computer, but she hadn't taken time to look for it. That task would have to wait for another day. She'd created a new file for unpaid invoices and put it with the other new file in the top drawer. Then she'd read through the message slips, putting Karen's messages to one side and ordering the remainder by date.

Her final task had been to clean the desk. She'd put the computer on the floor, thinking that she should dust that, too. "There must be furniture polish somewhere," she'd muttered to herself, opening the door to the bedroom. Barb had been right. The room was tiny, with barely enough room for a single bed. There was certainly no space for a dresser or even a bedside table. Instead, there were hooks attached to the wall in a neat row and a metal wall lamp. The walls themselves were painted light apricot and the bed was covered with an antique star-burst quilt. A hideaway within the Hideaway, Harry had thought, wondering how often Barb had used it.

She'd walked past the bed, opened the sliding door at the end of the room and found herself in the bathroom, amazed that it had been possible to cram a toilet, sink and shower stall into such a small space. The appliances and the walls were the same shade of apricot as the bedroom. She'd peeked behind the shower curtain, gratified to see a bucket of cleaning supplies, including a can of furniture polish. She'd taken it and a roll of paper towels and returned to the office, where she'd proceeded to thoroughly polish the desk. She'd glanced at the bookcase with some distaste, knowing that sooner or later she'd have to tackle it. Books and magazines were heaped on top of each other, piles of pamphlets and maps threatened to tumble to the floor, several mounds of old, yellowed newspapers looked about to crumble and yet more files as well as dusty knick-knacks and framed photographs were scattered throughout. She'd also spied and rescued two paper trays filled with books. Seconds later, they'd been washed in the sink in the bathroom, dried with a hand towel and installed on one corner of the desk.

Wonderful, Harry had thought to herself, sitting down behind the desk and surveying its shiny, pristine surface. Barb would have a good chuckle if she could see her desk now. "You're compulsive about dust," she always said whenever Harry visited. "Why, I could eat off your floors." Harry claimed it was because of her allergies while Barb maintained that the allergies were just an excuse. Harry had stopped arguing because she knew it was useless. Once Barb made up her mind about something, she wouldn't change it for the world. What a stubborn old duck Barb was, Harry thought. A sudden wave of sadness brought tears into her eyes.

But never mind; she still had work to do. She went to the filing cabinet to search for information on the Hideaway's suppliers, swiftly locating laundry bills and receipts for cleaning and catering services. It was after five, but much to her relief she reached the managers of all three services and was reassured that the usual cleaning of rooms and common spaces, the pick-up of soiled laundry, the delivery of freshly laundered sheets and towels and of food service for the continental breakfast would continue as before. She told the manager of the cleaning service to ask the cleaner regularly assigned to the Hideaway to drop by and say hello, and then hung up.

Finally, she shook herself mentally and decided that there was nothing else she could do this evening. She retrieved the telephone book from one of the shelves, looked up the number of the Southernmost Motel and asked for room 222, but there was no reply. Judy and Sarah had gone out for an early dinner, she told herself stoically. Either that or they were in bed and not inclined to be interrupted. She took Porter Ambrose's card from her purse and called him.

"I was just thinking about you," he said immediately.

"Are you busy?"

"Is the boyfriend of a doctor ever busy in the evening?" he replied rhetorically. "How about dinner?"

"Fine," Harry answered.

"I'll be there in half an hour," Porter said.

Harry hung up. How in the world could she run the guesthouse twenty-four hours a day? And what was going to happen once she returned to Montreal? Maybe Barb would come out of her coma before then, she thought as she rose from her chair. She picked up the computer and decided to wash it before she put it back on the desk. She might as well be like Nero, playing with her modern-day fiddle while Rome burned.

Some time later, after she'd painstakingly scoured the dirt-stained keys on the keyboard one by one and carefully wiped the screen, she turned on the computer and began to explore. She'd already used the reservation software, so she called it up and made notes on a lined pad. It was amazing how people came and went, she mused, looking at the list she had made. There wasn't a day this week when someone wasn't checking out.

"Aren't you ready yet?" Porter commented.

"Oh!" Harry started. "I didn't hear you come in."

"Obviously not," he said with a grin. He was nattily dressed in a tan suit and matching cap.

"Sorry," she said, glancing at her watch as she switched off the computer and stood up. "I completely lost track of the time."

"We're in no hurry," he assured her. "Monday nights aren't all that busy, so I didn't bother to make a reservation. I thought I'd copy Barb's power of attorney document and will for you, by the way."

"Thanks," Harry said, taking the documents from him. What should she do about the office while she was out? There was no way she could be there all the time, so the guests would just have to get used to it. She tore a sheet of paper from the notepad, wrote "Back at ten p.m." on it and stuck it on the door. "I hope no one gets upset, but there's nothing else I can do. Karen made it clear to me that she didn't want to help."

"Really," Porter said, surprised. "I thought she'd fight tooth and nail to keep you from getting involved in the day-to-day operations of the guesthouse."

"No such luck."

"Actually, don't knock it," he advised her. "This might be for the best. When you get back tonight, decide what hours you want to keep, type up a schedule, and tape it to the door. That way guests will know in advance when you're going to be here."

"That's a great idea," Harry responded enthusiastically. "Now why didn't I think of it? Still, that won't solve my other problems."

"Let's continue this conversation over dinner," Porter suggested. "I'll wait outside while you get changed."

"Fine," Harry answered, locking the office door behind them. "Enjoy your cigar."

"It hasn't taken you long to figure me out," he said with a laugh.

Twenty minutes later, Harry and Porter were seated in the garden at La-Te-Da on Duval Street sipping red wine. They had both ordered the green salad with house dressing while Harry, still feeling sated from her brunch at Pier House, had chosen a seafood pasta. Porter had ordered Italian sausage and pasta with tomato sauce, which, he assured Harry, was the best he'd ever eaten. Unfortunately, La-Te-Da's chef had vowed he would never reveal the recipe even under threat of death, as it was an old family recipe that had been passed down from generation to generation since before recorded time. Or so the chef said, especially when he was in his cups, Porter added.

"Where on earth do you get these stories?" Harry laughed. "No, don't tell me. There's a course in law school on how to entertain clients."

"Precisely. Now, fill me in on what's bothering you," said Porter as the waiter served their salads.

"Do you have all night?" Harry quipped. "For one thing, I'm completely overwhelmed by having to run the guesthouse, especially with Karen out of the picture."

"Just take it one step at a time, like deciding to set reasonable office hours." Porter refilled her wine glass. "Great wine, isn't it? I always order it when I come here."

"It's wonderful wine," Harry agreed. "I know that what you're saying is true, but some people study for years and then work their way up before they're ready to run a place like the Hideaway."

"Barb didn't," Porter pointed out.

"Yes, but she started small and learned as the business grew. And suddenly I'm stuck running a place with thirty rooms, even if it is temporarily."

"Just don't talk yourself into a real funk," he advised.

"You're right," Harry sighed, watching the waiter deftly remove their empty salad plates. "I'll start studying Barb's financial situation tomorrow and see where that leads me."

"That's better," Porter said soothingly. "You'll see, things will calm down after a few days."

"But the problem is that I have to leave Sunday," Harry pointed out.

Porter hesitated. "The police came to see me today," he said reluctantly. "They wanted to talk about you. I told them you had retained me in my professional capacity so I couldn't really help them. But I don't think you're going to be returning to Montreal until they make an arrest."

"I know. Detective Dovercourt gave me the fourth degree again this afternoon," Harry responded glumly. "I'm hoping they'll find the killer between now and then."

"Well, they've got lots of suspects."

"With me as number one," Harry interjected.

"Closely followed by Peter, Ross, Karen and Pearl," Porter added.

"The police don't know about it, but you can add Judy, Sarah, Alison Wheatley and Martin Culver to your private list," Harry said.

"What? Your lover is a suspect?" yelped Porter.

Harry swiftly told him about Judy and Alison's affairs with Barb, and Sarah's with Karen.

"How much more complicated can this get? And the police don't know?" Porter asked as the waiter approached.

"I doubt it," Harry said as the waiter served their pasta.

"Then they might not be asking the right questions," Porter commented as he sliced into a fat piece of Italian sausage. "Oh, how I adore this stuff. Why is it that everything I love to eat is bad for me?"

"Never mind," Harry said sympathetically, watching him savour his meal.

"Thank you," he bowed. "You only live once, so why spoil it with unappetizing food? But back to the business at hand. Shouldn't the police be informed about what you know?"

"I can't tell the police something which would put my lover under suspicion," Harry protested. Or even my lover's lover, she thought sourly, although she was sorely tempted. Alison Wheatley was another matter, but even then, it wasn't Harry's style to play confidante with the police.

"You're right," Porter said glumly. "Neither could I."

"The problem is that they all had opportunity, even Peter and Ross. And everyone has at least one motive, most of them two or three," Harry mused as she ate a shrimp and then sliced into a scallop. "Every time I manage to question someone, another motive or two pops up. It's driving me crazy."

"Do you think the attack was premeditated?"

"I don't know," said Harry. "Perhaps tempers flared and Barb fell and hit her head, although that doesn't explain the bruises around her neck. I just keep going around in circles. Sometimes I think it was an accident, other times I'm almost certain it was planned."

"In reality, we'll probably discover that it falls somewhere between the two," Porter said reasonably. "Perhaps there was a point at which her assailant could have stopped but didn't."

"You may be right," Harry agreed.

"What motives have you come up with so far?" Porter asked as he ate his last piece of sausage.

"Nothing stunning, I'll tell you that," Harry said, her tone self-deprecatory. "Greed or jealousy."

"Ah, greed," Porter nodded knowingly. "I know all about that. Lawyers always do. Somebody in desperate financial straits finds out they're going to inherit a bundle and they decide to give their benefactor a nudge toward the grave. Or someone doesn't have the patience to wait until a family member or friend dies a natural death. In Barb's case, we're talking about you, Karen Lipsky, Peter Fenton and Pearl Vernon. Of course," he added quickly, "I've only included your name for the sake being totally accurate."

"Of course. But if you really thought about it, you'd have to add Judy Johnson to your list of suspects, because of her relationship with me, and Sarah Reid, because she's a long-term lover of Karen's, and Ross Hunter," Harry said.

"You're right," Porter said with a grim nod. "Lovers have been known to take an interest in the large inheritances their partners are going to receive."

"And that doesn't even cover jealousy," Harry commented glumly. "If you factor in all the relationships people have with each other, everyone we already mentioned is suspect in one way or another, with the addition of Alison Wheatley and even Martin Culver. He could have been upset that Alison and Barb resumed their affair in Dallas last year."

"I suppose we could even put the two motives together," Porter said. "Someone who was jealous about one or another of Barb's affairs could also have benefited financially from her early death, either directly or indirectly."

They looked at each other and then Harry sighed. "It's really frustrating, in part because any one of them could have done it."

"And I suppose it isn't easy suspecting someone you care about," Porter commented.

"It sure isn't," Harry stressed. "Still, the worst thing is not being able to find out who attacked her. Porter, you must have a certain amount of leeway as an attorney. I was thinking that maybe it would be interesting to get everyone together for an evening. I mean, would it be a great imposition for you to invite them to a cocktail party at your house sometime soon? Like tomorrow night?"

"That sounds like a marvellous idea!" he exclaimed immediately. "Everyone would come to an innocent little soiree with plenty of things to nibble on and copious alcoholic libations."

"It might help to have them all together in the same room, without the police around."

"Of course it would!" he agreed enthusiastically. "Imagine how the sparks will fly when they start socializing with each other!"

"Some of them probably won't show up simply because of that," Harry told him.

"Ah, but you haven't taken my devious character into account," he said with a wily smirk. "I'll think of something so riveting to tell them that they won't be able to stay away."

"You devil, you," Harry grinned.

"All you have to do is come prepared to ferret out Barb's assailant," he said, signalling their waiter for the check.

"That's easier said than done," Harry warned. She watched him carelessly toss several twenty dollar bills on the table and return his wallet to his back pocket.

"Oh, I'm quite aware of that," Porter said with genuine jocularity. "But any old excuse for a party. Although Barb will be royally pissed when she finds out we had it without her."

"Naturally," Harry replied casually, although it hurt to respond so nonchalantly.

"Oh, fuck," Porter muttered under his breath. "I just wish she'd wake up and tell us who did it."

"You and me both," Harry sighed. As they left La-Te-Da, she said, "Look, I don't know how to thank you."

"You don't have to," Porter replied. "We both know what needs to be done. Meanwhile, I'll walk you back."

Harry weaved to the side of the street to avoid a pack of chattering lesbians. Duval was crowded with late diners and gay men and women going for a drink at one of the bars. She wished she was one of them, out on a carefree date with Judy, looking forward to a night of fun, their only quandary being which bar to privilege with their custom in a town full of gay establishments.

"There's no other city like this in the contiguous United States," Porter said, striking a match on his thumbnail and lighting a half-smoked cigar. "Non-contiguous either, for that matter."

"The world, even," Harry replied as she watched two young lesbians who could barely keep their eyes off each other stroll hand in hand, oblivious to everyone else. It had been a long time since she'd walked down the street like that. Far too long, she thought suddenly, feeling the weight of age and the cynicism of her relationships. Key West was no place to be estranged from friends or lovers.

"Tomorrow at seven?" Porter queried as they reached the Hideaway.

"Certainly."

"I'm sure none of them will refuse my invitation, especially if I tell them I have something confidential to impart."

"Is that ethical?" Harry couldn't stop herself from asking.

"Here's my address," Porter replied with a smile, handing her his card.

"I'll be there," Harry promised. She ran up the steps.

"And Harriet," he called to her as she opened the door.

"What?"

"If you do discover something significant between now and then, give the police a call."

"I will," Harry told him.

His duty done, Porter waved his cigar-laden hand at her and sauntered off. What a sweetheart, she thought.

She had just finished listening to the messages on the answering machine and typing out a list of temporary office hours on an index card (nine to noon; two to four; seven to nine, with the exception of tomorrow evening), when Pearl burst into the office.

"Where have you *been*? And what have you done to this office?" Pearl added, looking around.

"Not much," Harry responded, pushing past Pearl to tape the card on the door, affixing it at eye level so no one would miss it.

"I go fishing for half a day and when I come back, everything's changed," Pearl complained.

"Stop exaggerating," Harry laughed. "And I didn't know you liked to fish."

"There's lots about me you don't know," Pearl said with a flirtatious smile, lightly running her fingers up and down Harry's spine.

"Don't," Harry protested, twisting away. She felt slightly out of control in Pearl's presence and it made her tense.

"Are you rejecting me?" Pearl asked, perching on the edge of the desk.

"No," Harry responded quietly, sitting in Barb's chair. She glanced up and for a moment they stared into each other's eyes. Harry dropped hers first, afraid.

Pearl jumped down from the desk and opened the door to the small bedroom. "I'll be in here."

"Is that where you and ..."

"Mostly," Pearl said, and disappeared into the room.

"Shit," Harry muttered. She got up, locked the office door and went into the bedroom. It was in complete darkness. The curtains had been pulled and the lights were off. "Pearl?"

"Here," Pearl responded from the direction of the bed, a smile in her voice.

Harry stood still. Did she want this?

"Harriet?"

What a dumb question, she reflected. She had wanted Pearl ever since she'd first seen her in Barb's office, looking so tall and handsome and impossibly blond. "Coming," she muttered fiercely, launching herself at the bed.

"Let's get your clothes off," Pearl said, tugging at her tee-shirt.

"Why do you always call me Harriet?" Harry asked as she removed her earrings.

Pearl's fingers grew still and, seconds later, fell away. "Why do you ask?"

"Because so few people call me by my real name. I was named after a great-aunt and Harriet's quite old-fashioned. Harry's also a cute moniker for a dyke." They were so close that Harry felt Pearl stifle a sigh.

"You read the letter Barb left for me, didn't you?" Harry ventured.

"No."

"Don't lie to me, Pearl," Harry warned her softly. She reached up and turned on the wall lamp.

"All right, I did," Pearl whispered.

"When?" Harry asked. She climbed off the bed to put some distance between herself and Pearl's naked body.

"Barb came up to New York to visit me last month," Pearl said. "God! At times like this, I wish I still smoked. But never mind. She and Karen were going through a particularly bad time and she wanted to get away," Pearl continued as she slid down and pulled the covers up to her neck. "She didn't tell Karen where she was going. In fact, to this day I think Karen believes Barb went to Mexico on a retreat. Anyway, she stayed for a week."

"As your lover."

"You must have guessed by now that we never really stopped being lovers," Pearl said, giving Harry a kind look. "Whenever we were together, we started up where we had left off. It was nice to have her all to myself for once since she was rarely willing to leave the guesthouse for any length of time. I don't think she trusted Karen to take good care of it."

"Doesn't Karen do a lot of the work?"

"Karen *says* she does a lot of the work," Pearl responded, "but in reality, Barb's the one who runs this place. Oh, don't get me wrong, sometimes Karen knuckles down and puts in a lot of hours, but she's so moody that Barb never knows when she'll suddenly decide that the guesthouse is getting in the way of her precious art, which I've long thought was simply an affectation. I'll give her the benefit of the doubt and agree that she had talent when she was younger, but I don't think she had the discipline to develop it. Being a successful artist is a serious business, not a career for someone who's lazy. Or temperamental."

"I never really understood their relationship," Harry admitted.

"I don't think they had much of one," responded Pearl with a smile. "You see, I think Barb had a problem with intimacy, although she didn't like living alone."

"What?" Harry exclaimed, perching on the edge of the bed. "How can you even think that? Barb was intimate with more women than anyone I know."

"Having sex isn't necessarily the same thing as intimacy," Pearl pointed out.

"I know, but — "

"I think Barb preferred to be in a long-term relationship with someone she wasn't passionately in love with," Pearl interrupted. "Like me. Or you."

"Me?" Harry sputtered.

"You don't think she decided to leave you most of her estate because of the colour of your eyes, do you?"

Harry moaned and fell back on the bed. All those times Barb had given her that special look, all those times she'd said, "I love you."

"But we never had sex after we broke up."

"Don't be dumb," Pearl told her, cuddling up to her.

"You're right," Harry admitted. "That doesn't mean a thing, does it? But tell me the rest. Barb came to visit you in New York last month and showed you the letter she'd written to me. And then what? Did she show you her new will, too?"

Pearl's hand moved under Harry's tee-shirt.

"Stop trying to distract me," Harry said firmly. "Did she or didn't she?"

"Yes," Pearl said, her response muffled because her face was buried in Harry's neck.

There was nothing sexual about the tentative hug Harry gave Pearl then; it was too full of apprehension. Perhaps Porter's cocktail party wouldn't be necessary after all.

"She said she wanted me to know what she was planning to leave me," Pearl continued. "She also wanted me to meet you, although you might not believe that. Dammit, why doesn't she wake up? Then she'd be able to tell you that every word I'm saying is true. At any rate, that's why she gave me the cash to buy a ticket to fly here this week. She wanted us to be friends. Or whatever."

"She paid your way down?" Harry asked.

"Twice a year," Pearl replied. "Look, you may as well know that I'm flat broke most of the time. Without Barb's help, I'd have had to go on welfare more than once."

"But what do you do?"

"Not a hell of a lot, at least not now," Pearl said frankly, rolling over on her back. "But I spent quite a few years raising my kids."

"Your — "

"Four of them," Pearl said, giving Harry a shrewd look. "But that's all right. You don't have to hide your astonishment."

"I'm sorry," Harry squirmed.

"You're like most other lesbians who never took that route. When you meet a woman, you never assume that she might have married and had children," Pearl continued, ignoring Harry's apology.

"You were married?"

"Long enough to get pregnant four times," Pearl responded with a grim laugh at herself. "All girls, all grown up. The oldest is twenty-five, the youngest twenty. I left their father when he threatened to hurt Dina — she's the oldest — as well as me. But that's ancient history. Let's stop talking about me and get back to Barb."

"Was this in England?"

"Me and Barb? Yes. But I thought you knew that."

"No, I mean when you were married," Harry said stubbornly.

"Why can't you leave it be? It wasn't a very pleasant time in my life and I don't think about it often," Pearl responded. "But if you have to know about it, here it is, although it isn't very pretty. I had four young children to bring up and no money, so I found another man, one who didn't beat me, and he brought me to the United States. The only problem was that he was lazy and we were broke all the time. Eventually, when my kids were in their teens, we drifted apart."

"But you had stayed in touch with Barb all that time?" Harry asked.

"Yes," Pearl nodded. "We never stopped caring about each other. In the early years she didn't have much more than I did, but she sent me money whenever she could. Without her, my children and I would have starved. Once the Hideaway was up and running and she was bringing in more money than she knew what to do with, she invested a certain amount in a trust fund in both our names so that I could live on the interest. And over the years it grew until now I can live quite comfortably on it."

How much money would have to be in a trust fund to be able to live in New York on the interest alone, Harry wondered? Her heart skipped a bit when she realized that, since it was registered in both their names, Pearl would automatically inherit the capital if Barb died.

"You're very quiet," Pearl said, reaching out for her.

Harry went into her arms and kissed her fiercely.

"Hey!" Pearl laughed, sounding winded. "Don't you want to hear the rest of the story?"

Never, Harry thought, winding her arms and legs around Pearl. Since Pearl implicated herself every time she opened her mouth, and it was well neigh impossible for Harry to feel impartial about someone she wanted so badly, she'd make love now and think later. She knew she was betraying herself by succumbing to her own desires but she couldn't help it.

Their lovemaking was intense and powerful and just a little desperate, and only at the last minute did Harry rouse herself long enough to ensure that they engaged in safer sex. When it was over, she stretched out on her back and unwanted thoughts crept into her mind. Pearl stood to inherit the trust fund, which must be worth at least two hundred thousand dollars if she was able to live on the interest. She would also inherit another twenty thousand dollars from Barb's will. The question remained: Was Pearl desperate enough to assault a woman who had been her lover since university? Was she that greedy? So lacking in conscience?

"You think I attacked her, don't you?"

Pearl's hand lay on Harry's breast, her sweat was on Harry's body. This woman had made her cry out with pleasure so strong it almost hurt. But yes, Harry did suspect her. "How much money did Barb invest in the trust fund?" she said gruffly.

"There's a little over a hundred thousand in it now."

That was all? Harry was surprised.

"I did work once in a while, you know," Pearl told her, pulling away and turning on her side so that their bodies were no longer touching. "I have a Ph.D. in physics, which is essentially useless. I got pregnant during my last year and married straight out of university instead of getting a job, which meant that I didn't have the opportunity to keep up with advances in my field. But a Ph.D. can be useful in some contexts, and I've worked as a substitute and as an adult education teacher, especially once my children were old enough to look after themselves. So I never had to be totally dependent on the trust fund. In fact, sometimes I didn't even withdraw all the interest from it."

"But it made life a lot easier for you," Harry commented.

"Oh, hell yes. I'd admit that any time of the day or night," Pearl agreed at once. "But I didn't try to kill Barb. I loved her."

"I know," Harry sighed.

"Of course my motives for wanting her dead are essentially the same as yours," Pearl said sardonically.

Oh, great, Harry thought as strong hands pulled her down and skilled fingers moved yet again deep between her wet thighs, making her momentarily neglect her misgivings.

From the oppressive humidity in the morning air, Harry could tell that the weather was turning and a storm was brewing. She threw off the sheet, not surprised to discover that she was alone in bed. Pearl wasn't particularly coy, but she would be more likely than most to conceal her middle-aged morning face — especially if, like Harry's, it had ungovernable wrinkles, bushy eyebrows that had to be tamed and a slack muscle here and there. Harry rolled over and tried to go back to sleep, but her attempt was interrupted by the telephone. She pulled herself out of bed and picked up the extension.

"So, where are we having brunch this morning?" Judy asked.

"I don't know," Harry replied, waking up fast. "I hadn't really thought about it. Have you got somewhere in mind?"

"There's a Cuban restaurant that makes great French toast just up the street from the Hideaway," Judy replied.

"That sounds great," said Harry.

"I'll be there in ten minutes," Judy told her, and then she hung up.

Harry threw down the receiver and rushed back to her suite. She took a quick shower, dressed in fresh clothes and had just finished combing her wet hair when there was a knock on the door and Judy entered.

"Hi," she said, tossing her comb on the sofa.

"Hi, yourself," Judy smiled, giving her a hearty kiss. "How was your night?"

"Just fine."

Judy gave her a look but didn't say anything.

Stop worrying, Harry admonished herself. She couldn't possibly know.

"I wouldn't mind a good cup of coffee," Judy said.

"So would I," Harry responded.

As they were walking down Catherine Street, Harry realized that she should have inquired about Sarah. But it was too late now. "So how's Sarah?" she asked anyway.

"Fine," Judy responded, dodging tourists who were darting in and out of stores. She led Harry into a restaurant that smelled strongly of fried foods. "Why don't we sit over there?"

They took a table for two in the window and a young, Spanish-speaking woman placed menus on their table.

"We'll have French toast and coffee," Judy said, handing the menus back to her.

The waitress promptly returned with coffee. Harry added milk and sugar and took a sip. It was strong enough to dissolve the lining of her stomach, but she drank some more.

"I know we have to talk," Judy said as she stirred sugar into her coffee, "but I'm scared. What if we talk ourselves out of a relationship?"

"Is that what you think is going to happen?" Harry asked sharply.

"I don't know," Judy replied. They waited while the waitress served them plates piled high with French toast made from thick Cuban bread.

"That was fast. And what a daunting task," Harry commented.

"Dig in," Judy said, lifting her knife and fork.

Harry cut off a piece and stuffed it into her mouth.

"So, where do you want to start?" Judy asked.

"I don't think we should start anywhere," Harry responded. "Not right now, anyway."

"What?" Judy said with surprise. She put her knife and fork down on her plate.

"Aren't you hungry?"

"Actually, Sarah and I had something to eat earlier, before she went off with Karen," Judy said, an admission which instantly made Harry feel stupid for having concealed her night with Pearl. "But do I understand you correctly? You really don't want to talk about it?"

"Why don't we put it all behind us and go on from here?"

"I can't believe you really said that," Judy replied. "I mean, you're the one who always wants to talk things to death."

"Could we have more coffee?" Harry asked the waitress as she rushed by, plates of scrambled eggs, French toast and fried eggs with Cuban sausages piled high up her arm.

"Si, si," the waitress responded breathlessly. "Uno momento, por favor."

"I not only said it, I meant it," Harry said, turning her attention from her French toast to her lover. "I don't think it'll serve any purpose for us to dissect every little misunderstanding or to explain why we didn't mean to hurt each other. I think we already know that."

"You're right, of course," Judy said thoughtfully.

"We love each other, and that should be enough," Harry added.

Judy blinked.

"Oh, forget it," Harry muttered as the waitress refilled her coffee cup.

"You slept with Pearl, didn't you?"

"Yes," Harry responded evenly. "But that doesn't matter."

"So you say. But you've always been capable of a certain equanimity once you've had a little on the side," Judy said with a tinge of bitterness. "You should watch that — it's a dead give-away. Besides, you never feel the same way a few days later."

"You're not listening to me," Harry contended.

"You're not listening to yourself," Judy retorted. "Do you really think we can go on as if nothing's changed?"

"Yes. No. Oh hell, I don't know."

"I mean, what would we do with our lovers, or even our impulse to have them?" Judy asked.

"I don't know," Harry said, trying not to sound upset. She kept her mouth shut and studiously added milk and sugar to her coffee, stirred it and took a sip. It was even stronger than her first cup. At this rate, she'd be fortunate to fall asleep without artificial help, like a sleeping pill the size of a small bomb or a tap on the head with something solid. Then she remembered what had happened to Barb and her stomach turned over. "Look," she said, "why can't we just go back to the way we were?"

"I do love you, you know," Judy replied.

Harry shook her head impatiently; she knew Judy well enough to realize that this comment was the overture to a negative response.

"But I'm too confused to make any decisions right now," Judy continued. "I thought you would feel the same way, and it surprises me that you don't."

"Never mind," Harry responded glumly.

"Are you certain?"

Was she ever? Harry mused even as she nodded.

"The truth hurts, doesn't it?"

"Yes," Harry admitted, looking up as she felt a hand lightly touch her shoulder.

"Hi," Sarah said. "Judy told me you'd be here. Do you mind if I join you?"

Harry resisted the urge to close her eyes. "You won't like the coffee," she warned.

"It won't be the first time," Sarah said, giving Harry a fleeting smile and sitting down.

What had she done to deserve this, Harry wondered. The waitress swooped down on them. "More coffee?" she asked brightly.

"Si," Harry responded against her better judgement. She could always take some antacids when she returned to the guesthouse. The waitress removed a cup and saucer from a nearby table, plopped it in front of Sarah and filled it. Then she refilled Harry's coffee cup for a third time and gave her such a flirtatious look that Harry was unable to ignore it. "Gracias," she said with a nod.

"De nada," the waitress murmured, hovering for a few seconds longer than necessary before she hurried away to serve another table of starving tourists.

"Lucky you," Judy murmured, an amused look on her face.

"I thought you were with Karen," Harry said to Sarah, ignoring her lover.

"She's at the hospital visiting Barb, so I took the opportunity to drop by," Sarah replied. "Look, are you all right?"

Harry waited for Judy to respond and then realized that Sarah was talking to her. "Me?" she asked, suddenly tongue-tied.

Sarah looked to Judy for direction, but Judy was communing with her pancakes.

"Look, you're not the only one who doesn't know how this is going to work out," Sarah said.

"Is that meant to be reassuring?" Harry asked, ignoring Judy's snort.

"I don't understand," Sarah replied uncertainly.

"Well, in the first place, I've got a relationship with her, and I'd like to assume it's going to last," Harry explained, gesturing at Judy.

"In fact, I'm kind of insistent about it lasting, since I've put a lot of love, time and energy into it over the past twelve years."

"But I love her, too," Sarah claimed, pushing her untouched coffee away from her.

"Would you mind participating in this discussion?" Harry asked Judy.

Judy smiled and pointed to her inflated cheeks to indicate that her mouth was full of pancake.

"We'll wait," Harry assured her.

"I realize this isn't easy," Judy said after she had swallowed her food and wiped her mouth with a napkin.

"Tell me something I don't know," Harry retorted, and then she felt sorry that she'd responded so harshly. "It's not entirely your fault," she conceded to Sarah.

"So blame it on me, then," Judy said, resigned.

Harry didn't want to blame it on anyone; she just wanted it to go away and for life to return to normal.

"But no matter what you think, I didn't do it on purpose," Judy continued. "It just happens to fulfill a need."

And there it was, Harry reflected. If she tried to force Judy back into a monogamous relationship, she'd lose her. "But what about Karen?" she asked Sarah.

"We're just good friends," Sarah insisted, suddenly discovering her coffee.

"I've heard it was more than that," Harry remarked.

"Harry!" Judy protested.

"No, it's all right," Sarah said with a dull smile. "There's no reason why she shouldn't know about it."

Harry finished her coffee and resisted the urge to burp. If she never had another drop of caffeine, it would be too soon.

"Another refill?"

Harry looked up at the waitress. "No, thanks."

"I get off at four," she murmured in Harry's ear.

Oh, great, Harry thought, feeling chagrined when Judy smirked at her. "This is my girlfriend," she announced. And her girlfriend, who also has a girlfriend. And after that, who knows? The goddess, maybe, but don't count on it.

"Your loss," the waitress said with a casual shrug. "I'll bring the check."

"This is futile," Sarah said, dropping a dollar bill on the table.

"What did you expect?" Harry asked.

"I thought that what happened to Barb might change how you looked at things," Sarah responded. "I thought that you and I might be as comfortable around each other as we used to be."

Harry was silent. She'd been tried and found wanting and she didn't like the feeling.

"Perhaps it wasn't meant to be," Sarah said brusquely.

"So tell me it's all my fault," Harry blustered. "The next thing you'll be saying that I'm responsible for what happened to Barb."

Silence reigned. When Sarah glanced at Judy, Harry began to feel frightened. "Judy?"

"I've got to go," Sarah said.

"Me, too," Judy added. "You don't mind, do you? I'm giving up my room at the Southernmost Motel today, so I have to go check out and then I'll be moving back in with you. Unless you have other plans, that is."

"Of course I don't," Harry replied at once.

"What about Pearl?" Judy ventured.

Harry shrugged, not because she felt nonchalant but because she bloody well didn't know about Pearl.

"We could connect at Porter's tonight," Judy said, bending down and kissing Harry lightly on the lips. "Do you believe him, actually?"

"Who could?" Harry fibbed. "Did he say the same thing to you as he did to me?"

"That he had an inside track on the police investigation which he wants to share with us?" Sarah responded.

Oh, that wicked, wicked man, Harry thought. "That's precisely it," she smiled.

Ah, Key West, Harry ruminated as she watched Judy follow Sarah from the restaurant. Duplicity, deviousness, deceit, deception. Or vice versa. And she was stoned on caffeine, which was a distinctly dangerous feeling. It was all she could do to stop herself from picking up the Cuban waitress, just out of spite, but she paid the bill and left, telling herself that being cautious didn't mean that she was a wimp. Taking a perfect stranger to bed wouldn't redeem her wounded ego. Besides, what would she do once the sex was over? Perhaps that was an old-fashioned way of looking at things. Rumour had it that perfect strangers were capable of rising from a sweaty mattress, getting dressed and leaving without recriminations.

Duval Street felt competitive. It was overrun with tourists scurrying like rats to finish their shopping before it rained. Harry dodged them all the way back to the guesthouse, hopped into her car and drove to the hospital. Fat raindrops spattered on the windshield just as she pulled into the parking lot, and by the time she had pushed through the entrance doors, the pavement was wet.

"How is she today?" Harry asked the nurse. The same somnambulant police officer was seated in her chair in the corner, but the second she saw Harry enter the room, she stood up and approached the bed. Harry decided to ignore her no matter how much energy it took.

"She's a little better," the nurse replied.

"You mean she's coming around?"

"No, sorry, I didn't intend to mislead you," the nurse said hastily. "I meant that her vitals are better."

"Oh," Harry said, turning her attention to Barb. She leaned over the railing, wishing Barb's eyes would open. "I'm back," she said cheerfully. "How've you been, anyway? Have the nurses been treating you right? Any of them coveting your bod yet? Hey, I bet you've been trying to figure out which one to flirt with, but why bother? They all look pretty good to me. Even this cop would do in a pinch," she added, stifling a grin when the police officer didn't blink.

"I just had brunch with Judy and Sarah at that Cuban place on Duval — that's right, with both Judy and Sarah. Well, that's not precisely true, Sarah only joined us for coffee, but as you can imagine, that was enough. You know me. A jealous bitch if there ever was one. What stinks about the whole thing, besides the fact that Judy spent last night with Sarah, is that they both suspect me of having put you here," Harry said, glancing at the police officer. She was studying her long, blood-red fingernails.

"I bet you can't guess what I did last night. Or maybe I should say what Pearl and I did last night. And don't ask why it took so long for us to get around to it, you know perfectly well that I don't jump into bed with every pretty face I see even when you orchestrate our introduction. Besides, pretty faces don't habitually ask," Harry said, ignoring the police officer's reddening cheeks.

"I'm so damn lousy at carrying on one-sided conversations. I wish you'd wake up so we could talk about all this," she said fervently. "There's so much I have to tell you — "

"Good afternoon, Ms. Hubbley," Detective Allan said.

"We've been looking for you," Detective Dovercourt added. "We have a few questions to ask you."

"Certainly," Harry replied. "But not here," she added, glancing at Barb.

They went to the cafeteria, where Detective Allan poured three cups of coffee and placed one in front of Harry. She studiously ignored it.

"We'd like you to go over everything again," Detective Allan requested, flipping open his notebook.

"Starting where?"

"Well, first of all, why did you decide to come down here this year?"

"But I've already told you that," Harry groaned audibly.

"And we'd like to hear it again," Detective Dovercourt responded.

Harry took a deep breath and began a long monologue which was punctuated by questions from both detectives. She talked about her life in Montreal and described the planning phase of her trip. After that she provided them with some sanitized details about why Judy had been travelling with Sarah and not with her. Then she went through her arrival, check-in, conversations and dinner with Barb, and her subsequent tryst in the patio with Pearl. Finally, she included Alison Wheatley's arrival.

"Is there anything else?" Detective Allan asked, finishing his coffee.

"Not really," Harry responded.

"What do you mean, not really?" Detective Dovercourt asked suspiciously.

"I mean, no," Harry stated.

Detective Allan rubbed his chin and stared at her.

"Do you have a problem with that?" Harry asked him after a lengthy silence.

"I've been checking up on you," he said finally. "This isn't the first time you've been involved in a murder investigation."

So the long arm of the law had finally reached from Florida to Cape Cod to Nova Scotia. "That's right."

"Apparently you were lucky enough to solve a murder in Canada," he continued. "But I, for one, am not interested in having an amateur detective involved in this case."

"Especially a suspect," Detective Dovercourt added.

This good cop, bad cop routine was getting on Harry's nerves, although she had to admit Detective Dovercourt was damn good at it. "But I didn't do it," she insisted.

"I can't believe that you were in the room next to Ms. Fenton's and you didn't hear a thing," Detective Dovercourt commented.

"Believe what you like," Harry retorted.

"And it's inconceivable that you knew nothing about Ms. Fenton's will."

"I already told you that I didn't," Harry insisted.

They stared at each other but Harry refused to back down.

"Fine," Detective Allan eventually remarked apropos of nothing. "But if you do happen to discover something important, don't forget that it's your duty to report it to us."

Harry nodded. They knew everything that she knew — except about the more secret love affairs: Judy and Barb, Karen and Sarah, Alison and Barb. And then a new thought hit her: If they did happen to uncover the truth about Judy and Barb, would they think that she, Harry, had attacked Barb because she'd been jealous?

"Ms. Hubbley?" Detective Allan persisted, as if he sensed there was something else on her mind.

"What?"

"Are you certain you haven't got anything to tell us?"

"Quite certain," Harry said firmly.

"We'll be in touch," Detective Dovercourt said curtly.

"I'm sure you will," Harry said with more equanimity than she felt. She watched detectives Allan and Dovercourt leave the cafeteria and wondered for the first time if she was being foolish in thinking that the cocktail party at Porter's was going to create anything except more confusion.

"Darling!" Porter enthused as he opened the front door.

Harry was hovering under the porch light, her puny umbrella unable to deflect the heavy, wind-blown rain from her body. She had parked her rental car in front of Porter's house, nosing it close to Pearl's moped, which she recognized by its distinctive licence plate, but the cascading rain had still coated her jeans and sweatshirt with a sheen of moisture. "What a storm!" she exclaimed, following him inside.

"That's what always happens," Porter said as he took her umbrella from her. "The heat and humidity build up day after day and then suddenly a storm sweeps through and dumps a ton of rain on us. It has something to do with low fronts and high fronts banging into each other, or so one of my meteorologist friends tells me."

"Sounds sexy," Harry commented as she took a tissue from her purse and wiped rainwater from her face.

"Don't be naughty," Porter laughed.

"Is your boyfriend here?" Harry asked.

"Jock? No, unfortunately, although everyone else is," Porter responded, leading her into the living room. It was a large room with a high ceiling, and the walls were covered with gold flecked wallpaper. Three black leather sofas formed a conversation pit on one side of the room while a piano and two upholstered wingback chairs were grouped on the other.

"This is lovely," Harry told him, wanting nothing more than to sink into one of the leather sofas and chat with Porter for the rest of the evening. "But where is everyone?"

"Haven't you noticed that people tend to gravitate in the kitchen?" Porter asked with a chuckle. "I suppose it's the booze and the munchies."

"You're right," Harry told him.

"Actually, they seem to be determined to eat and drink me out of house and home, probably because they're not pleased about having been duped," he chuckled, sounding pleased with himself. "Ross accused me of getting them here under false pretenses and that Wheatley woman threatened to sue."

"But no one left?"

"Of course not," Porter replied. "They may be annoyed with me for promising them information I didn't have, they may not particularly like each other, but none of them seems to be in a hurry to hightail it out of here. And although they would never admit it, there is a certain camaraderie in all this."

"Because they're all suspects."

"Yes. But we should get you into the fray. Just follow me," he said, opening a door which led to a spacious dining room containing an oak table surrounded by ten matching chairs. The only other furniture in the room was a massive oak hutch. "It was my mother's and her mother's before her," Porter explained. "If I'd sold it, I could have probably put myself through law school on the proceeds, but neither of us could bear to part with it."

"I don't blame you," Harry responded, running her fingers lightly along the polished oak.

"The kitchen's this way," Porter said, pointing at a closed door.

Harry moved past him and opened it, pausing when she heard voices.

"No, I tell you, we're definitely going to sue if Barb dies and that Hubbley bitch gets it all," Ross insisted.

"I don't blame you," Alison Wheatley said. "But I still think she did it."

"Let's be perfectly honest with each other: who the hell knows who did it?" Ross responded.

"She had the motive and the opportunity," Martin Culver pointed out.

"If only Barb would wake up," Peter said. "Then she'd be able to tell the police who attacked her."

"And we could give her bloody hell for changing her will," Ross added.

"I'd just be relieved that she was going to be okay," Karen said.

Harry pushed open the door and entered the kitchen. "Wouldn't we all," she said, looking around. Porter's kitchen was one of the largest Harry had ever seen, with floor to ceiling glass-doored wood cupboards, a double refrigerator-freezer and patio doors leading to a deck and yard overlooking the ocean. Alison, Martin, Peter and Ross were holding court over the square butcher's block in the middle of the room while Karen, Sarah and Judy were standing near the patio door and Pearl was searching through the fridge for something.

"Harry," Alison responded with barely concealed hostility. Harry moved between them and poured herself a rum and Coke.

"How are you?" Peter asked.

"Fine," Harry responded, giving him a warm smile.

"I suppose you've already discovered that Mr. Ambrose deceived us," Pearl commented.

"Really?" Harry responded, pretending to be surprised.

"When he called me, he said he had new information about the police investigation," Sarah said.

"Yes, that's what he told me, too," Harry fibbed. "Do you mean he actually doesn't?"

"Oh, he rambled on about this and that, but it was nothing we didn't know already," Ross grumbled, pouring himself another shot of scotch.

"What I don't understand is why he wanted us to come here if he didn't have anything useful to contribute," Judy remarked.

"Why don't you ask him if it bothers you so much?" Martin suggested. He was leaning over the butcher block, methodically drinking his way through a bottle of rye.

"Never mind," Judy said, giving him a distasteful look and turning back to Sarah.

What now, Harry wondered as she joined Peter and Ross, ignoring the inhospitable look on Ross's face. "Have you been to see Barb today?"

"Just before we came here," Peter replied.

"I was there earlier," Harry said.

"Do you think she's going to come out of it?" Peter asked.

"Of course," Harry asserted.

"Ever the pollyanna," Ross said derisively as he took a large swig of scotch. "You can see for yourself what condition she's in."

"People have been known to recover from comas weeks, months, even years later," Harry told them.

"How depressing," Ross commented. He gave Peter a look Harry couldn't decipher and joined Alison, Martin and Pearl, who were engaged in a loud discussion about which was the best seafood restaurant in Key West.

"He certainly doesn't like me very much," Harry said to Peter.

"It doesn't really have anything to do with you — he isn't all that fond of women in general," Peter confided. "I'm afraid he's had bad experiences with them, especially his ex-wives."

Harry moved closer to Peter and asked, "Were you two really together the night Barb was attacked?"

Peter fidgeted with his glass, finished his drink and poured himself another. Like Ross, he was drinking scotch straight up.

"You weren't, were you?" Harry pressed as he drank half of the amber liquid in his glass. "What happened? Did Ross wander off during the tea dance?"

"And he didn't come back until early morning," Peter murmured plaintively, glancing nervously at his lover and then relaxing when he saw that Ross was talking to Martin. "I mean, he's not supposed to do that. We agreed that it wasn't safe, and yet I have the devil of a time getting him to use a condom."

"Where was he?"

"He said he was with another man," Peter whispered vehemently.

"Do you think he was?"

Peter shrugged uncomfortably.

"Do you think he might have attacked Barb?"

"I don't know," Peter sighed. "He's always vague when he's been with someone else."

"Does he do that often?"

"Not any more," Peter admitted, "although Key West is always such a temptation. There are so many men on the make, you see."

Peter had just destroyed his own alibi as well as Ross's. "If Ross didn't do it, then perhaps you did," she suggested provocatively, "especially since you didn't know that Barb had changed her will."

"I did no such thing!" he hissed, looking around to assure himself that no one was listening to their conversation. "I might not be the best brother in the world, but I love my sister! And no, I didn't know anything about her new will, but I didn't know anything about her old one, either. How could I? Barb didn't exactly confide these things in me."

Harry put a restraining hand on his arm but he angrily shrugged it off.

"It's true that I'm always bugging her for more money, but I wouldn't harm a hair on her head," Peter said. "She's the only relative I have left. I know Ross thinks Barb should leave everything to me, but I'm more realistic than he is. I haven't added it all up, but Barb's given me plenty over the years."

Harry believed him. Peter was weak and vacillating and likely somewhat in awe of Barb, perhaps even a bit afraid. Ross was another matter, though.

"Time for a refill," Judy stated. She plunked her empty glass on the butcher block and half-filled it with scotch.

"I though you were never going to drink again," Harry commented, taking a sip of her rum and Coke.

"Never mind," Judy retorted with a sheepish grin.

"It's nearly stopped raining," Harry said, followed her lover to the patio doors. They stood close together and stared out.

"But the lightning is quite fierce out to sea," Judy commented as several bolts flashed simultaneously.

"I wouldn't want to be out on a boat in that," Harry said.

"This is a fantastic house, isn't it?"

"I haven't seen all of it yet."

"I got here a bit early, so Porter took me on a tour," Judy said. "He's quite a nice man."

"That he is," Harry answered.

"Although I don't understand why he decided to throw this party and why he lied to get us here. You wouldn't happen to know anything about that, would you?" Judy asked.

"What on earth are you talking about?"

"He said that I should tell you what I know about the attack on Barb rather than fencing with you," Judy replied.

"And what do you know?" Harry inquired, putting her arm around Judy's shoulder. Maybe if they kept their heads close together, people would think they were having a private chat and wouldn't interrupt.

"Barb was in love with Pearl, but Pearl wouldn't commit herself to a long-term relationship," Judy said in a low voice.

"How'd you find that out?"

"Karen told Sarah, and Sarah told me," Judy responded. "Apparently Pearl borrowed a lot of money from Barb and never paid it back. But because Barb cared about her so much, she never made an issue of it. Needless to say, Karen was not thrilled."

"How much did she borrow?" Harry asked, wondering whether Barb had told Karen that the hundred thousand dollars she'd put in a trust fund for Pearl was a loan.

"Karen didn't tell Sarah the precise amount," Judy replied. "All she said was that it was a lot."

The interpretation of "a lot" was relative. It would depend on one's perspective, Harry reflected, which would hinge on the size of one's salary or the balance in one's bank account, trust fund, retirement savings plan, and so on. "So we don't know whether Karen was talking about a thousand bucks, ten thousand bucks or a hundred thousand bucks," she said to Judy.

"A thousand dollars isn't a lot. Be honest about this, Harry — you just don't want Pearl to have done it."

"But I know you must feel the same way about Sarah, and she must feel the same way about Karen," Harry couldn't help but reply. "And then, of course, I feel the same way about you, even though the police likely suspect you because you're my lover. And they'd suspect you even more if they knew you were Barb's lover ..."

Judy shifted, forcing Harry to remove her arm. It soon became apparent that she had no intention of answering the question Harry had left hanging. Instead, Harry was going to have to ask whether Judy's affair with Barb had been a one-shot deal or whether they had picked up where they left off when Judy and Sarah had come to Key West. "It looks like the rain's completely stopped," Harry commented. "Why don't we go outside?" They stepped onto the deck and she closed the sliding door behind them. The air had turned much cooler after the rain, and tendrils of fog rose slowly from the sea and probed the shore.

"Were you and Barb lovers this time around?"

"Yes," Judy whispered.

"Are you in love with her?"

"Love?" Judy barked as she walked down the stairs. "I wouldn't exactly call it that."

"Did Sarah know about you and Barb?" Harry asked, not especially interested in knowing what Judy would call it.

Judy's look of surprise turned to wariness. "She didn't do it. And anyway, she's got an alibi."

"Karen," Harry surmised as she stepped gingerly on the wet grass.

"That's right. They spent the night together in Karen's suite."

"We spent the night together, too," Harry reminded her. All of them had alibis, she reflected dourly, although they weren't worth a plugged nickel. And perhaps Judy hadn't realized it, but by telling her that Sarah had been with Karen the night Barb had been attacked, she'd just put Sarah across the hall from the scene of the crime rather than in a motel room across town.

"Do you think Sarah did it?" Judy asked. "Or Karen?"

"I have no idea," Harry responded honestly as she reached the edge of the grass. A stone wall had been constructed between the garden and the beach with three steps leading to the sand. "You went next door to see Barb the night she was attacked, didn't you?"

"Of course I didn't," Judy protested with an uncomfortable laugh. "I was with you, for god's sake."

"And I fell asleep," Harry responded quietly.

"Come on, Harry, don't be such a bitch."

"What time did you leave?"

Judy stared at Harry and then shrugged. "Around two in the morning."

"And?"

"And nothing."

"What do you mean? Wasn't she there?"

"Of course she was," Judy responded. "She answered the door right away, but she looked disappointed. She was obviously expecting someone else."

Pearl? Alison Wheatley? Karen? "Did she invite you in?"

"Yes," Judy answered. "But she didn't want me to stay. So I chatted with her for a little while and then I left."

"You didn't come back to our room, though, so where did you go?"

"I went out to the patio and sat down in a deck chair," Judy replied. "I must have fallen asleep, because the next thing I knew, it was nearly dawn and I was freezing. I went into the kitchen to make coffee, and that was when the police arrived."

"And yet you said nothing to them or to me," Harry said stonily.

"Because I didn't want you to find out about my relationship with Barb," Judy responded. "Not like that, not through the police. I realized that I'd have to tell you, but I wanted to do it in my own good time."

It was a reasonable response, but it didn't assuage Harry's misgivings. Her first lover and best friend had been attacked and nearly killed, and here she was, suspecting both Judy and Pearl of being her assailant. They both had the motive, they both had the opportunity, and they had both lied to the police. In addition, Judy had visited Barb that night.

"I think I'll get another drink," Judy said.

"I'll be in soon," Harry said.

"Don't stay out here too long — it's starting to rain again."

"I won't."

Judy reached out and touched Harry's shoulder. "It'll be all right."

"When?"

Judy's frown revealed to Harry that she didn't know either.

It rained lightly for a couple of minutes and then stopped. Harry paced the beach, her thoughts racing. Not one of them had a reliable alibi. Ross had abandoned Peter and stayed out all night, while Judy had secretly visited Barb a few hours before she'd been attacked and Sarah had been with Karen in her suite in Barb's building. It was like Harry had said to Porter over dinner the night before: The more she probed, the guiltier they all seemed.

"Hello, sweetheart. I've been looking for you," Pearl said as she hurried across the lawn and joined Harry on the beach.

"Hi."

"I think Alison hates me," Pearl said conversationally, linking arms with Harry and pacing in stride with her.

"You slept and ran," Harry said succinctly.

"How right you are," Pearl replied with a chuckle. "But she didn't want me, anyway — I was just a stand-in for Barb."

And vice versa, perhaps. "You went to Barb's apartment after Alison fell asleep, didn't you?" Harry asked with sudden illumination.

"What are you talking about?"

"Nobody makes love all night long. So once Alison fell asleep, you got up and left," Harry speculated.

"And what if I did?"

"Perhaps she was expecting you," Harry continued. "Maybe you had a date."

"Don't be silly," Pearl protested. "If I'd had a date with Barb, I certainly wouldn't have been cruising you, and I wouldn't have bedded down with Alison."

She'd been compared and found wanting, Harry reflected, refusing to take umbrage. "Perhaps you were worried that Barb would be with someone else. Judy, perhaps. Or me. Or even Karen."

"Are you implying that I was jealous of Barb's other lovers? Don't be so naive, Harriet."

She was right, Harry thought. "But you did go to Barb, didn't you?"

"Do you really think I would flit from one lover to another during the same night?"

"It's been known to happen," Harry responded dryly, "although I'm not necessarily implying that you and Barb made love."

"Well, we didn't," Pearl retorted.

"So you were there."

"Yes," Pearl admitted. "But I didn't attack her."

Harry was glad it was dark, because she was terrified that she'd see another truth in Pearl's eyes.

"She was already unconscious when I got there," Pearl sighed. "But how did you know?"

"Your alibi leaks like a sieve, just like mine. Everyone was with someone that night, but we all fell asleep at one point or another," Harry responded.

"Of course," Pearl said. "I should have known. Well, it was late by the time Alison dozed off. I sleep very little, even at the best of times, which this wasn't. And no, don't ask, because I won't tell you. I got up and put my clothes on and went out to the patio. And then I heard something, although I don't know what it was. I decided to go back to my suite, so I let myself into the building. I was about to open my door when I noticed that Barb's was open. I went in and found her lying on the bedroom floor. At first I thought she was dead, but when I discovered she wasn't, I went out and called the police from the pay phone across the street."

"So you were the anonymous caller," Harry said. "But why didn't you tell them who you were?"

"I was scared," Pearl replied. "I thought that they'd arrest me for attacking her, what with the trust fund and the twenty thousand dollars in the will. So I disguised my voice and went back to my room as soon as I hung up the telephone. I don't think anyone saw me. I was so upset at that point that all I did was pace back and forth. It seemed to take such a long for the police to arrive that I'm surprised I didn't wear a path in the carpet. I know it looks bad, but I swear to you that I didn't do it."

"The police will find out about the trust fund, you know," Harry told her. "They're investigating everything about us. By the time they're finished, they'll know stuff about you that you forgot a long time ago."

"I suppose you're right," Pearl conceded.

"You should tell them what you've just told me. It would be better if you volunteered the information before they find out on their own," Harry proposed.

"You're in a bit of a quandary, aren't you?" Pearl said absently, bending to give Harry a dispassionate kiss. "Damned if you tell them, damned if you don't."

"I don't know what you mean," Harry bluffed.

"Yes you do," Pearl sighed.

"Did you attack her?" Harry asked suddenly.

"Oh, god," Pearl groaned. "I knew you were going to ask."

"I wish we'd never slept together," Harry said bitterly.

"Don't say that," Pearl retorted, sounding angry for the first time. "I guess I was a fool to trust you," she added, turning and rushing up the beach.

"Pearl!" Harry shouted, hurrying after her. She banged her shin on the stone wall, cursed under her breath and clambered over it, not slowing down until she reached the patio door. She leaned against it and stared toward the ocean, but the fog had claimed the beach and was threatening the bottom slope of the lawn. Pearl was nowhere in sight.

"What on earth?" Porter exclaimed as he opened the patio door and Harry stumbled backward into his arms. "You're bleeding," he added, glancing at her shin.

"I had a slight disagreement with your stone wall," she croaked, relieved to see that no one else was in the kitchen. "Porter, I think Pearl might have done it."

"Really," he responded. "Where is she?"

"She was down on the beach," Harry responded, grasping his arm when he moved toward the door. "Don't bother. You'll never find her in all this fog."

He glanced indecisively at the deck and then closed the patio door with a slam and locked it. "Well, at least the little plan you hatched worked. But hadn't we better call the police?"

"I don't know," Harry admitted, walking over to the sink. She reached down and widened the tear in her jeans, exposing a jagged, two-inch cut along her shinbone. It was bleeding freely, so she appropriated the dishcloth, soaked it in cold water and dabbed gingerly at her shin.

"What do you mean, you don't know?" Porter asked, sounding confused.

"I'm just not certain. I mean, she said she didn't do it," Harry responded lamely. "She said that she found Barb after she'd been assaulted and made the anonymous call to the police, but that she didn't attack Barb."

"And you believed her?" he retorted incredulously, grasping the portable telephone in one hand and punching numbers with the other.

"I guess I'm a fool," she said. Porter was right; the evidence pointed to Pearl. The trust fund over which she'd have total control if Barb should die, the twenty thousand dollars in Barb's will, the fact that Pearl admitted to having left Alison's suite in the middle of the night, that she was at the scene of the crime and that she'd called the police to report the crime but hadn't given her name. Unfortunately, it all fit together. She wiped away the blood and held the dishcloth over the gash.

"Give me the police," Porter said, and then he was speaking rapidly into the phone, giving his name and address and saying, "Yes, that's correct. We know who assaulted Barbara Fenton. Yes, it was Pearl Vernon." He added a few more details before switching off the phone and returning it to its cradle.

"They're going to search for her and a couple of detectives will meet us at the hospital for questioning," he told Harry. "Now take the dishtowel off the rack and wrap it around your leg. You obviously need a few stitches, and the sooner the better."

"Where is everyone?" Harry asked as she did as he suggested.

"Peter, Ross, Alison and Martin left together as soon as they'd emptied my bottle of best scotch," Porter replied. "I think they were going to dinner. Karen, Judy and Sarah left a few minutes ago. They said they were going to the hospital, so we'll likely run into them there. Now, let's get a move on."

Harry hobbled after him and then waited for him to reset the security system and lock the front door. It had started to rain fairly hard again. "Pearl's moped is gone," she told Porter.

"I'm not surprised," he replied. "But don't worry, they'll find her."

"Harry!" a woman's voice called. "I have to talk to you!"

"We must get to the hospital," Porter said as Sarah Reid came into view. He used his remote control to open the doors of his car and then got in. "Your leg needs medical attention."

"Please," Sarah said, holding out her hands.

"I thought you went to the hospital with Judy and Karen," Harry commented.

"I begged off at the last minute because I wanted to speak with you," Sarah explained. "It's important, Harry."

"Come with us, then," Harry suggested, getting into the back seat and leaving the door open for Sarah.

"But what I have to say is confidential," Sarah protested with a glance at Porter.

"It's all right, he's my lawyer," Harry assured her.

"I don't like it," Sarah muttered, but she got in.

Porter ignored her complaints, reached back and closed the door. Then he stepped on the gas.

"Where are you going in such a hurry?"

"I had a slight accident and Porter thinks I need a few stitches," Harry responded, wondering what had become of Pearl. Perhaps she'd headed back to the guesthouse. Or maybe she'd rushed to the hospital to try and finish what she'd started. Then again, she could already be off the island. The police would think of all those possibilities and more, Harry mused, saddened that she'd made love with the woman who'd attacked her best friend. But there was a hell of a lot of rationalization going on in this untidy little group, Harry thought wearily as she banished such depressing thoughts from her mind. "You were with Karen the night Barb was attacked, weren't you?"

"I was in her suite, but she wasn't there all night," Sarah responded, her voice so low that Harry could barely hear her over the rhythmic swishing of the windshield wipers and the hiss of the tires over wet pavement. "That's what I wanted to talk to you about."

"Do you know where she was?"

"No," Sarah responded with a shake of her head. "Look, it was a lousy evening all around, starting with the fight Judy and I had over dinner."

"She was upset about you and Karen," Harry inferred.

"Yes," Sarah answered, "although I thought she was being unreasonable. She's involved with you, after all, and I knew she was also carrying on an affair with Barb, so how could she be jealous about Karen?"

Jealousy was intrinsically so illogical that Harry sometimes suspected it had been secretly cast upon unsuspecting human beings from outer space as a cosmic joke of sorts.

"Anyway, we'd planned to go to one of the bars after we left the tea dance at La-Te-Da, but Judy changed her mind. She said she wasn't in the mood, that she was going to pack up her stuff and move back with you a little early," Sarah continued.

"So you called Karen," Harry surmised.

"No. I went to the bar by myself. Actually, that wasn't the first time and it won't be the last," Sarah responded dryly. "You might not have noticed, but there haven't been a hell of a lot of women in my life."

Then why did you have to take mine, Harry wanted to ask.

"I went to the Club International bar on Simonton Street, where I met some women and ended up having a couple of beers with them," Sarah continued. "They eventually left, but I didn't feel like going back to Alexander's alone, so I called Karen. She told me to come over."

"And you stayed there for the rest of the night."

"That's right."

"When did you realize that Karen had gone out?"

"I'm not sure," Sarah replied. "I assumed she was checking someone in or something like that. But she was gone for a long time. Hours, actually. I've lived alone for a long time, so I'm quite conscious of someone else being in bed with me to the point that I wake up when they leave. After Karen left, I couldn't get back to sleep, so I got up and read. I grew drowsy around dawn and went back to bed, and when I woke up, Karen was there beside me."

"But you didn't hear her come back in," Harry commented.

"No."

"Where did she say she was?"

"She didn't."

"What?" Harry exclaimed. "You didn't ask?"

"It didn't occur to me to ask; I thought she was working," Sarah responded. "And then suddenly the police were there questioning us and Karen told them that we'd been together all night."

Like everyone who'd ostensibly spent the night with someone else, Harry mused. It didn't mean a blasted thing. And they'd all lied to the police.

"How could I contradict her in front of the cops?"

Harry knew precisely what she meant because she'd initially acquiesced when Judy had pulled the same number on her. "Did you ever tell the police the truth?"

Sarah sighed and shook her head. "I wanted to. But once I'd lied, I didn't know how to take it back. I had to tell someone, though," Sarah added. "And Judy mentioned how you'd solved the murder of your classmate last summer, so I thought I'd confide in you."

Oh, great. "Thanks," Harry replied, trying not to sound glum.

"So what are you going to do?" Sarah asked.

What *was* she going to do, Harry wondered as Porter pulled into the hospital parking lot and backed his car into a space near the door. Not that it mattered, she thought as she stifled a sigh. Not with all the incriminating evidence she'd uncovered against Pearl. "Telling me doesn't absolve you, you know," she said to Sarah more curtly than she had intended to.

"I know. I guess I'd better call the police," Sarah said, opening the door and sliding from the car.

"Wait!" Harry shouted. But by the time she'd plucked her purse from the floor and got out, Sarah had disappeared. "She's gone!" she said to Porter.

"Never mind," Porter said soothingly. He took her arm and led her into the hospital. She ignored the gusting rain which infiltrated her clothes, ran down her neck and thighs and moistened the freshly coagulated scab which had started to form on the cut on her calf.

"The emergency department's over there," an orderly told them once he'd spied the blood on her leg.

"Thanks," Harry replied, pulling Porter in the opposite direction.

"What are you doing?"

"Humour me, will you? I have this feeling Pearl's in Barb's room," Harry replied.

Visiting hours were over, but there were few staff about, and no one stopped her from pushing through the padded doors leading to the intensive care unit and making her way to Barb's room. Pearl was bending over Barb's immobile form.

"Get away from her!" she ordered Pearl.

"I wondered how long it would take you to get here," Pearl replied calmly, backing away from the bed as the confused police officer jumped to her feet and approached them.

"You shouldn't all be in here," the officer remarked tensely.

"We have reason to believe this woman was responsible for the attack on Ms. Fenton," Porter said, pointing at Pearl.

"No one's said anything to me about that," the police officer responded, perplexed.

"I just finished telling Barb what a good detective you are, how you'd already signed, sealed and delivered my fate," Pearl said brightly. "In fact, I was telling her she'd better wake up or I'm likely to go to jail for quite a few years for something I didn't do, but she doesn't seem inclined to listen. And without her to testify that I'm not guilty, that it was her idea to set up the trust fund and to leave me twenty thousand dollars because she happened to love me, no one's going to believe a word I say."

"What trust fund?" Porter asked, looking at Harry.

"Never mind," Harry sighed.

"Actually, I'm surprised the police haven't already arrived," Pearl remarked.

So was Harry. Not only that, but the hurt look in Pearl's eyes confused her.

"Would you mind moving further away from the bed?" the police officer asked, definitely worried now.

"I didn't do it, Harriet," Pearl said, her voice tight with repressed anger. "I love her, for god's sake. You know that. All the riches in the world couldn't fill the void her death would leave in my life."

"Then why did you come here tonight?" Porter asked sharply. "Were you planning to kill Barb?"

"No!" Pearl proclaimed. "I wanted to see her, to speak to her."

"To say good-bye," Porter surmised.

"Yes, although I suppose that admission further seals my fate," Pearl said.

Detective Dovercourt walked into the room, giving the dithering police officer a withering stare. "Would you mind stepping into the hall with me? All of you? Detective Allan is waiting for us. Now."

Pearl glanced at Harry, despair in her eyes, and trailed after Detective Dovercourt.

"How's your leg holding out?" Porter asked.

"It hurts like hell," Harry admitted, limping after Pearl. "But let's get this over with."

"You don't sound very pleased," Porter commented.

Should she be pleased that a woman she liked enough to make love with was about to be arrested for assaulting her best friend?

"You're under arrest," Detective Dovercourt said to Pearl.

"You can't be serious," Pearl said with an uncertain laugh.

"I'm afraid so," Detective Allan piped up.

"You have the right to remain silent, to — "

"Never mind," Pearl interrupted mildly. "I've heard it often enough on TV to know it off by heart."

"That doesn't matter," Detective Dovercourt maintained. "I still have to tell you."

Pearl closed her eyes and let Detective Dovercourt read her her rights and then handcuff her. "Do you believe this?" she said to Harry and Porter, a curious smile on her face. "Especially since I didn't do it."

"Tell that to the judge and jury," Detective Dovercourt responded stalwartly.

"Bitch," Pearl said conversationally.

"Do you need a statement from my client this evening?" Porter asked. "She had an accident on the beach and we're on our way to the emergency room for repairs."

"Made a bit of a detour, did you?" Detective Allan commented once he'd inspected Harry's leg. The blood trickling down her calf had soaked her sock and was collecting in her running shoe, but she ignored both the detective's comment and her throbbing leg.

"Do you need her at the station tonight?" Porter asked again.

"No," Detective Allan replied. "We've got more than enough to book Ms. Vernon on suspicion of attempted murder, including a witness who saw her make a call at four-thirty in the morning from the phone booth across the street from Isadora's Hideaway to report the attack on Barbara Fenton, an attack she made herself."

Pearl's shoulders sagged.

"I'll see you in the emergency room before you leave. And I expect you to come down to the police station tomorrow morning and make a complete report," Detective Allan added, emphasizing the word "complete" as he stared at Harry.

Harry nodded and watched as the two detectives and the uniformed police officer led Pearl down the hall and toward the bank of elevators.

"I'm just going to see Barb for a second," Harry said.

"I'll wait here," Porter told her. "But don't be long. You should get that leg taken care of before you lose too much blood."

Harry bent over Barb, reaching down and pulling the sheet from her arm. "I can finally touch you," she whispered as she slid her hand under Barb's, being careful not to disturb her IV lines. Barb's hand was warm but limp and unresponsive. "It's hard for me to believe that Pearl attacked you even though the evidence is so damning," she murmured. "Can't you tell me what happened? Did she really do it? Are my instincts that bad?" But Barb didn't budge.

So this was a coma, Harry reflected, staring so hard at Barb's inert body that her eyes began to play tricks on her and she was practically certain she'd seen Barb move. She forced her eyes to momentarily scan the ceiling and then pounce on Barb, as if she was trying to find her out in a lie. But no such luck. Barb was as still as a dormouse. So it wasn't a test, she thought; Barb hadn't been pretending to be in a coma so she could judge her lovers.

"Harry," Judy whispered as she glided into the room.

Harry slid her free arm around Judy's waist and drew her to the bed.

"Let's go home," Judy whispered.

Visions of Montreal filled Harry's head. "I'm not sure that Pearl did it."

"Oh, god," Judy responded. "Why can't you face reality? Porter told me that the police had enough evidence to arrest her. And what happened to your leg?"

"I tangled with a stone wall. But you should see the wall," Harry said with an attempt at humour, but Judy wasn't having any.

"You're going to need stitches."

"That's what everyone says," Harry grunted. She removed her hand from beneath Barb's and straightened up, stretching to remove the kink from her back. "Let's go down to emergency and get it over with. I'll be back," Harry said to Barb. They left the room and found Porter leaning against the wall, an unlit cigar dangling between his fingers.

"Here, here, what are you doing?" a man in a dingy lab coat asked, glancing at Harry's bloody leg. "You should be in the emergency room getting that stitched up, not wandering around in intensive care. How on earth did you get here?"

"I guess we got lost," Harry lied. She felt tetchy. The cut on her calf was like the bites of a dozen freshwater leeches — bothersome and hideous but not dangerous or life-threatening, although it hurt like hell.

"I'll show you where it is," he volunteered, staring at them suspiciously.

They followed him downstairs to the emergency room, where business was slow and Harry was immediately seen to. She was taken into a tiny cubicle, told to remove her running shoe and sock and to sit down on the gurney. Then a nurse came in and said, "I hope you don't mind if I cut off your jeans at the knee."

"Go ahead," Harry answered. Not being an admirer of patches, she had planned to throw them out, anyway.

"This won't take long," she was told as the nurse methodically cleaned her calf with something which felt cold on her skin and then plunged a needle into her leg. Moments later the flesh around the wound grew numb.

"Shit," she muttered under her breath as she fell back on the gurney.

"Do you feel faint?"

"No," Harry replied. "I just don't like watching."

"It won't be long, now."

The local anaesthesia soon deadened her calf from knee to ankle. The doctor arrived and sewed her up, but all she could feel was a strange but painless pressure along the sides of her cut. She closed her eyes to escape the glare of the florescent lights and breathed deeply. Had Pearl attacked Barb? So many of the suspects had just as much opportunity as Pearl, and none of them had an alibi worth mentioning. In the end, it all came down to who had the strongest motive, and Harry hadn't been able to make heads or tails of that.

"There," the doctor's brisk voice interrupted her musings. "You're all stitched up."

"Thanks," Harry responded.

"Now I want you to rest for a couple minutes, and then you can go," he told her. "Your doctor can take your stitches out in a week."

"Great," she replied absentmindedly. If Pearl hadn't assaulted Barb, who had?

Motives, motives and more motives, she thought, and not only economic ones. Add jealousy, possessiveness and the web of emotional and sexual relationships amongst them, top it up with the spurned Alison Wheatley and her jealous boyfriend, and what did she have? Not a clue.

Harry sighed and sat up, disgruntled that it had to be any of them. Why couldn't Barb's assailant have been a total stranger rather than someone she knew, someone she liked, maybe even someone she loved? The question now was whether she should trust her instincts and go with her growing, uneasy suspicion that Pearl might be innocent, or whether she should accept Pearl's guilt.

Some choice, she reflected. If Pearl was guilty, she'd slept with someone who'd attempted to murder her friend and lover. And if Pearl was innocent, then she was still trapped in the web of deceit the real assailant had created. Had it been a crime of jealousy or of greed? Or both?

Judy walked into the cubicle, staring at her bandaged leg. "Detective Allan's come to see you."

"Wonderful," Harry responded.

"Does it hurt?" Judy asked. "How many stitches did they put in?"

"It doesn't hurt right now, but it's likely going to smart like hell once the anaesthetic wears off," Harry responded, looking with distaste at her bloody sock. "I don't know how many stitches there are — I didn't ask."

"Did you get something for the pain?"

"No," Harry replied. She probably should have, but she hadn't thought of it. She stepped down from the gurney, used a towel to wipe the blood from the inside of her running shoe and then slipped it on and laced it up. She planned to throw it out as soon as she got back to the guesthouse, but for now, she needed something to wear. "Why don't you and Porter wait for me in the front lobby? I'll try to keep it short."

"Fine," Judy replied. "You can always plead exhaustion, or something."

"I'll just wave my leg in his face," Harry said as they left the cubicle.

"Ms. Hubbley," Detective Allan said, standing up. "Perhaps you'd join me for a coffee."

Did she have a choice, Harry wondered wryly as she followed him from the emergency ward to the nearly deserted cafeteria.

"Did you know about the trust fund Ms. Fenton set up for Ms. Vernon? And that Ms. Vernon had been the anonymous caller who reported the attack on Ms. Fenton to the police? And that they'd been lovers for over thirty years? That Ms. Vernon rarely worked long enough to support herself?"

"Yes," Harry admitted.

"And you didn't think to tell us about any of this," he commented, looking like he wanted to give her a good shake. Instead, he sat back in his chair.

"I didn't discover everything at once. And I told her she should tell you," Harry said, trying not to sound defensive.

"Well, she didn't," he remarked. "I'm sure you realize that there were a lot of suspects in this case, and it took us a while to complete our investigation. But now it's over. When you come to the station tomorrow morning, I expect you to tell us everything you know, and I mean *everything*. And between now and then, why don't you spend some time seriously thinking about what obstruction of justice means?"

He couldn't have been any clearer than that, Harry reflected as she watched him walk away. She couldn't straddle the fence forever, he wasn't going to let her. She abandoned her half-filled coffee cup and walked out of the cafeteria, avoiding the front lobby by taking the back stairs. She wanted to see Barb one more time tonight before she returned to the guesthouse.

"What are you doing here?" Karen exclaimed, jumping back from the bed, a pillow in her hands.

"The same thing you are," Harry answered, baffled by Karen's reaction. "Where is everybody?"

"The nurse asked me to keep an eye on her while she spent some time with a new admission down the hall," Karen said, hugging the pillow against her chest. "I was just trying to make her more comfortable," she added, placing the pillow against Barb's side and giving it an awkward pat.

It was all a lie, Harry realized, her suspicions growing as she looked around the room. "Who turned all the machines off?" she asked, pointing at the silent heart monitor.

"The nurse, I suppose," Karen said casually. "Or one of the doctors. They're always changing things. Anyway, don't you ever stop asking questions? I'm not a doctor, so how the hell should I know?"

"You came in and found the police officer gone, so you were going to kill her, weren't you? That's why you were holding that pillow in your hands. You were intending to smother her, so you disconnected the monitors so none of the alarms would go off," Harry said swiftly.

"Don't be silly — I met Porter downstairs and he told me that they'd already arrested Pearl for attacking Barb," Karen said with an unsteady laugh. "And it serves her right, the bitch. Imagine leaving Alison's bed to come looking for Barb. Didn't she know when she had a good thing going for her? She couldn't keep away from Barb even when she was screwing someone else."

"What?" Harry asked sharply. She was rooted to the spot. If Karen had seen Pearl that night, then she'd been in Barb's suite. "You were there, weren't you? You and Barb fought and you attacked her."

"Of course not," Karen blustered.

"And you came here tonight to make sure she couldn't wake up and tell the police that you were the one who'd assaulted her," Harry continued.

"You're nuts!" Karen said scornfully.

"How did you know Pearl was in Barb's apartment if you weren't there yourself?" Harry asked.

"I don't remember," Karen replied, her eyes sliding away. "And anyway, what difference does it make?"

"You could have seen her in the patio, when she was on her way to call the police from a pay phone on the street. Or maybe it was when she came back from phoning the cops and crossed the patio to return to her room," Harry said swiftly.

"I don't know what you're talking about. I never left my room that night," Karen bluffed. "Actually, that's when I saw her — when she walked down the hall."

"What, were you sitting there with your door open at that time of night just waiting for someone to pass by?" Harry said, disbelief plain in her voice.

"So what if I was?" Karen said with a smug smile.

"And you mean to tell me that Pearl didn't see you?"

"Maybe she needs glasses," Karen smirked. "None of us is getting any younger, you know."

"That's a load of bull," Harry retorted. "Perhaps you don't know this, but Sarah woke up when you left and read until dawn. If you'd been sitting in your living room with your door open, she certainly would have noticed."

Karen's expression changed, but she didn't back down. "You've got quite a fertile imagination."

"Pearl didn't see you because you were hiding in Barb's suite," Harry said.

"Oh, come off it," Karen retorted scornfully.

"Where were you, Karen?" Harry asked. "In the closet? The bathroom? The kitchen? You had to hide somewhere when Pearl came in and found Barb, didn't you?"

"I didn't realize you were so fond of fairy tales," Karen laughed.

"You tried to strangle her, but she was too strong and she managed to get away. But then she lost her balance and you gave her a push. She must have just fallen and hit her head when someone knocked at the door. The only option you had was to hide," Harry persevered. "And that's when you saw Pearl."

"Why don't you leave it alone, Harry?" Karen said suddenly. "It's all just a lot of conjecture, anyway."

"Barb decided to tell you about the changes she made to her will, didn't she? And you couldn't stand the idea that after fifteen years, she would leave nearly everything to someone else," Harry continued, knowing she was on the right track.

Karen's face was stony.

"At first I thought the fact that you didn't inherit the bulk of Barb's estate made it unlikely that you would attack her," Harry said.

"And you were right. I didn't," Karen insisted.

"But it was too much to take, wasn't it? Your pride was hurt, and you lost your temper," Harry added.

"You're too smart for your own good," Karen said, her face suddenly twisted with bitterness. "Just like Barb. She stood there that night like the sanctimonious bitch she could be sometimes, telling me she had decided to leave everything to you except for twenty thousand dollars and half the guesthouse. She didn't even leave me enough cash to buy you out, for god's sake! For years I put up with her lording it over me because she was smarter than me, sexier than me, richer than me. So how did you think I'd react? Step up and give her a big kiss? Thank her? Give me a break."

"Why did you put up with it if you felt that way?"

"We'd been together for fifteen years," Karen responded.

"You still could have gone on to build another life for yourself," Harry said.

"And leave everything?" Karen protested. "I would have had to go to court and sue her, and what were the percentages in that? Besides, I have hardly anything put away."

"But how could you possibly hurt someone you loved?"

"Love?" Karen asked, a look of surprise on her face.

Poor Barb, Harry thought involuntarily. She could have done so much better.

"You're one dumb bunny, aren't you?" Karen said with a shrewd smile. "She was planning to cheat me out of what was rightfully mine. I'd put up with her affairs and I'd worked my butt off, and for what? To have to share it with someone else? No way. She was trying to make a fool of me. When she asked me to come over that night, I told her I was busy. But then I thought maybe she'd grown tired of Pearl and Judy and wanted a change, so I called her and told her I'd drop by as soon as Sarah fell asleep. When I found out that you were going to get nearly everything, I went crazy. I jumped her and began to strangle her before she knew what had happened. She was stronger than me, though, and she threw me off. I came back at her, and that's when she lost her balance and fell. And now, I'm out of here," Karen said, brushing past Harry, who automatically recoiled at her touch.

"Stop!" Harry shouted.

"Oh, she's not going anywhere," Porter announced as he backed Karen into the room.

"You turn up at the most propitious times," Harry commented as she reached under the sheet, found the buzzer and pressed it.

"Surveillance 101," Porter responded with a smug grin.

"Another obligatory course, I presume."

"Precisely," he replied as a nurse rushed into the cubicle and all hell broke loose.

"Porter's suggested we meet this evening at Mallory Square and watch the sunset together," Harry said to Judy as they sat in the office of the guesthouse. Harry waved at one of the guests as she hurried down the hall, obviously on her way somewhere important.

"Do you think the young woman you hired can handle things by herself?" Judy asked.

"Hilde? Yes," Harry answered. "She'll be okay. She's smart enough to take a message if she doesn't understand something."

"And your leg?"

"It's stiff, but I'm fine," Harry assured Judy, reaching out and capturing her hand. "I'd like to go. It's for Barb, after all."

"Let's get changed, then."

Half an hour later, Judy pulled into the parking lot off Front Street.

"There's a spot," Harry pointed through the front windshield.

"I see it," Judy responded, pulling swiftly into the parking space.

"This must be the only one left in the whole lot," Harry commented, opening the door and rising stiffly to her feet. Sometime during the night the local anaesthetic had worn off and her wound had started to throb. Over-the-counter pain killers had helped, but the ache never entirely faded.

"Are you sure you're up to this?" Judy asked as Harry limped toward the dock.

"I wouldn't miss it for the world," Harry said, linking her arm through Judy's as she thought back to the visit she had paid to the hospital less than an hour ago.

"She's really all right?" she'd asked Dr. Albertini yet again, needing to confirm and reconfirm that Barb hadn't been harmed when Karen had disconnected her IV and various monitors.

"She's fine," Dr. Albertini had replied. "The monitors are just machines, none of them are keeping her alive. They simply tell us how she's doing. Although she's being hydrated and fed through the IV, it wasn't disconnected long enough to do any damage."

"So how are you today?" she'd said as soon as the doctor left the room. "Everybody's rooting for you to get better, to wake up and return to the world of the living. I guess you know what happened last night, since you were here through a lot of it. Porter and I decided to try and flush out your assailant by inviting everyone to a cocktail party at his house. But all we managed to do was to place suspicion on the wrong person, and that's why they arrested Pearl. I never really thought it was her — well, maybe for a few minutes — but my instincts were leading me in another direction. The trouble is, I didn't trust my instincts. And I know what you'd say about that, so never mind. The thing is, Karen was planning to finish you off last night because she was afraid you'd wake up and tell the police that she attacked you. I guess her resentment built up over the years, and when she found out about your new will, she just lost it. I'm sure it wasn't premedicated, but she compounded it by not going to the police right away. She's being charged, of course, and Sarah's hired a lawyer who's trying to get her out on bail. I hate to tell you this, sweetie, but as one friend to another, you could have done better. Anyway, we're all waiting for you to come home. And you don't have to stay in a coma any longer because we know Karen did it. You don't have to protect her any more."

But Barb had slept on. Harry had chatted for a while longer, and then she'd returned to the guesthouse, where there was no lack of work to be done.

"It's a wonderful evening," Judy commented as they walked slowly through Mallory Square to the dock. "That's new since we were here the last time, isn't it?" she added, pointing to the Shipwreck Historeum.

"Yes," Harry agreed. "Let's come back and go through it when my leg's better."

"Have you decided what you're going to do about your job?" Judy asked.

"I've thought about it and thought about it, and I just can't leave with Barb still in a coma and Karen in jail," Harry said. "I'm going to call the school board the first thing tomorrow morning and ask for a leave of absence."

"You mean that you're going to stay here and run the guesthouse?"

"I know it'll be difficult, but what else can I do? Barb did give me power of attorney, and I accepted the responsibility. I can't let her down now," Harry said, glancing nervously at Judy.

"How are you planning to live without working?"

"Porter said that as long as Barb's in a coma, I can charge a monthly fee for running the Hideaway and administering the estate. I can live free of charge in the guesthouse. I might have to stay on even after she wakes up, depending on whether she needs to spend some time in a rehab centre. And there's going to be a lot for her to catch up on when she does get back on her feet," Harry replied.

"Not to mention dealing with people who are pissed off with her because of her will," Judy commented.

"There's that, too," Harry laughed. "But I imagine one of the first things she'll do when she wakes up is rewrite it."

"You've got it all figured out, haven't you?" Judy asked, her voice troubled.

"It won't go on forever," Harry assured her. "If Barb doesn't wake up in a couple of months, I'll hire someone to run the guesthouse and Porter can watch over things. I trust him implicitly. But I'm sure she'll recover long before then and give me hell for cleaning up her office and messing up her business. But even if she stays in a coma for a long time, I've got to learn the ropes myself, otherwise I'll never be able to supervise anyone else. In the meantime, I'll travel back and forth between Key West and Montreal quite often, and you can fly down — "

"I have a job," Judy interrupted.

"I know," Harry admitted. "But I've got to do this."

They reached the dock and walked slowly through the throngs of people gathering for the sunset ritual. The bagpiper was playing a Scottish reel, while the juggler was surrounded by an enormous crowd.

"It hasn't changed much, has it?"

"No," Judy replied.

They strolled past displays of tee-shirts and jewellery being hawked by local dealers until the tantalizing odour of conch fritters drew Harry like a bee to honey.

"So here you finally are!" Alison Wheatley exclaimed.

Harry paid for her conch fritters and turned around.

"You walked right by without seeing us," Alison complained.

Hell and damnation, Harry thought as she bit into a fritter, determined not to share them with Alison or Martin.

"I was beginning to think we were the only ones who were going to show up," Alison protested.

"I'm sure the rest of them will be here soon," Harry remarked, and then she sneezed. "Don't mind me, but your perfume's aggravating my allergies," she told Alison, moving away after she devoured another fritter.

"You'd think people would be on time," Martin Culver remarked with a glance at his watch.

"What's the big rush?" Judy commented. "The sun won't go down for quite a while yet."

Martin looked displeased, but he didn't say anything.

Harry ignored them and concentrated on eating her conch fritters. A few minutes later, Porter hurried up to them, followed closely by a burly man with a shock of unruly black hair. "Harriet Hubbley, I'd like you to meet Jock MacLeod," Porter said.

"I've heard a lot about you," Jock said, giving Harry's hand a hearty shake and then passing on to Judy.

"Are you being naughty?" Porter asked, pointing at the empty conch fritter container Harry was still holding.

"I decided I deserved it," Harry said, grinning at him. "Sorry I didn't save you any."

"I'll bet," he said dryly.

They gravitated toward the edge of the dock and stood staring out to sea as the sun sank toward the horizon. Harry crushed the greasy cardboard container in her hand, looking for a garbage can. There was one close to the fritter stand, so she left the group and walked over to it, not seeing Pearl until she was beside her.

"Hi," Harry said, tossing the crumpled container and her napkin into the overflowing can. She hadn't been looking forward to this moment, and now that it had arrived, she didn't know what to say. "Look, I'm sorry."

"It's okay," Pearl replied.

"No, it's not," Harry sighed.

"You're right, it's not," Pearl said. "But we hardly know each other, do we? And maybe it's better if it stays that way."

Harry felt real regret. "Can we talk about this later?"

"I'm going back to New York early tomorrow," Pearl said.

"Come on, the sun's going down," Peter urged as he and Ross sauntered by. Harry turned and followed them.

"Where's Sarah?" Porter asked Judy.

"Visiting Karen," Judy responded.

Their group had been mortally truncated, Harry reflected. One of its members was lying insensate in a hospital bed, another was in prison for having done the unthinkable, a third was voluntarily absent because of divided loyalties, others were alienated and distrustful.

The sun slowly began its descent. Harry stood between Judy and Porter, facing the Gulf of Mexico, watching the molten orb slip behind the horizon. Red flames shot into the sky and lit up the clouds. Where are you, Barb? she wondered as the piper began to play "Amazing Grace" and the crowd grew quiet, nearly reverential. Tears gathered in her eyes and spilled down her cheeks but she made no effort to hide them. She felt Judy grasp her left hand, and then Porter's larger one enveloped her right.

"Things are never going to be the same again," she said under her breath.

"You're right," Peter said, his voice melancholy. "They're not."

"That's not necessarily a bad thing, though," Porter responded.

"But it's scary," Judy commented, giving Harry's hand a gentle squeeze.

"I don't know what you're talking about," Alison complained, making Harry smile through her tears.

"Change," Pearl answered impatiently.

"That's all?" Martin asked.

"That's enough," Harry insisted.

"No, I mean that," Martin said, gesturing toward the crimson sky.

"Spoil-sport," Porter chided.

"Change," Harry said more to herself than anyone else.

"Yes," Judy responded.

"Then call me Harriet," she said as the clouds turned orange.

More Critically Acclaimed Books
by Jackie Manthorne

Deadly Reunion: A Harriet Hubbley Mystery

"Manthorne has a clean, crisp style and a heroine likeable enough to create something of a following." *Bay Windows*, U.S.A.

ISBN 0-921881-32-0 $10.95

Ghost Motel: A Harriet Hubbley Mystery

"Manthorne knows how to keep the action moving." *The Globe and Mail*

ISBN 0-921881-31-2 $9.95

Fascination and Other Bar Stories

"A brilliantly crafted collection." *Time Out*, U.K.

"A funny and hot collection from the smoky heart of the Montreal bar beat." *Sinister Wisdom*, U.S.A.

ISBN 0-921881-16-9 $9.95

Without Wings

"Manthorne's community of characters calls to mind Armistead Maupin's *Tales of the City*." *1994 Canadian Book Review Annual*

"Written with skill, depth and credibility and informed with a feminist sensibility." *Bad Attitude*, U.K.

ISBN 0-921881-29-0 $9.95

Jackie Manthorne is the author of two collections of short stories, *Fascination and Other Bar Stories* and *Without Wings*, as well as the recent Harriet Hubbley Mystery Series (all from gynergy books). Her writing has appeared in numerous magazines and anthologies, including *Lesbian Bedtime Stories II* (Tough Dove Books) and *By Word of Mouth: Lesbians Write the Erotic* (gynergy books). She is also the editor of *Canadian Women and AIDS: Beyond the Statistics* (Les Éditions Communiqu'Elles). She lives in Toronto, where she writes full time.

Best of gynergy books

Bordering, *Luanne Armstrong*. Louise is "bordering": on coming out as a lesbian, on imagining her future, on leaving the small town that keeps her pinned down. But before she can cross over to a new life, she must face up to the old.
ISBN 0-921881-35-5 $10.95

By Word of Mouth: Lesbians Write the Erotic, *Lee Fleming (ed.)*. "Contains plenty of sexy good writing and furthers the desperately needed honest discussion of what we mean by 'erotic' and by 'lesbian.'" *Sinister Wisdom*
ISBN 0-921881-06-1 $10.95/$12.95 U.S.

Lesbian Parenting: Living with Pride & Prejudice, *Katherine Arnup (ed.)*. Here is the perfect primer for lesbian parents, and a helpful resource for their families and friends. "Thoughtful, provocative and passionate. A brave and necessary book." *Sandra Butler*
ISBN 0-921881-33-9 $19.95/$16.95 U.S.

To Sappho, My Sister: Lesbian Sisters Write About Their Lives, *Lee Fleming (ed.)*. This one-of-a-kind anthology includes the stories of both well-known and less famous siblings from three continents, in a compelling portrait of lesbian sisterhood.
ISBN 0-921881-36-3 $16.95/$14.95 U.S.

Triad Moon, *Gillean Chase*. Meet Lila, Brook and Helen, three women whose bonds of love take them beyond conventional relationships. *Triad Moon* is an exhilarating read that skilfully explores past and present lives, survival from incest, and healing.
ISBN 0-921881-28-2 $9.95

gynergy books titles are available at quality bookstores. Ask for our titles at your favourite local bookstore. Individual, prepaid orders may be sent to: **gynergy books**, P.O. Box 2023, Charlottetown, Prince Edward Island, Canada, C1A 7N7. Please add postage and handling ($3.00 for the first book and 75 cents for each additional book) to your order. Canadian residents add 7% GST to the total amount. GST registration number R104383120. Prices are subject to change without notice.